WITHDRAWN

Large Print Mar
Maron, Margaret.
Up jumps the devil

STACKS
JUN 1 2 1997

NEWARK PUBLIC LIBRARY
NEWARK, OHIO

GAYLORD M

UP JUMPS THE DEVIL

Also by Margaret Maron in Large Print:

Fugitive Colors

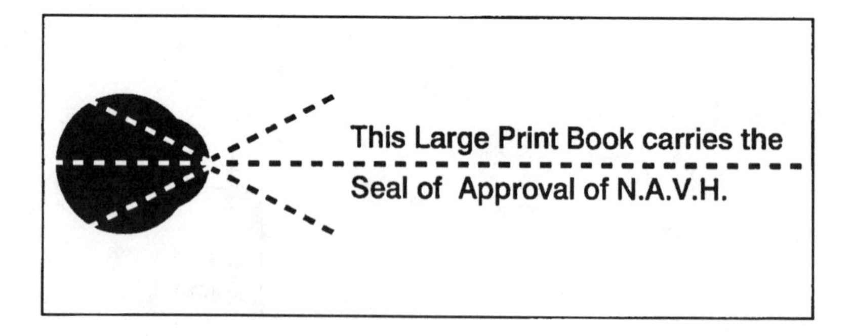

UP JUMPS THE DEVIL

Margaret Maron

Thorndike Press • Thorndike, Maine

Copyright © 1996 by Margaret Maron

All rights reserved.

This is a work of fiction. Names, characters, places, and incidents either are the product of the author's imagination or are used fictitiously, and any resemblance to actual persons, living or dead, events, or locales is entirely coincidental.

Published in 1997 by arrangement with Warner Books, Inc.

Thorndike Large Print ® Cloak & Dagger Series.

The tree indicium is a trademark of Thorndike Press.

The text of this Large Print edition is unabridged.
Other aspects of the book may vary from the original edition.

Set in 16 pt. Bookman Old Style by Rick Gundberg.

Printed in the United States on permanent paper.

Library of Congress Cataloging in Publication Data

Maron, Margaret.
Up jumps the devil / Margaret Maron.
p. cm.
ISBN 0-7862-0882-1 (lg. print : hc)
1. Large type books. 2. Knott, Deborah (Fictitious character) — Fiction. 3. Women judges — North Carolina — Fiction. 4. North Carolina — Fiction. I. Title.
[PS3563.A679 U6 1996d]
813′.54 — dc20 96-34447

For Sara Ann Freed,
now my nurturing editor,
but years ago the friend who first said,
"Why don't you write another book
about North Carolina?"

ACKNOWLEDGMENTS

As always, I am indebted to many for their technical advice or help, in particular: District Court Judges Shelly S. Holt, John W. Smith, and Rebecca W. Blackmore of the 5th Judicial District (New Hanover County, NC) and former Special Agent Henry Lee Poole of the State Bureau of Investigation. David Brown shared the memory of his one moonshine run, Linda Bryan Murphy gave me her father's deer story, Ann R. Stephenson tries to keep me accurate, and Susan Dunlap and Joan Hess let me bounce ideas. Thanks, guys!

All chapter captions have been taken from a pamphlet published anonymously in 1773 by "Scotus Americanus": *Informations Concerning the Province of North Carolina, Addressed to Emigrants from the Highlands and Western Isles of Scotland, by an Impartial Hand*, courtesy of the North Carolina Collection, Wilson Library, University of North Carolina, Chapel Hill.

NEWARK PUBLIC LIBRARY
NEWARK, OHIO 43055-5087

Large Print Mar
Maron, Margaret.
Up jumps the devil

436 2092

1

Surely if these people, artless and undesigning as they are, could mean to deceive, it must be reckoned a very uncommon and most unnatural deception . . .

"Scotus Americanus," *1773*

Most of my brothers —

Most of my respectable brothers, that is —

(Which also includes the ones that've sowed all their wild oats and are now settling into gray-haired middle age and trying to pretend they've been respectable all along.)

(When you have eleven older brothers, it's sometimes hard to keep straight which ones have walked the line their whole lives and which ones are newly whitened sepulchers.)

Anyhow, most of my brothers say I don't think long enough before I go rushing off half-cocked.

Usually I'll argue their definition of what's half-cocked, but every once in a while I have to admit that they may have a point.

If I hadn't rushed out to do the right thing when Dallas Stancil got himself shot and killed in his own backyard, I wouldn't have been left looking like a fool.

("Don't bet on it," says Dwight Bryant. He's the deputy sheriff here in Colleton County and might as well be another brother the way he feels free to smart mouth everything I do, even though I'm a district court judge and higher up in the judicial pecking order, technically speaking, than he is.)

What happened was I'd been holding court in the mountains near Asheville for a colleague who got called out suddenly for a family emergency. His elderly mother had wandered off from her nursing home and stayed missing two nights before they found her in a homeless shelter more than a hundred miles away in Atlanta, Georgia, alive and well and not a single clue as to how she got there.

It was early October and there'd been enough cool nights up in the mountains to color all their leaves; but down here in Dobbs, our flatland trees were just beginning to get the message that summer really was over.

I stopped by the courthouse that Wednesday evening to see if I was still scheduled to hold a commitment hearing the next morning out at Mental Health. A couple of white bailiffs were standing by my car when I came down the sun-warmed marble steps and one of them who knew I'd been away asked if I'd heard about the shooting.

"Past Cotton Grove on Old Forty-Eight," said the bailiff who also knew that some of my daddy's land borders that hard road south of Cotton Grove.

"Two niggers out from Raleigh killed a man as wouldn't let 'em hunt on his land," his fat-faced colleague interjected with relish.

I put my briefcase in the car, then turned and read the name tag pinned to the man's brown uniform shirt.

"Niggers, Mr. Parrish?" I asked pleasantly. I was born and raised here in Colleton County and will no doubt die here, too, but I swear to God I'm never going to get used to the casual slurs of some people.

The other bailiff, Stanley Overby, gave me a sheepish smile as I said, "Use that word again, Mr. Parrish, and I'll have your job."

A dull brick red crept up from his tight collar, but I'm a judge and he's not and the hot ugly words he really wanted to say came out in a huffy "Y'all excuse me. I got to get on home."

As we watched him cross the street to the parking lot, Overby hitched up his pants around his own ample girth and said, "Don't pay him any mind, Judge. He really don't mean anything by it."

I liked Overby and I knew he could be right. Parrish was probably nothing more than an equal opportunity bigot. Most of our bailiffs are like Overby — good decent men, augmenting a retirement pension that's sometimes nothing but a social security check. Every once in a while though, we'll get a Parrish, who, after a lifetime of taking orders himself, will put on that brown uniform and act like he's just been put in charge of the world.

Black or white, at least half the people

who get summoned to court through speeding tickets, misdemeanor subpoenas, or show-cause orders are there for the first time. They come in worried and unsure of themselves, they alternate between nervousness and embarrassment, and they certainly don't know the procedures. It doesn't help when the first person they approach with their timid questions is a surly-tongued white bailiff who either won't give them the time of day or else treats them like chicken droppings.

Happily, someone overly officious doesn't last too long. Not if Sheriff Bo Poole catches them at it.

"So who was it got himself shot?" I asked, not really concerned. If it'd been blood kin or a close friend, somebody in the family would've called me long before now.

"A Stancil man. Drove one of them big tractor-trailer trucks and —"

"*Dallas* Stancil?"

"You know him?"

"What happened?" I asked, too surprised to answer his question.

"Way I heard it, he went out to get in his truck yesterday morning and a couple of black fellows come up in a red pickup — Ford or Chevy. She couldn't say which."

"She?"

"His wife. She said it was the same two as he'd chased off his land Monday evening. She said they was talking and she commenced to make a fresh pot of coffee and then she heard gunshots and that pickup went screeching out of the yard. When she run out, he was laying dead next to his rig. Sheriff's got a call out on the pickup but she couldn't tell him a license plate or nothing."

Again he looked at me curiously. "Did you know him, Judge?"

"A long, long time ago," I said.

I should've either let it go, or phoned around my family for more solid information; but it was October and even if our trees hadn't yet flamed red and gold, fall was in the air, and could be stirring up the ashes of things I'd just as soon my family didn't remember.

Leaving Overby in the parking lot, I walked down the back stairs of the courthouse to the Sheriff's Department, but Dwight wasn't there. Nor was Sheriff Bo Poole.

I did ask a deputy if there'd been any development in the Stancil shooting, but he shrugged. "Last I heard, the body's still over in Chapel Hill. Don't know why it's taking 'em so long. Two barrels at close range, what the heck they think killed him?"

What indeed?

Aunt Zell's big white brick house sits on a quiet residential street six blocks from the courthouse. It was silent and empty when I let myself in a few minutes later because blues were running down at the coast and she and Uncle Ash had gone down to Harkers Island for a week of fishing. They'd taken Hambone with them, so I didn't even have a dog to greet me.

Didn't matter. I dumped my garment bag and briefcase on the deacon's bench inside the door and headed straight down the hall for the deep freezer on the side porch. Like most women around here, Aunt Zell keeps two or three casseroles on hand at all times for emergencies, and the top one was baked chicken, garden peas, sliced hard-boiled eggs and mushroom soup with a drop-biscuit topping. She had thoughtfully printed the heating instructions on the outer layer of tinfoil in case the bereaved had too much perishable food on hand and wanted to wait till the next day to serve it.

I stuck it in an ice chest, which I carried back out to the car. On my way out of town, I stopped off at a 7-Eleven for a bag of ice and a couple of liters of chilled Pepsis and ginger ale. So many people always gather at the home of the deceased that they usually run out of drinks and ice halfway through the evening.

The preacher that lurks on the outer fringes of my mind nodded approvingly as I added my purchases to the ice chest, but the cynical pragmatist who shares headspace with him whispered, *"Don't you reckon Dallas's wife might appreciate a pint of your daddy's peach brandy more than a liter of Pepsi?"*

"Unkind and unworthy," murmured the preacher.

I only knew Dallas's third wife, his widow now, by that sort of snide hearsay.

Hearsay said she'd been waiting tables at a truck stop in north Florida when Dallas pulled off I-95 for a late night hamburger about six or seven years ago.

"Hamburger?" one of my cattier sisters-in-law had snorted at the time. "That's a new name for it. Big hair, big boobs, skinniest bee-hind I ever saw."

"It's them leopard print stirrup pants," another sister-in-law said.

They were giggling about leopard pants when I came into the room.

"Who y'all trashing now?" I asked curiously.

They glanced at each other, then, careless-like, one said, "You remember that Dallas Stancil? He went and got himself a new wife with two half-grown young'uns. Third time lucky, maybe."

I suppose they told me all the gossip they'd heard, but it barely registered.

Did I remember Dallas?

Oh, yes.

And as I drove through the gathering dusk of early October, I remembered him again.

Twelve or fifteen years older. A hard-drinking, hard-driving roughneck. Not the kind of man any of my brothers would want me associating with.

And maybe he did drive me to the devil, but hey, I was raring to go, wasn't I? Begged him to take me, in fact.

And to do him justice, he went in and picked me up and drove me out again before I got more than just a little singed around the edges.

Did I remember Dallas Stancil?

Enough that I owed him at least the ritual of paying my respects by taking his widow a casserole.

The moon was rising fat and orange in the east, nearly full when I passed through Cotton Grove and headed south on Old Forty-Eight. The road gets rural real quick once you pass the last streetlight — big empty fields and thick woodlands with only a few house lights shining from yards back off the road. So far, most of the growth has been on the other side of Possum Creek where New Forty-Eight cuts a nearly straight line between Cotton Grove and Makely. The original highway meanders along the west bank and follows every bend and crook of the creek. I could almost drive it blindfolded.

Or without headlights, which is the next thing up from a blindfold on a moonlit night like this.

I don't know what it is about those lazy S-curves where the road dips down into the bottom between stands of oaks and poplars and sweet gums, but I can never drive through them without automatically speeding up. I haven't had a speeding ticket in four years, but there are two places in Colleton County where I'm bound to hit 80 even if I know there's a trooper with a radar gun behind every tree. One of them's that deserted stretch that crosses Possum Creek.

I cut off my lights and started down the long curving slope, my foot easing down on the accelerator as my eyes adjusted to the moonlight. By the time I hit the bottom where the air flows sweet and cool even on the hottest summer nights, the needle was on 78 and still climbing.

At the far end of the sharpest curve, on the right-hand side just before the bridge, an anonymous dilapidated mailbox — no name, no box number — stands beside a dirt lane that winds up through the underbrush, over a low ridge and then down to the homeplace. When I go home, and if nobody's coming from the other direction, I bank off the left side of the blacktop, accelerate again as the turn tightens, then, at the last possible moment, I take my foot off the gas and let momentum carry me halfway up the lane. Even my little Firebird will kick up a wide arc of dirt if I've cut it sharp enough, but it takes a longbed pickup to sling a really good nasty.

Daddy used to growl about the ruts the boys made fishtailing their trucks in and out of the lane, but all his life he'd slung too many nasties of his own not to let them get away with it most of the time.

Tonight I had the road to myself, and I wasn't going home. Instead I banked on the curve, gave it enough gas to corner sweetly, and raced across the bridge doing close to 85.

A few hundred feet past the bridge, I saw headlights in the distance and reluctantly took my foot off the gas pedal and switched my own lights back on. As I flicked them back to high after the other car roared past, I caught a glimpse of fluorescent orange ribbons tied to a stake on the opposite ditch bank and I almost stood on the brakes.

Surveyor's ribbons.

Oh, shit. Not out here, too.

I tried to remember whose land this was. I could hope it was merely someone selling off his timber, but I've seen too many of those orange ribbons across Colleton County these last few years not to realize that they could signal yet another new subdivision.

Ever since I-40 came through, linking Wilmington, North Carolina with Barstow, California, not to mention putting much of Colleton County within forty minutes of the Research Triangle, more and more of our fields and woodlands have been bulldozed under for cheap housing.

No, I don't want us to go back to 1910 or to mules and wagons that took six hours to haul a load of watermelons to Raleigh, but damn I hate how cars and highways are destroying the places where I grew up.

I'd have to worry about it another time though because I was coming up on Dallas Stancil's house. Since I hadn't given it much thought in the last few years, I had to look sharp or miss the turn-in — especially since my headlights didn't seem to be as they should be even though I'd had a new battery installed less than a month ago.

First comes Mr. Jap's trashy, unlovely place — a boarded-up cinderblock garage set back from the road in a grove of oaks. Moonlight glinted dully on the old tin roof. In summer, shoulder-high hogweeds disguise the rusted hulks of junker cars out back, and curtains of kudzu and Virginia creeper swing over the tumbledown sheds where more derelicts sit on concrete blocks. In winter, when all the weeds die and the vines wither, the place is a true eyesore; but there aren't any zoning laws out here nor many neighbors to complain about Jap Stancil's mess.

I saw lights at the rear of the old man's house and several cars and pickups were parked by his back door.

That surprised me a little. I'd have thought he'd be on down at his son's house, grieving with his daughter-in-law.

Whose name, I suddenly realized, had fled from my mind.

A couple of hundred feet further along, past a thicket of sassafras, wild cherries and scrub pines, was the mailbox with Dallas's name painted on it and I turned in.

And there I got another surprise.

A house of bereavement is normally lit up like a Christmas tree. Cars come and go, men stand around in the yard talking, and women stream in and out of the house bearing enough food to get Moses halfway to the Promised Land.

Not here.

The front part of the brick house Dallas had built for his second wife — one of the Otlee sisters from Makely — was dark and unwelcoming. As I drove around to the back (out in the country, some front doors haven't been opened in ten years), only the kitchen and porch lights were on. Dallas's rig was parked off to the side underneath one of those tall security lights, and yellow crime scene ribbons marked the place where he must have died.

Further up the lane, another security light guarded a black Nissan pickup and a single-wide mobile home. I'd heard that Dallas had let his stepdaughter move her trailer in when her husband lost his job at the lumber yard in Makely. A blue Toyota truck and a white Ford sedan were parked in the carport and a black-and-silver Jeep Cherokee stood near the back steps.

For a moment, I was tempted to turn around and drive right out again, wondering if those bailiffs were mistaken about who'd been shot.

But then I remembered the sheriff's deputy. They couldn't all be wrong.

I got out of the car with more confidence than I felt and carried Aunt Zell's casserole before me like a shield against awkwardness. I figured whoever walked me back to the car later could carry in the ice and soft drinks.

The inner door was open on this warm evening and as I came up onto the porch, a plump young woman with lots of curly brown hair got up from the table and met me at the screen door. Dallas's stepdaughter?

I didn't know *her* name either.

This was getting to seem more and more of a bad idea, but I took a deep breath and gave her my best politician's funeral smile, half friendly, half mournful.

"I'm Deborah Knott," I said. "I used to be a neighbor of Dallas's."

She wore green biker pants that were two sizes too small for those hefty thighs and a ruffled pink-and-green striped top that was so loose I couldn't tell if she was pregnant or merely overweight. Her eyes were swollen and her round pink face was blotched from crying as she held open the screen. "Ma's over there."

The large L-shaped kitchen was as much dining room and den as a place to cook and every surface gleamed with vinyl wax and lemon polish. I could have eaten off that white tile floor it was scrubbed so clean.

At the long end of the L, a plum-colored sectional set of couches and recliners wrapped around the corner and faced a color television that could be viewed from the dining table as well.

Football players grappled each other on the screen. The sound was turned off but it still held the attention of a hulking young man who sat at the table and munched on a drumstick from the biggest bucket of the Colonel's take-out chicken. From his looks, he and the young woman had been fished up out of the same gene pool. Both had fair skin and thick heads of lustrous brown hair, both had eyes that shifted away as soon as they met mine, and both could have stood to lose a fourth of their body weight.

Their mother, on the other hand, was so thin as to be almost gaunt. She still had big hair — thicker, browner and curlier than her daughter's — but the big breasts that had impressed my sisters-in-law were no more. Her many rings — diamonds? zircons? crystal "ice"? — slid loosely on thin workworn fingers as she poked at her hair. Beneath those towering curls, her face looked haggard despite a generous layer of pink blusher, bright red lipstick and dark blue eyeshadow.

She perched on the edge of one plum-colored couch at a right angle to a black couple who sat just as stiffly on an adjacent section of the couch. It might have been my imagination, but it seemed as if all three looked at me in relief as I approached, still bearing Aunt Zell's frozen casserole.

Either my name hadn't registered on the daughter or she simply lacked the social skills needed to introduce me, so I said, "Deborah Knott, Mrs. Stancil. I grew up down the road from here and used to know Dallas when I was a girl. I was so sorry to hear about him."

"Mr. Kezzie Knott's daughter?" she asked in a voice husky with cigarettes.

I nodded and looked at the black couple inquiringly.

The man came to his feet and put out his hand. "I'm Fred Greene, Miss — Knott, was it? And this is my wife Wilma."

They looked to be about my age, mid-thirties, and both were as formally dressed as if they'd just come from church.

I balanced the casserole in my left hand and shook with each of them, apologizing for my cold fingers.

"You want Ashley to take that for you?" asked Mrs. Stancil as she straightened the rings on her fingers and pulled a cigarette from a gold leather case. "Ashley, honey, put that in the refrigerator, would you?"

From the pile of red-tipped butts heaped in the cut-glass ashtray on the couch beside her, she was working on her second pack since the tray was last emptied.

I handed Aunt Zell's casserole to Ashley and explained how it could go in the freezer if they didn't need it right away.

"That'll be nice," said Dallas's widow. "We're much obliged." She inclined her head toward the Greenes. "They brought us some chicken and we surely do appreciate that, too. There's no way I feel like cooking since everything happened."

"It was nothing," Mrs. Greene murmured. "We just hate it so bad about your husband."

Fred Greene continued to stand and I looked at him closely. There was something awfully familiar about his face, but I couldn't think in what context.

"You wouldn't happen to be kin to Maidie Greene that married Cletus Holt, would you?" I asked.

"No, ma'am," he answered politely. "My family's from Pitt County."

My brain made a template of his face and slid it across a wide variety of places and events. A desk? Law?

"Were you ever a guardian *ad litem* down in Lee County or maybe a parole officer?"

"Sorry. I install mufflers over near Garner."

"I'm sure I've seen you before," I insisted.

"A lot of white folks tell me that," he said, and something about his stony manner made me wonder if he'd ever stood up before me in court.

I would've dropped it at that point, but his wife came to her feet anyhow. "Since Miss Knott is here to visit with you, Mrs. Stancil, we'll go on now. We just wanted you to know that all your African-American neighbors in the Cotton Grove community really hate what's happened. If we can do anything to help you identify those two cowards who shot Mr. Stancil in the back —"

The widow exhaled a long stream of smoke. "I appreciate you saying that, but you tell your people not to worry. We know it's not anything to do with anybody 'round here. Dallas got along real good with everybody, I don't care if they were green or purple. He always said, 'I treat everybody decent, Cherry Lou, and long as they treat me decent back, we won't never have any trouble.' That's what he always said and that's how he always did. But if I think of anything else, I'll let y'all know."

After putting the casserole in the freezer compartment of the refrigerator, Dallas's stepdaughter had joined her brother and that cardboard bucket of fried chicken at the table; and since their mother remained seated as well, the Greenes nodded good-bye to me and saw themselves out.

As soon as she heard their car engine turn over, Cherry Lou Stancil stubbed out her cigarette with angry, jerky motions.

"Can you believe the nerve of them?" She turned her head closer to mine and I caught the rich burnt sugar smell of bourbon mingled with her cigarette.

"Dallas not even in his coffin yet and

they come in here bold as brass, telling me that the *African-American community,* if you please, wants to help bring his killers to justice. What were they driving? What were they wearing? What did they look like? Like you can tell one nigger from another when they're both black as the ace of spades like them two were that shot him."

"Mrs. Stancil —"

"Call me Cherry Lou, honey. If you knew Dallas, you don't need to be a stranger."

"Your sisters-in-law sure had her number," muttered the pragmatist inside my head.

"Now, now," said the preacher. "She's a poor soul who just lost her husband. You can't be hard on her for reverting to stereotype."

I swallowed my distaste and said, "Were the Greenes friends of Dallas's?"

She shrugged. "Never saw them before. He says he's a deacon in the Tabernacle down the road, but Dallas knew lots of people I didn't, what with him gone so much. Left me stuck out here with nobody but the kids to talk to half the time. Now that he's gone, I guess I'll sell this place and move back to Florida."

"Sell? But I thought this was Mr. Jap's farm."

"Nope. He messes with a little corn and vegetables, but no, he signed everything over to Dallas years ago, before we was even married. The government was about to take it for taxes or something. I reckon it'll be mine, now that Dallas is gone."

When she said that, I remembered hearing my daddy talk about the hole Jap Stancil got himself in with the IRS over some used cars he'd sold without paying taxes on his profits.

Mr. Jap was a self-taught mechanic who liked to tinker with anything that had a carburetor. Some of my brothers got their first cars from him and he showed them how to keep those old engines running with cuss words and socket wrenches. He could do anything with a motor, but he probably never finished sixth grade and he wasn't much for keeping books, much less for reporting all his income. It was a cash-and-carry business and according to my daddy, "He couldn't come up with the cash he owed 'em, so the government carried him off to jail for six months."

Before they'd actually arrested him though, he gave the farm to Dallas and declared personal bankruptcy. After he got out of prison, he only worked on cars in somebody else's backyard so far as the tax people knew.

"What'll happen to Mr. Jap?" I asked.

"He can always have a home with me, if he wants it. Don't you know he'd just love Disney World?"

That was something I'd almost pay to see. Jasper Stancil's nearly as old as my daddy. I hadn't seen him in two or three years, but even though I knew he and Daddy still fished together, I couldn't picture either one of those octogenarians at Disney World.

"I've been out in Asheville all week," I said. "Didn't get back to Dobbs till this afternoon, so I'm not clear about what all happened. Did you see it?"

"Not really. It was yesterday morning a little before eight o'clock, about thirty minutes after the school bus run. Dallas told me 'bye and said he was on his way. I was fixing Bradley his breakfast and Ashley and Tig didn't eat yet either —"

"Tig?" I murmured.

"Ashley's husband. They usually bring Michelle down to catch the school bus

— she's in kindergarten this year — and then they stay and eat breakfast with Bradley and me most school mornings. Anyhow, I was over there at the sink and could see the truck out the window and Dallas just had the door open good and was about to climb in when up drives this red pickup and these two niggers get out.

"I says to Tig and Bradley, 'Y'all better go out there and see if Dallas needs any help because I believe them's the same ones he chased out of his woods yesterday.' "

"That was odd, wasn't it?" I asked. "Most hunters respect those posted signs."

(The signs say "No Hunting — Possum Creek Hunt Club." Every year, hunters out from town with their shotguns and rifles will knock on the door at Daddy's or Mr. Jap's or over at Leo Pleasant's and meekly ask if they can join. The three old men solemnly take down the applicants' names and promise to put them on the waiting list. Of course, there is no waiting list. No hunt club either, for that matter. Daddy long ago noticed that most men, the same men who won't think twice about trespassing onto posted land, do seem to respect a hunt club's lease.)

"Them people don't respect nothing," said Cherry Lou.

Her son had stopped eating and now lit up a cigarette as he half-turned in his chair to follow his mother's words.

"I didn't have my shoes on," he told me, "so Tig stepped out on the porch by himself."

"But it was like they never knew he was there," said Cherry Lou. "Or didn't care. 'Cause the next thing I knew, I heard both barrels of a shotgun go off and when I ran back to the window, that green Chevrolet was halfway down the driveway."

"Ford," said her son.

"I thought you said it was a Chevy."

"No, I told you it was a Ford. Bright red."

"I was never one for knowing the makes of anything," Cherry Lou told me.

"It was a full-size red Ford pickup," said Bradley, "and they were flying out the yard on two wheels by the time I got out there. Dallas was laying half in and half out of his truck with a big hole in his back. Blood all over the yard, all over the truck."

"On you, too, I reckon when y'all ran to help him."

An embarrassed look crossed his chubby round face. "Well, naw, I could see he was beyond help. It was awful. I just ran back in and told Ma to call the sheriff."

"So you actually never saw the men that shot him?"

He shook his head as if he'd flunked a test of personal bravery.

"Then it's a good thing your brother-in-law got a good look at what happened."

"Yeah. They took him over to Dobbs so he could help some artist draw one of them —" He hesitated, not quite sure of the term. "Like when they don't have a real picture?"

"A composite drawing?"

"Yeah, that's it."

"But he's been gone ever since eleven-thirty this morning," Ashley burst out. "What you reckon's taking so long?"

"Ashley, honey," said her mother, "I believe I could eat a little piece of white meat if there's any left. And a glass of tea? How about you, Deb'rah? Tea? Something to eat?"

"Tea would be great," I said. And in

truth, I needed cool liquid to my throat because all three of them had lit up again and the air around us was turning blue.

As Ashley reached into the cupboard to get me a glass, her hand slipped and the glass crashed to the floor in a zillion shards.

Her brother started yelling because he was barefooted. She yelled back that he hadn't got up off his fat butt all evening so he could just sit there a little longer till she got the broom. Cherry Lou yelled at both of them to hush up before they woke the baby.

Too late.

Above the din came a child's fretful wail and a sleepy-eyed little girl in Mickey Mouse pajamas stumbled down the hallway, squinting against the light.

"Now see what you did!" said Ashley.

"*Me?*" protested her brother. "You're the one broke the damn thing."

While they bickered, Cherry Lou darted across the room and snatched up the child before she could get near the glass and cut her feet.

"I'll get her back to sleep," she told us and carried her granddaughter down the hall, crooning soothing noises to the child as they went.

I held the dustpan while Ashley swept up the glass. She kept glancing anxiously at the clock above the kitchen sink.

"I just don't know why they don't let Tig come home," she said again. "I called over to Dobbs about an hour ago and they wouldn't even let him talk to me. Said they still had things to ask him about. That don't mean they think *he* shot Daddy Dallas, does it?"

"Of course not," I assured her. "They always question the family first. Doesn't mean a thing. They've probably got him looking at mug shots."

Uneasily, I remembered that I'd been in the sheriff's office an hour or so ago and neither the sheriff nor Dwight Bryant had been there.

"You sure they took him to Dobbs and not just up the road to Cotton Grove?"

She was positive.

"Well, you did say your husband was the only one to see the actual shooting, right?"

Brother and sister nodded vigorously and both seemed anxious to go over the whole incident again, explaining why neither had happened to be looking out the window at the time. Curious, I asked them every question about those hunters I could think of, yet they couldn't seem to come up with a single new detail. They were just two big black men in a red pickup. A full-size Ford.

"Ma keeps getting it mixed up, but it was a Ford alright. About three years old."

Cherry Lou returned to report that she'd finally gotten her granddaughter back to sleep. "Poor little thing. Keeps asking me where's her Paw-Daddy. That's what she calls Dallas. And he was just as foolish about her. Brought her a stuffed animal every time he come home from one of his long hauls. You can't hardly get into her room over yonder at their trailer for all the rabbits and teddy bears. Some of them's bigger'n she is, aren't they, Ashley?"

She suddenly noticed my empty hands. "Didn't you get you any tea yet? Ashley, where on earth's your manners, girl?"

Dry as my throat was, I declined politely, expressed my condolences, promised to attend the funeral, and got out of there as quickly as I could because I'd suddenly remembered where I'd seen Fred Greene before.

When I pulled up at Jasper Stancil's back door, that black-and-silver Jeep Cherokee was parked alongside the other vehicles.

Surprise, surprise.

I slammed my car door and stomped into the kitchen without knocking and there were the "Greenes" with Sheriff Bo Poole, Dwight Bryant, and SBI Agent Terry Wilson, all with big gotcha grins on their faces. The only person not there was Jap Stancil and I later heard that Daddy'd taken him over to his niece's house.

In the middle of Mr. Jap's eating table was a radio receiver and a tape recorder and I could hear Ashley's voice wailing, "They know Tig did it, they *must* know or why else won't they let him come home?"

"They don't know shit," her brother said. "You keep your mouth shut and Tig stays cool, we'll all be back in Florida before Christmas."

"No thanks to you two," came Cherry Lou's voice. "Won't for me getting the gun and Tig pulling the trigger, we'd all be out on our tails without a dime."

"Bingo!" said "Wilma."

"Fred and Wilma *Greene?*" I rolled my eyes at the two black SBI agents, who tried to look innocent. "Why didn't you use Flintstone and be done with it?"

"Sh-sh!" said Dwight as he concentrated on the bickering voices their bug was beaming over from Dallas's house.

Terry Wilson tried to give me a hug. "Sure do 'preciate you going in there and asking all those questions for us. We didn't get doodly with ol' Fred and Wilma here."

"Go to hell!" I flared. "What's my Aunt Zell going to say when I tell her one of her best chicken casseroles is sitting down there in a murderer's refrigerator?"

2

. . . nor will it be easy to explain how they should all conspire in the same tale, and, without varying, stumble upon the same favorable accounts.

"Scotus Americanus," *1773*

It was almost Halloween before the worst of the kidding died down.

Cherry Lou Stancil and her son-in-law Tig Wentworth were sitting in jail waiting to be formally arraigned on first-degree murder charges. Both were going to be under such high cash bonds that neither would be able to raise it. Cherry Lou's main collateral was the farm, but Mr. Jap had retained John Claude Lee, my cousin and former law partner, to roadblock her putting any liens on the land till after the trial. Under North Carolina's Slayer Statute, she'd forfeit any claims to Dallas's estate if convicted as a principal or accessory, and since Dallas had no children from his first two marriages either, John Claude was pretty sure he could get the farm reverted to Mr. Jap as Dallas's closest blood kin.

Turns out that the land may have triggered the shooting. A local speculator offered Dallas a hundred thousand for his place. Soon as Cherry Lou heard that, she got visions of returning to Florida in glory.

Maybe they'd even buy a house right next door to Disney World.

"In your dreams," Dallas told her.

From that day forward, according to Mr. Jap, she was at him like a hound dog after biscuits — just wouldn't let it alone — till one day Dallas looked around and realized he was supporting a wife, a stepson, a stepdaughter, a stepson-in-law and a step-granddaughter. And he didn't really like a single one of them anymore except for maybe the little girl. Mr. Jap said Dallas told Cherry Lou he was going to see a lawyer about a divorce when he got home from his next run to Galveston. In the meantime, he wanted Ashley and Tig's trailer off his land. Ashley, Tig, and Bradley, too, for that matter.

Three days later he was dead.

Cherry Lou's two children had been charged with conspiracy, but at their probable cause hearing, the DA cut them a deal when they agreed to testify for the prosecution. They were out on relatively small bonds, secured by Bradley's truck and Ashley's trailer.

Tig swore he'd kill them both if he ever got turned loose and he kept badgering his court-appointed attorney to forget about murder charges for a minute and start filing divorce papers on Ashley. "And put in there that I want sole custody of my little girl. Ain't no fit momma that'd tell on her baby's daddy."

Cherry Lou had disowned the whole bunch. She admitted buying the shotgun the day Dallas told Mr. Jap he was going to divorce her — how could she not with her signature on Kmart's credit card receipt? — but it was supposed to be a Christmas present for Dallas, she said. Along with a box of shells, she said. She didn't know why Tig decided to try it out on Dallas two months early.

"Trick or treat maybe?" Dwight suggested.

* * *

They buried Dallas at Sweetwater Missionary Baptist Church, next to his mother, who'd been the only churchgoing person in the Stancil household. She was a Yadkin though and her niece, Merrilee Yadkin Grimes, Dallas's first cousin, made all the funeral arrangements for Mr. Jap, right down to picking out the music, "This Little Wheel's Gonna Turn in Glory," and the text, Ezekiel 1:21 — *"And when those were lifted up from the earth, the wheels were lifted up beside them; for the spirit of the living creature was in the wheels."*

The preacher was good with metaphors, but even he seemed to have a right hard time stretching that particular text to fit the occasion. Merrilee was pleased with the sermon though. "Dallas loved trucking and I thought Ezekiel was real appropriate for a truck driver."

The words of the Old Testament prophet must have touched Mr. Jap more than Merrilee could've hoped for. Or maybe it was losing his only child like that.

Anyhow, the next thing I heard was that Mr. Jap had got religion and painted a purple cross on his front door right above the words "Holyness Prayr Room."

Daddy said he had about twenty pictures of Jesus tacked up on the walls and he'd made a simple cross out of two tobacco sticks and some baling wire. "Other'n that, the living room looks just like it did when Elsie was living, 'cept now Jap sits in there and reads the Bible to a couple of Mexicans that show up every Sunday morning."

"You, too?" I asked, knowing Daddy seldom stepped inside any kind of a church except for weddings and funerals.

"Be different if he'd just read," Daddy said regretfully. "Jap and me, we been knowing each other our whole lives, but I never much cared for being preached at."

3

. . . but, in the month of October, there cannot be a more temperate air, and finer climate, than here, the weather being mild and dry for the space of forty or fifty days.

"Scotus Americanus," *1773*

By the middle of October, I get pretty tired of any leftover summer dregs — the midday heat, the dust, the grasshoppers, the dogflies from hell. I'm usually ready for some serious rain and a killing frost. Especially one that'll kill dogflies.

(Takes a sleet storm to kill grasshoppers. They just hunker down in the broom sedge and wait for sunshine. I've flushed grasshoppers five inches long on a sunny January day.)

So far, the nights had been cool enough to start coloring leaves and brown off most of the weeds, but one last dogfly had somehow managed to survive and it had been circling my head for several minutes, eluding my flailing hands and waiting for me to lower my guard long enough so it could land on bare skin and dig in.

Exasperated, I started to duck into a thicket of hollies to get away from it, then recoiled in automatic reflex.

Hanging upside down between two young holly trees was a spider that looked like a tiny yellow-and-white hard-shell crab, and I had almost put my face through its large delicate web. One minute the dogfly was following my head. The next minute it was entangled in the sticky strands. The more it struggled, the tighter it was held and already the spider was hurrying over, playing out more sticky threads of silk to tether those kicking legs and buzzing wings before they could break loose.

"Hey, cute trick!" said Kidd. "I never saw anybody do that before."

If a man thinks you've deliberately maneuvered a pesky winged bloodsucker into a spiderweb, why tell him it was a pure accident? Can it hurt to have him think you're uncommonly clever in the ways of the wild? Especially when he's so crazy about the outdoors himself?

Picture six feet three inches of male lankiness. Long skinny legs. Flat belly. A face more homely than handsome. Crinkly hazel eyes that disappear when he laughs.

Kidd Chapin.

How I Spent My Summer Vacation.

You know how you'll see pretty shells lying on the sandy beach, cast up wet and lustrous from the ocean floor, so colorful you can't resist picking them up? You know how, months later, you find them dry and dull in a jacket pocket or stuck down in a desk drawer, and you wonder what on earth made you bring them inland?

Kidd Chapin's a wildlife officer. I found him down at the beach back in the spring.

So far, I haven't once wondered why I brought him home with me.

Not that I have, actually. Not in the literal hang-your-jeans-in-my-closet sense. For starters, he has his own house on the banks of the Neuse River above New Bern, and he's assigned to cover an area down east.

"Inland" is complicated by the fact that I live in the middle of a small town with an aunt and uncle. My own quarters are relatively separate, with a private entrance which I seldom use, and no, I don't think Aunt Zell would get out her scarlet thread and start embroidering my shirts if I chose to let Kidd use that entrance. I don't know if it's manners, my abiding awareness that it *is* their house, or an active neighborhood watch system (made up of active voters, be it stipulated) that keeps me from giving him a key.

If I were eighteen years old again, maybe I would. Maybe I'd even stand on the front porch and make a speech about hypocrisy and honesty, about personal freedom and modern morality.

But I'm a district court judge. I know the value of hypocrisy. I've also learned a little bit about discretion as I've passed thirty and race toward forty: *don't do it in the road and scare the mules.* I don't want to watch Aunt Zell and Uncle Ash struggling to be broadminded and tolerant, and I certainly don't want judgmental neighbors putting my morals on the ballot come the next election.

If Kidd's still around after Christmas,

I may finally think about getting my own place. In the meantime, instead of taking him into my bed like a mature woman whenever he drives over, we sneak around Colleton County like a couple of horny teenagers. His new minivan has four-wheel drive, tinted windows and seats that let down flat, and it's been up and down just about every secluded lane and byway along Possum Creek.

Kidd and I were out on the back side of my daddy's farm that warm Sunday afternoon. We'd been to church that morning with Nadine and Herman, the brother who worries most about my soul. We'd eaten dinner with Minnie and Seth, the brother who cuts me the most slack. (Being the closest thing I had to a campaign manager, Minnie's also the sister-in-law who's least interested in seeing me married. She'd rather see me in the state legislature.) Now we were out running a pair of young rabbit dogs Kidd had just bought. They were barely past puppyhood and eager to please, but they didn't have a clue and if you didn't watch them every minute —

Well, let's just say we both got distracted for maybe a bit more than a minute. By the time we came up for air, the dogs had got into the woods and across the creek and sounded as if they were heading for Georgia.

Kidd whooped and hollered, but they were too excited to mind and there was nothing for it but to jump back in the van and go chase them down. We both had our heads out the windows, listening for the dogs, when we rounded a corner of the field and surprised a huge flock of blackbirds. As one, they rose from the earth in a great rush of wings to settle raucously in the trees around us.

All through spring and summer, grackles and starlings are little-noticed birds. In the fall, though, they band together by the thousands in flocks so large that it can take a full two minutes for them to cross the sky. Their chatter was so noisy that the dogs could have been just beyond the trees and we wouldn't have heard them.

When we got to the homemade bridge across the creek, Kidd wasn't sure he wanted to risk his van on something built out of hickory logs and some scrap two-by-fours.

"It's strong enough to hold a tank," I

assured him. "Shorty and Leonard and B.R. drive over it twice a day."

"Who're they?" Kidd asked as we crept across, going maybe half a mile a minute.

"Some of Daddy's old tenants from when he was still suckering tobacco by hand. He lets them live rent-free on our side of the creek, but they work for part-time wages at Gray Talbert's nursery and this is their shortcut."

Kidd breathed easier when his back wheels were on firm dirt again. Not me. I'm never comfortable on Talbert land.

G. Hooks Talbert is head of Talbert International and a power player in the reactionary right wing of North Carolina's Republican party. He has a hundred-acre country estate near Durham with a private airstrip and a couple of Lear jets. He also has two sons: one's a grasshopper with the morals of a cowbird; the other's a conscientious ant whose morals are probably whatever G. Hooks tells him they are.

When G. Hooks needed to stand the grasshopper in a corner, this little piece of land he'd inherited through his mother's side was the corner he chose. Gray Talbert raised a lot of hell at first, then, to everybody's surprise, he seemed to settle right down. Repaired the greenhouses. Started a profitable nursery.

According to Daddy, who twisted a knot in G. Hooks's tail over that nursery, it's totally legitimate these days, if maybe not quite as profitable as back when Gray was running it unsupervised.

Nevertheless, I was glad when Kidd stuck his head out the window again, heard the dogs, and said they'd veered off to the east. We doubled back along a lane that followed the creek bank and soon passed the iron stake that marked the corner between our land, G. Hooks's, and Mr. Jap's. One of those ubiquitous orange plastic ribbons was tied around the stake and the loose ends fluttered in the breeze.

Kidd slowed down to a crawl when he saw me twist around to stare out the back window. "Something wrong?"

"Just wondering who's surveying what," I said.

Sighting back along the Talbert line, I could see more orange ribbons tied to a distant tree at the edge of the creek bank.

"My daddy has a standing offer to buy this piece of land, but G. Hooks would dig up the whole forty-six acres and ship it to China before he'd let Daddy have a square inch. If he's getting ready to sell, you can take it to the bank that he's found a buyer he thinks'll give Daddy grief."

"Why should your dad care who Talbert sells to?" asked Kidd. "He's already got a mile-wide buffer around his house."

An exaggeration, but not by much.

Daddy's always happiest when he can put a little more land between himself and the outside world and he's been adding to it ever since he was a boy of fifteen. He and my brothers own at least twenty-five hundred acres between them. A hundred or so of those acres are mine.

Some people spend money on fancy cars and lavish houses or expensive toys. We Knotts like to put our spare change in land. As Daddy always reminds us, it's not like God's making any more of it.

We cleared the trees and there, blocking the lane, was a shabby black two-ton farm truck with bald tires and home-made wooden sides to the flatbed. A wiry young white man in blue jeans, a faded red T-shirt, and a green John Deere cap leaned against one of the fenders as he talked with Mr. Jap. Beside the lane was a nice patch of bright orange pumpkins that looked big enough to harvest even though the vines were still green.

I hadn't seen Mr. Jap since the funeral, so I motioned for Kidd to stop and got out to say hey.

He looked old and frail standing there with the sun beating down, as if Dallas's death had drained off ten years of energy, and he didn't seem to place me till I mentioned Daddy, introduced Kidd, and explained why we were there.

Then he smiled and said, "Oh, yeah. A pair of hounds went streaking past here about two minutes ago. I wouldn't be surprised but what that rabbit's holed up down yonder at the sheds. You just go ahead, but try not to run over no pumpkins if you can help it."

"I'm glad you reminded me," I told him, "because Aunt Zell asked me to bring her a dozen ears of your corn if I was out here before Halloween."

Mr. Jap was never much of a farmer,

not even in tobacco's glory days. He so preferred working on cars that he rented out his acreage and even let some of his fallow fields go back to nature. A few years ago, though, when the influx of new people started and those newcomers couldn't seem to get enough of the ornamental corn he brought to the crossroads flea market, Mr. Jap planted a couple of acres so he could pay for his winter heating oil. Now, to my surprise, he seemed to be in farming with both feet. Except for that small pumpkin patch, the whole back side of his farm was covered with broken stalks and culled ears.

"Billy here picked it last month and it's stored in that barn back of Dallas's house."

Mr. Jap had always grown a strain that he swore had been handed straight down from a great-great-grandmother who befriended an Indian woman who gave her some seed stock in return. The colorful red, black, orange, and yellow ears were small and perfectly shaped, "and them fools over'n Cary and North Raleigh'll hang it on anything that opens or closes," he told Daddy gleefully. "Hell, they even buy corn shocks and hay bales and stick 'em all over them fancy yards they got."

He'd shaken his head at the folly of city folks, but he was happy to take their cash. And was evidently eager for more.

"Billy here and me go halves on it," Mr. Jap told us now, which explained the larger crop.

"Billy Wall?" I asked the young man. "Troy Wall's boy?"

"Yes, ma'am," he said shyly.

"I didn't know your daddy farmed."

"He don't. But I've always wanted to ever since I was a little boy."

Troy Wall had been five or six years ahead of me in school and this boy, about twenty I'd say, was his spitting image. "What's your dad up to these days?" I asked.

"Oh, not much. He lays floor tile for Carpet Country when his back don't act up on him. They got the contract to do all the houses in Mr. Sutterly's new subdivision over on New Forty-Eight."

Dick Sutterly was the developer who'd tried to buy the farm from Dallas.

Mr. Jap dropped his cigarette, ground it out with the toe of his brogan. "That's the old Holland homeplace," he said. "Used to be one of the prettiest farms around, yes, it was. And James Holland always had the best yield of sweet potatoes of any man in the township. It's a downright sin to put houses on such mellow land."

"Been mine, I'd have never sold it," Billy said wistfully.

"Well, everybody ain't as willing to work as hard as you, boy. No, they ain't." Mr. Jap shook his head. "I reckon some folks would sell their soul if you offered 'em enough."

I didn't know if he meant the Holland heirs or his daughter-in-law sitting in the jailhouse over in Dobbs, and for a minute I thought he was going to launch into a discussion of sin and redemption. Instead, our conversation turned to crops and the weather.

Billy had come over today to see if Mr. Jap wanted some help getting up his pumpkins, which the old man peddled out of the back of his pickup at the flea market. Otherwise, he was going to bring out a crew this week to ready another load of ornamental corn for market. I gathered that it was a matter of carefully pulling back the dried shucks, tying them in bunches of threes, and then packing them into crates. Mr. Jap thought they might have a thousand dozen all told.

"Been such a good year, I'm a mind to run a load up to Washington," said Billy. "I think I can get a dollar and a half an ear up there."

A couple of short rows were still standing next to the pumpkin patch. Although some of the colorful ears had been nibbled down to the cob by squirrels and coons or carried off by crows, we found more than a dozen nearly perfect specimens for Aunt Zell, who was in charge of decorations for the County Democratic Women's November meeting. Kidd loaded them in the van while I tried to pay Mr. Jap, who put his hands in his pocket and said, "Even if it won't Sunday, I couldn't take no money from Kezzie's girl. 'Sides, y'all better go on and get them fool dogs 'fore that rabbit takes 'em across the road."

In the distance we could hear the dogs yipping like crazy, so I thanked him and climbed back in the van. We drove on around the edge of the big cornfield, through a stand of pines and straight across a fallow pasture, through chest-high hogweeds, cockleburs, and bright yellow camphorweeds till we could actually see the two pups.

Whatever they'd been chasing had gone to earth somewhere beneath the tumbledown outbuildings there on the edge of Mr. Jap's farm. The young dogs were running in and out and underneath the sagging wall of an old log tobacco barn, trying to figure out exactly how to get at their quarry.

We hurried over to them and Kidd had to speak smartly to them before they'd listen long enough for us to each grab a collar while he snapped on the leads.

Shelters with dull tin roofs shedded off three sides of the barn, which had almost disappeared under a tangle of kudzu vines. Hundreds of tobacco sticks were bundled and stacked under one; five old wrecked vehicles, four cars and a pickup, were nosed up under the other two shelters. They were dirty and covered with bird droppings, but their windows weren't broken and they didn't seem to be as rusty as the half-dozen that had been left to the weather out behind the shelters.

"Well, would you look at this!" Kidd said. He ducked beneath the kudzu vines and walked around to the front of a sporty little car with a smashed-in rear. "A 1967 Ford Mustang. That was my first car."

"Was it red, too?"

He nodded.

"First boy I ever went steady with drove an old Mustang. Candy-apple red." (Benny Porter. He'd had great potential till that warm spring night when four of my brothers boxed us in with their cars and trucks at the drive-in.)

Kidd smiled as his hand touched the frisky little grille ornament. "Y'all make the horse buck?"

"Why, Mr. Chapin," I drawled. "What kind of a young girl do you think I was?"

(My brothers had kept their eyes on the screen and didn't say a single word, but poor old Benny was so intimidated that he would barely kiss me after that and we broke up before school was out.)

"I bet you were hell on wheels."

I laughed as he caught my hand and pulled me to him. The pups yipped and strained against their leads.

They barked again and we heard a deep male voice say, "Can I help y'all with something?"

Standing out in the sunshine was a heavyset muscular man with a thick mop of straight brown hair just beginning to go gray. He had a strong nose and square chin and his mouth was curtained by a salt-and-pepper mustache that bushed out over his upper lip.

Kidd and I were at the rear of the shelter, in deep shadow, of course, and the man squinted against the bright sunlight, trying to make out our features. We still had our arms around each other and Kidd gave me an inquiring glance. When I shrugged my shoulders to show I didn't recognize him, Kidd stepped forward, looping the leads around his hand so the over-friendly pups couldn't jump up on the stranger.

The man wore sun-faded jeans and a brown leather vest over a blue plaid shirt. The big buckle on his belt was enameled green-and-white and shaped like the logo of a popular motor oil.

I took a longer, harder look and my heart sank straight to the bottom of my stomach as I mentally shaved off that thick straight mustache and lengthened the hair into a ponytail. And maybe it was my imagination, but I could almost feel a tingle in my left shoulder where I'd once carried the tattoo of a small black star. Cost me a bunch to get the damn thing lasered off. When this man turned his left hand, I saw the mate of my black star on his palm and I knew that if he took off his shirt, there'd be a red, white, and blue American flag on one deltoid and a pair of black-and-white checkered flags on the other. (Not to mention a couple of raunchy tattoos on more intimate parts of his anatomy.)

He had to be at least fifty now, but he squatted down on the heels of his cowboy boots as easily as a teenager and rubbed the dogs' ears. Suspicion was still in his eyes. "Y'all ain't friends of that Tig Wentworth, are you?"

The name of the man that'd shot Dallas Stancil meant nothing to Kidd and he shook his head. "No. My dogs got across the creek and we came over to get them. Then I saw this old Mustang and had to take a closer look."

He stretched out his hand. "I'm Kidd Chapin. From down east."

"Allen Stancil," said the man, sticking out his own hand as he stood up again. "From out near Charlotte."

They both turned to me and since the *Enterprise* hadn't suddenly beamed me off the planet like I'd been praying the last forty seconds, there was nothing for it but to come out of the shadows from behind the wrecked car and say, "Hello, Allen. What're you doing here?"

"Well, I'll be damned! Debbie?"

"Don't call me Debbie," I snapped automatically.

"Y'all know each other?" asked Kidd.

I hesitated and Allen Stancil said smoothly, "Yeah, I used to do a little work for Mr. Kezzie. He's sure looking good these days to be as old as he is. You, too, Deb."

"Don't call me Deb," I said, enunciating each syllable through clenched teeth. "And just when did you see my daddy?"

"Coupla days ago. I was driving into Uncle Jap's yard while he was driving out. I throwed up my hand to him, but I don't guess he knowed who I was."

A damn good guess. If Daddy knew Allen Stancil was anywhere within a hundred miles, he'd have told me. Assuming he didn't shoot the bastard first as he'd once threatened to.

All through Dallas's funeral, I'd been thinking about Allen, wondering if he'd show, wondering what I'd say if we came face-to-face before I could slip away. And here he'd jumped up like the devil when I least expected him.

"How long you planning on staying?" I asked.

He shrugged. "Long as Uncle Jap needs me, I reckon. Dallas getting hisself killed sort of knocked the fire out of him, didn't it?"

"Or put a different kind of fire into him," I said, thinking of that Holyness Prayr Room. "We just saw him over at his pumpkin patch with Billy Wall."

"Dallas and me, we was more like brothers than first cousins," Allen said mournfully. "I'm gonna have to be Uncle Jap's son now."

That pious tone made me snort, but it was drowned in the yips and yells as the dogs got loose again.

Once Allen quit paying them any mind, they lost interest in him and suddenly remembered the rabbit that was hiding somewhere under the shelter. Their lunge caught Kidd off guard and the leads slipped from his hand. An instant later they dived under an old Chrysler that was sitting up on blocks. I saw the rabbit squeeze underneath the side wall and light out for the tall weeds, but the pups never missed him. They just kept on yipping and whining around the cars until Kidd stepped on one lead and Allen got hold of the other.

And when Kidd opened the door of the steel cage in the back of the van, Allen hoisted up the dogs and helped get them inside. I could see him sizing Kidd up as they talked dogs a minute or two before getting off on cars again.

"I'd forgot about all the old beauties Uncle Jap has sitting round this place," he said. "There's a 'sixty-one Stingray and a straight-eight 'fifty-nine Packard Clipper. And you're probably too young to appreciate it, but damned if he ain't got a 'forty-nine Hudson Hornet setting over yonder beside the feed barn."

"I know a doctor down in New Bern with a classic Stingray," said Kidd, "but I don't think I ever heard of a Hudson Hornet. Good car?"

"Good car? Hell, bo, it was just the prettiest aerodynamic body anybody ever saw," Allen said. "Had this incredible overhead cam in a one-eighty-two horsepower engine. I tell you, around here, Hornets flat-out *dominated* stock car racing in the late forties. Then along came the Olds Eighty-eight and after that the Hornet was finished. Hudson merged with American Motors and now the Jeep's about the only thing Chrysler kept when they took over AMC."

He pulled a crumpled pack of cigarettes from his shirt pocket. He knew better than to offer me one, but he did hold out the pack to Kidd, who shook his head.

There was a faraway look in Kidd's eyes, as if seeing something wonderful and long gone. "My dad used to have an old 'fifty-two Thunderbird," he said.

"Man, they were something else!" Allen agreed as he took a long drag of smoke and exhaled it through his nose. "Don't suppose he still owns it, does he?"

Kidd gave a rueful shrug. "Mom made him sell it when my little brother came along. She couldn't hold both of us on her lap anymore."

"Too bad. A 'fifty-two T-bird in good shape, it'd be worth a bundle now."

"That's what my dad keeps telling her," Kidd said with a wide grin.

Car talk bores the hell out of me. I've never felt the allure of carburetors, rings and spark plugs and whether an engine's a V-6 or a V-8. All I care about is how it looks and whether it's got decent acceleration. Long as it's not too shabby, long as I can turn the key and get to court on time, what difference does it make how big the engine is or how many cylinders it has?

My brothers spent half their growing-up years with their heads under the hood of some old broken-down piece of junk. Any time one of their friends drove over, the first thing they'd do is troop out to look at the new set of chrome-plated exhaust pipes or marvel at the size of the big wheels somebody'd just put on his truck.

I can still hear my mother: "You boys change clothes before you go crawling up under that car. You get grease on those school shirts, it'll never come out."

While Kidd and Allen talked Cougars, Impalas, and Goats and the pleasures of a manual transmission over an automatic, I sat down on the back of the van and let the hatch shade me like a beach umbrella. The pups nuzzled my fingers through the steel wire for a few minutes and then went to sleep.

Eventually, Allen glanced over at me and, casual like, said, "Last I heard, Debbie —"

He caught himself and my name came out "Debbierah."

He must have remembered what happened the last time he called me Debbie.

I'm not a cupcake and nobody shortens my name too many times. *Nobody.*

"I heard you're a lawyer."

"Used to be," I admitted.

"So what're you doing now?"

"I'm a district court judge."

"A *judge?* Really? Hey, way to go, girl!"

Was it my imagination or were his congratulations a bit forced?

"How 'bout you, bo?" he asked Kidd. "You in the law business, too?"

Kidd propped one foot on the back of the van next to me, leaned an elbow on his knee, and gave Allen a lazy smile. "You could say so. I'm a wildlife officer."

"A game warden?" Allen shook his head. "A game warden *and* a judge? I better watch my step, hadn't I?"

"And what are you doing these days?" I asked suspiciously.

"Oh, some of this and a little of that. Still messing around with cars." He held out his big square work-stained hands. "Ain't got all the grease out from under my nails yet."

"Still hanging around racetracks?"

"You race?" asked Kidd, showing me a whole different side that I hadn't seen in the six months that we'd been together.

"Not anymore," Allen told him. "It's a young man's game and I ain't got the reflexes I used to have."

He'd heard the quickened interest in Kidd's voice and was giving back a regretful nostalgia for races run, for records set, for roses and beauty queen kisses in the winner's circle. Charlotte and Rockingham were in his drawl. Maybe even Daytona and Talladega, too, for all Kidd knew. But unless things had changed a hell of a lot in the last few years, Allen himself had never raced on any track longer than a half-mile and had never won a purse larger than three or four hundred dollars.

"These days I do a little pit crewing to keep my hand in. Mostly though, I'm moving into restoring classic cars. Like your daddy's T-Bird," he told Kidd. "Or like that little Mustang there."

His eyes moved speculatively from the dilapidated outbuildings to a cinder-block building sitting halfway between us and the road. It was encircled by even more wrecks rusting away in a thicket of ragweeds and sassafras trees.

"In fact," said Allen, "I was thinking I might even open up Uncle Jap's old garage. All these new houses going up,

I bet Jimmy can't keep up with them."

He had that right. Bad as my battery needed checking, I'd have to call Jimmy first and make a real appointment and I kept forgetting.

I've been taking my cars to Jimmy White ever since the white Thunderbird my parents gave me for my sixteenth birthday slid into the ditch on the curve in front of his newly opened garage. He was standing right there in the open doorway, and after he made sure I wasn't killed, he went and got a tow rope, pulled my T-bird over to his garage and hammered out the dent in my fender.

"You going to tell my daddy?" I asked.

"Ain't Mr. Kezzie's car, is it?" said Jimmy as he handed me his bill for fifteen dollars. " 'Course, I see you take that curve that fast again, I might have something to say to my Uncle Jerrold."

Jerrold White was one of the first black troopers in North Carolina and I knew if I got another speeding ticket, Mother and Daddy would take away my keys for a month.

So I still go slow when I drive past Jimmy's and I still bring my car to him even though he has so many new customers I can't just drop in and get it fixed while I wait anymore.

Intellectually, I know that people (and their cars) have to live somewhere, but selfishly I can't help feeling that way too many houses are sprouting up on our fields and in our woods. All these new people looking for the good life — crowding up against us, taking up the empty spaces — they're changing the quality of *our* lives.

That's why I flinch every time I see orange ribbons. Seems like they're all followed by dozens of Dick Sutterly's For Sale signs.

"Gracious Southern Living in a Spacious Sutterly Home."

Right.

Twelve-hundred-square-foot cardboard boxes slapped down on a bare acre lot and built cheap enough to compete with double-wide trailers.

Car keys jingling in his hand, Kidd straightened up and said, "Well, I reckon we'd better roll if I want to make it back to New Bern before dark. Nice meeting you, Stancil."

"Same here," Allen told him. To me he said, "Now don't you be a stranger, Deb'rah."

* * *

With the dogs and the ornamental corn giving off familiar earthy smells, we drove down the rutted lane to the road and headed back to Dobbs.

"Stancil seems like an interesting guy," Kidd said.

I made a noncommittal sound.

"Nice of him to come spend some time with his uncle."

I was wondering about that myself, but all I said was, "Uh-huh."

Kidd glanced over at me. "Been a long time since you last saw him?"

"Years," I said.

"So how come you're still so pissed at him?"

"Marriage'll do that," I said.

"Marriage?" he asked blankly. Then it registered, and the van suddenly veered so far into the passing lane that one wheel hit the shoulder and Aunt Zell's corn went flying. "You were *married?* To *him?*"

"What happened to 'interesting' and 'nice guy'?"

He was too steamed to smile. "The whole time we've been together and you never found a spare minute to say 'Oh, by the way, I used to be married to some redneck speed jockey'?"

"I thought we agreed not to talk about past relationships."

"Relationships, yes, but marriage is more than a one-night stand. Wasn't I up front about Jean and Amber?"

"You were married for twelve years," I said. "And you could hardly keep Amber a secret. Sooner or later I was bound to wonder why your spare bedroom's done up in ruffles and lace."

Kidd's fourteen-year-old daughter is very retro-feminine.

"It's not funny, Ms. Judge. Is there a kid you forgot to mention, too?"

I was starting to get a little steamed myself. "Does it matter?"

"Jesus Christ, Deborah! Of course it matters. I thought we had something open and honest here. I thought —"

Both hands clenched the steering wheel and he drove in moody silence.

This had the makings of Our First Fight and I was bedamned if it was going to be over Allen Stancil.

"Look," I said, twisting around till I was sitting on my left leg and facing him across the width of the van. "If you really want to know why I don't talk about it — why I try to not even *think* about it —

it's because Allen Stancil's the stupidest thing I ever did in my entire life."

My internal preacher gave my conscience a jab and I amended, "Well, one of the stupidest, anyhow. Sometimes I still can't believe I was ever that messed up. My only excuse is that Mother had just died. I was eighteen and a freshman at UNC-G, away from home for the first time. I was mad at God, mad at Daddy, not talking to at least eight of my brothers, even mad at Mother for dying."

The van suddenly felt hot and stuffy. I cracked the window and took several deep breaths. "Running off to a Martinsville magistrate with Allen seemed like a way of getting some of my own back. Of course, we hadn't been married twenty minutes when I knew it was a mistake, but by then I was so high on pot and tequila, I didn't really give a damn."

I lowered my window all the way and cool wind whipped my hair into tangles.

Kidd reached over and laid his hand on my drawn-up knee. "You don't have to tell me any more if you don't want to," he said gently.

"There's not much more to tell. About a week after we married, he went and called me Debbie one time too many. I was slicing limes with a rusty old butcher knife and I guess I overreacted. Scared the hell out of me. I got him to the emergency room before he bled to death, and then I just walked out the door and kept walking."

"Home?"

"No. There were some other girls. Women. Race car groupies," I said vaguely. "I crashed with them."

I don't like to think of that brief period. It had seemed like an eternity when I was living it — terrified that Allen might die, then scared he might live and have me arrested for trying to kill him. I freaked and crawled inside a tequila bottle carrying my saltshaker. To this day I still can't look a margarita in the eye.

"Dallas was the one who'd given us a ride up to Martinsville and when he heard what happened, he came looking for me and tried to bring me home, only I wasn't ready to come back and be preached at. I did let him take me on up to my Aunt Barbara's house in Maryland, and while I was there, Daddy and my cousin John Claude — the one that's a lawyer over in Dobbs? They had the marriage annulled before half my brothers were even aware I wasn't still at school. It was over two years before I finally came home, so I doubt if there's ten people outside my family that know it ever happened."

"Eleven now," said Kidd.

I slid across the wide seat and tucked myself under his free arm. "I said *out*side my family."

4

It is indeed astonishing, how far ignorance, partiality, and prejudice will often carry people.

"Scotus Americanus," *1773*

As so often happens, I no sooner meet someone than he appears in my courtroom.

Wednesday morning, the first day of November, I looked up from the papers before me to see young Billy Wall called to the defendant's table for issuing worthless checks. A very young, very pregnant woman with short brown curls sat on the bench beside him and she gave his arm an encouraging pat as he stood up and came forward.

The prosecuting witness was Curtis Thornton, a cheerful balding man who owned Thornton Tires, a truck and tractor tire service between Dobbs and Cotton Grove. Mr. Thornton is no stranger here. He's one of those easy-going businessmen who freely extend credit, accept anybody's check, and then use district court as their collection agency when the check bounces or the debt isn't paid.

There's been some talk about changing the setup and requiring such businessmen to hire private collection agencies or pay the court a fee, but until the laws are changed, all I can do is lecture the Thorntons of the world about their trusting natures and order the defendants to make restitution or go to jail.

Thornton took the stand and testified that this was the second time Billy Wall had made payments with a bad check. "Much as I hate to press charges against such a hardworking young man, Your Honor, you know I do have a business to maintain."

Speaking in his own defense, Billy Wall was clearly embarrassed to be standing before me so soon after we'd met out at Jap Stancil's pumpkin patch. He'd crammed his Royster fertilizer cap in the hip pocket of his jeans and his knuckles were rawboned as he leaned his hands against the table. He looked so much like one of my nephews as he earnestly explained how he'd gotten a little behind this fall that I couldn't help feeling sympathetic toward him.

"My truck needed some work and a set of new tires, too, if I'm going to haul corn up to Washington, and then I had to pay my labor cash or they wouldn't ready the corn. I swear I'll give him his money soon as I get back next week, but, Judge, I just ain't got it till then."

I could have laid a fine on him in addition to court costs and restitution, but it seemed to me that if Mr. Thornton was going to keep on handing out credit so freely, he could just wait another week for the sixteen hundred dollars Billy Wall owed him. "But I don't want to see you back in here with Mr. Thornton again," I warned.

"No, ma'am," he promised. "Thank you, ma'am."

As he turned away, his young wife stood up to meet him with a relieved smile, and she, too, murmured thanks to me.

I smiled back and handed the judgment papers over to the clerk, then looked expectantly at Tracy Johnson, the assistant district attorney who was prosecuting today's calendar. She seemed to be in yet another whispered conference between two attorneys. Court's busy enough without these constant interruptions.

"What's the holdup, people?" I asked impatiently.

"Sorry, Your Honor," said Tracy, without a smidgin of sorrow in her tone as she reached for the next shuck. She's been an ADA about a year longer than I've been on the bench. Tall, blond, knockout gorgeous. Or would be if she'd take off those ugly oversized glasses. She thinks they make her look more professional.

I shifted my gaze to the two attorneys who'd taken advantage of the six-second break that occurs when I sign a judgment and hand the paper over to the recording clerk. Sometimes there are legitimate and urgent reasons for a lawyer to speak with the ADA while court's in session, but sometimes it's just a matter of the lawyer's convenience. Give them too much leeway and they'll wind up conducting a lot of their business on your time.

"Mr. Whitbread? Mr. Stephenson? Either of you have clients on this morning's calendar?"

Reid Stephenson's my own cousin and former law partner and he was too familiar with my testy tone not to say "No, ma'am" and sit himself down, but Edward ("Big Ed") Whitbread thought he had enough charm to get away with it. He gave me an ingratiating smile as he continued to lean over Tracy's shoulder. "Your Honor, if I could just —"

"Unless this pertains to the next case, I suggest you speak to Ms. Johnson when we recess," I said crisply. He probably had business elsewhere and hoped to clear up a small but crucial point with Tracy so he wouldn't have to wait around till I was ready to recess.

"Sorry, Your Honor." He lumbered over to squeeze his ample backside in between Reid and another colleague on the attorneys' bench.

"Call your next case, Ms. Johnson."

The next thirty-five minutes moved briskly as we disposed of some more guilty pleas. Pimply-faced black and white kids of both sexes stood penitently before my bench, nervous that they were about to lose their driver's licenses before they'd even worn the new off. Unless they've done something really stupid like passing a stopped school bus, roaring through a residential section, or deliberately running a red light, I usually enter a prayer for judgment continued so that they don't get points against their insurance or licenses.

At ten-thirty, a grandmotherly white woman came forward with a timid air. She didn't look like a leadfoot even though she was charged with doing 57 in a 45 mph zone. Probably hadn't noticed when a 55 zone changed to a 45.

"How do you plead?" I asked.

She hesitated nervously and seemed to be on the edge of blank panic.

I leaned forward and spoke as gently as I could. "Guilty or not guilty, ma'am?"

"Guilty," she blurted. "But I'd sure appreciate it if you could offer up a prayer for my redemption?"

The attorneys and law officials seated on the side benches burst into laughter and I couldn't stop my own lips from twitching as I said, "You haven't been with us before, have you, ma'am?"

Bewildered, she shook her head.

I explained what a prayer of judgment was (basically a suspended sentence —

the temporal equivalent of "go in peace and sin no more"), entered hers, then announced a fifteen-minute recess.

Three lawyers swarmed toward Tracy.

As I stepped through the courtroom door and out into the corridor, I, too, was waylaid by people who wanted my signature on various documents. I signed a search warrant, a couple of show causes, and a temporary restraining order against a well-known merchant here in Dobbs who always treats his wife with old-fashioned courtesy. At least, that's how he always treats her in public. According to her attorney, he'd broken her nose last night. For the second time in two years.

I haven't been on the bench long enough not to still be surprised by the violence that can rage behind a lovely facade of heirloom silver and Queen Anne mahogany.

Eventually I made it to the rest room off the small office assigned to me this week, and when I emerged, I found Merrilee Yadkin Grimes clicking up and down in turquoise high heels in front of the bare desk. She's a Clairol auburn, a perfect size four body inside that turquoise suit, and five or six years older than me.

("Than *I*," comes Aunt Zell's voice in my head. Aunt Zell fights a losing battle with my grammar.)

"Hey, Merrilee, what's up?" I asked. Dallas's cousin works in Raleigh, a middle manager of something with the Department of Transportation, and would normally be in her own office on a Monday morning.

"It's not what's up, but what's out," she said, her little Yadkin eyes flashing.

I suddenly remembered that today was finally supposed to be the probable-cause hearing for Cherry Lou Stancil and Tig Wentworth.

The wheels of justice turn slowly in a death penalty case, which was what Douglas Woodall, our district attorney, said he was going for. It had been set back twice now. First, Doug was waiting for results from the SBI lab, then Cherry Lou's court-appointed attorney had to argue a case in federal court.

"Don't tell me Judge Longmire didn't find probable cause," I said.

"Oh, they've both been charged with first-degree murder all right," Merrilee said angrily, "but he turned *her* loose on bail."

"How'd she raise it? I thought John Claude —"

"Not on the land," said Merrilee. "On Dallas's rig. He bought it brand-new three years ago and her lawyer argued that it's community property till they prove her guilty. *And* she gets to stay in the house and use Dallas's bank account till then, too."

"The law does say innocent till proven guilty, Merrilee."

"Innocent?" She was outraged. "When everybody in Colleton County *knows* she bought that shotgun just to kill poor Dallas?"

"Did he set bail for Wentworth?"

"No. Mr. Woodall said he'd made enough threats against Ashley and her brother to be a danger to society and that even if he didn't kill somebody else, he'd probably try to run off, so they're going to keep his sorry tail in jail with no bail."

All those -ail words brought a rueful smile to her lips and made her face look five years younger under its artful makeup.

I glanced at my watch. I'd been out of

the courtroom nine minutes and I still didn't have my cup of coffee. Interesting as all this was, I could probably hear the rest of the details over lunch with Roger Longmire.

"I'm sorry, Merrilee," I said, "but if you're wanting me to do something about Cherry Lou's bail —"

"No, no, it's not that. What I really stopped by for was to see if there's some way to put a stop on Uncle Jap's bank account. Maybe get them to give me his power of attorney or whatever you call it before all his money's gone?"

For a moment I wondered where Jap Stancil got enough cash money for Merrilee to worry about. Then I remembered the ornamental corn and how his share was probably going to bring him five or six thousand.

"Oh yes. I saw him with the Wall boy a couple of weeks ago. He sounded pretty cogent to me about their business deal."

"I don't mean Billy Wall even if Uncle Jap hasn't seen a penny of the sales yet. The way he's carrying on though, it's just as well. Every penny'd be right down the drain."

"Don't tell me he's started drinking

again? I thought he swore off for good at the funeral."

Jasper Stancil had pulled some monumental drunks in his day, but Daddy said he'd already tapered off even before Dallas was killed.

"Allen's got him started again," said Merrilee with returning anger. "You know Allen Stancil, don't you? Uncle Jap's brother's boy?"

She paused and I could almost see her mind grasp at the tendrils of old gossip. "In fact, didn't you date him or something once?"

"Water over the dam," I said hastily. "What's he done now?"

"I thought he was just here for a sympathy visit, but he's settled into Uncle Jap's spare room like he's here to stay. He's got Uncle Jap drinking, got him fixing up that old repair shop, got him thinking he's forty again. Petey and I stopped by last week on the way to church to take Uncle Jap a plate of my fresh ham and sweet potatoes. Half the time he forgets to eat. I signed him up for meals-on-wheels so he'd get lunch through the week, but I like to make sure he eats on the weekend, too. I thought sure Allen would have gone by now, but there he was, cleaning out that garage — on *Sunday*, too! — like he owned the place. He's just as sorry as he ever was and I wish there was some way to get him to leave before he drags other people down with him."

High heels clicking on the bare tiles, Merrilee was back pacing again.

It didn't take me but a moment to understand the real reason for her agitation. Like Allen and Dallas, Pete Grimes also had a rough, hardscrabble childhood, only there had been no Miss Elsie to mitigate his father's drunken rages or to comfort him with a mother's pitying love. Pete's trashy mother had fought his even trashier father for the last drink in the bottle and it never worried either of them if the kids went off to school hungry, dirty and ragged. They didn't care if the kids went to school at all, long as they weren't being pestered by truant officers.

Even though he drank too much and drove too fast and ran with a rough crowd after he grew up, Pete was never as bad as some of those older Grimes boys and he had a gruff charm that convinced Merrilee he was worth saving. Must be something in their blood that makes Yadkin women such redemptionists: first Miss Elsie, then Merrilee. On the other hand, there's a reason why so many country songs tell of wild men tamed by the love of a good woman, and Pete Grimes isn't the first roughneck to run through a couple of bad marriages before taking happily to a well-ordered life. Such a man appreciates regular meals, a tidy house, and a woman who can lead him to Jesus.

In fact, Pete thinks Merrilee's a saint for loving him and he'll tell anybody who'll listen how grateful he is to her. "She raised me up," he says. "I'd be in jail or dead by now if it wasn't for her."

But Merrilee lives in fear that Pete might backslide and she tries to keep him away from bad influences like Allen.

"And now Uncle Jap's saying he's going to hire Charlie Holt to come fix that old hydraulic lift like he's got half the wealth of the world and he doesn't, Deb'rah. Except for a little bitty Social Security check, all he has is his corn money and what he picks up selling pumpkins and turnip salad at the flea market. But Allen's going to use him just like he uses everybody and what's poor old Uncle Jap going to do if he has to go in a nursing home or something? Last time he got to drinking so bad, the doctor said his liver couldn't hold out much longer."

She didn't wait for my answer. "So what I want you to tell me is, how can I get Uncle Jap's power of attorney? Or maybe get me named his guardian?"

"You can't," I said bluntly. "Not unless he agrees to it or you can show that he's mentally incompetent. And even that might not do it if his nephew wanted to fight you for it. After all, he's Mr. Jap's closest kin. You're only related through Mr. Jap's wife and she's dead."

"But I was blood kin to Dallas and I'm the one that's been looking after Uncle Jap for years," Merrilee argued. "Ever since Aunt Elsie died, whenever Dallas went on the road, he went easy, knowing I'd check on his daddy while he was gone. Even after he married Cherry Lou and brought her back here to that nice house he built for Mary Otlee, I'm the one Uncle Jap always called if he needed anything, not her. And certainly not Allen Stancil. What's *he* ever done his whole life but crash in on Dallas and Uncle Jap every time he gets fired or wrecks his car or needs to hide out from some woman?"

"Everybody knows how good you've been to Mr. Jap," I assured her, "but unless you can show that he's no longer competent, he can stand on top of the courthouse and fling his money to the four winds if he wants to and there's nothing we can do about it."

Merrilee looked horrified at the thought.

I looked at my watch.

I'd been out fourteen and a half minutes, so no coffee for me this morning.

Darned if Allen wasn't doing it to me again.

By lunchtime, we'd disposed of all the Guilty pleas and made a start on the Not Guiltys.

Administering justice is like shoveling smoke. Justice Learned Hand said that.

Shoveling smoke. That's exactly what it seems like sometimes — the same petty offenses over and over, and yeah, I got caught but here's why it's not really my fault, Your Honor: I was just going with the flow; my speedometer was off; somebody was tailgating me and I had to keep out of their way; that stop sign

I run was hid behind some bushes/too far off the shoulder/won't there the last time I come through that crossing; if that lady didn't slam on her brakes, I wouldn't have rear-ended her; the only reason the officer stopped me is because I'm black/a teenager/a senior citizen/driving a red sports car.

Actually, I'm always just a little sympathetic to that last excuse. Ask any cop. A bright red car is four times more likely to get pulled for speeding than a nondescript blue one. I myself haven't had a single ticket since I smartened up and reluctantly traded my red Corvette for a dark green Firebird.

Of course, except for the Possum Creek bottom and one other back-country stretch, I've pretty much quit speeding since I came to the bench. And for the record, no, I never asked anybody to fix a ticket for me before that. You can't preach responsibility to others and then weasel out of the consequences of your own actions.

Unlike our new "family values" congressman who washed in on the ultraconservative tidal wave last year.

When his car passed another in a no-passing zone and caused an oncoming van to flip over, he swore to the patrolman that his wife was driving, even though five witnesses had him behind the wheel and two more said they saw him changing places with her immediately after the accident. The DA kindly offered to let him plead nolo contendere and he took the deal because, and I quote, "I didn't want to spend the next six months proving that my wife was guilty," which, I suppose, says something about family values?

Some local wags said his greatest fear was that Jesse Helms would find out he'd been caught going left of the center, while others went out and made up a bumper sticker that said MY WIFE WAS DRIVING.

Fortunately, I didn't have anything quite that colorful on the day's docket. We finished up shortly before four and I went looking for Dwight Bryant. He's not seeing anyone right now and with Kidd a hundred miles away and most of my women friends tied up at night, I'm usually at loose ends during the week, too.

I found him at his desk in the sheriff's department. "Want to drive over to Raleigh and catch the early show at the Longbranch?"

"Can't. I'm overseeing security at East Dobbs's football game tonight. It's a makeup game."

As Sheriff Bo Poole's chief of detectives, Dwight wasn't exactly earning a shabby salary and I raised my eyebrows. "Moonlighting?"

"Yeah," he said dejectedly. "Got a call from Jonna last week. Cal's front teeth are coming in crooked and he's going to need braces."

Braces on top of the maximum child support for his income bracket? Wasn't going to leave him much walking-around money. Most of Dwight's friends think Jonna took him to the cleaners in their "amicable" divorce, but we never hear him gripe about it.

I was ready to gripe for him. "Cal inherits her teeth, and she can't pay for the braces?"

He shrugged. "What can I tell you? C'est la damn vie."

Sitting in domestic court a few days later, I thought of Dwight as I listened to a long string of excuses from the men who'd been hauled before me because they refused to recognize their responsibilities toward the children they had fathered. One man with a half a pound of gold around his neck and wrists explained that he'd gotten behind on his child support because he had to buy a new suit and a plane ticket to California. His brother was getting married and he was the best man.

Best man.

Right.

Three more said they'd been laid off. No jobs, no money.

I could have sent them to jail, but why should taxpayers support them and their kids, too? Instead, I've picked up on something a colleague over in Goldsboro's been trying. When deadbeat dads (and the occasional deadbeat mom) quit paying because they aren't working, the Honorable Joe Setzer fills their days with community service. They get to sweep gutters, pick up litter, rake leaves, mop floors, or wash windows — eight hours a day, zero pay. After a few days of working for free, most of these young men miraculously find jobs that let them resume their child support obligations.

Along with everything else today, I also had a contested paternity suit from a few weeks earlier. Clea Beecham, the mother; Timothy Collins, the alleged father; and Brittany Beecham, a perfectly adorable two-year-old baby girl.

The young mother swore that Collins was the only man she'd been with for six months before the baby was conceived.

Collins admitted that he'd lived with Ms. Beecham during the pertinent time period, "But I'm not the first guy she ever slept with and I certainly wasn't the last. That's why we broke up. She was seeing the same guy she'd been with before me."

As is not unusual in proceedings like this, both parties had insisted on blood tests and I'd agreed to the postponement. My good friend Portland Brewer was representing Timothy Collins and from that kitten-in-cream look in her eye this morning, I didn't really have to hear the testimony to know that the blood test had turned out well for her client. She stepped forward now to question the witness, a qualified technician from one of the medical labs in the Research Triangle who had taken the stand with a thin manila folder.

Mrs. Diana Henderson was in her early forties. She wore a black skirt and a white silk blouse that was neatly knotted at the neck. Despite her businesslike air of competence as the clerk swore her in, Mrs. Henderson hadn't entirely forgotten she was a woman. Her blouse was demurely styled, but so sheer that when she twisted around to retrieve a dropped document, I could clearly see the lace on her slip and even a dark mole on her left shoulder blade. That plain black skirt did nothing to disguise her slender hips, and her black patent T-straps had three-inch heels that drew attention to her slender ankles. Ash blond hair fell softly around her thin face.

Not the most attractive face, unfortunately. She had nice eyes, but her nose was too long and her chin was almost nonexistent.

Her voice was music though — soft, yet every word distinct and deliberate as she told in measured tones how she'd taken blood samples from Mr. Collins and Ms. Beecham and the baby girl. She described the tests she'd performed and explained how the results proved conclusively that Mr. Collins could not possibly be this baby's father.

Ms. Beecham's attorney gamely tried to get the technician to admit that the tests weren't absolutely positively one hundred percent accurate, but Mrs. Henderson wasn't having it. "While they can't prove conclusively who the father *is*," she said authoritatively, "they do prove who the father *isn't*. There is no way that the man who provided this blood sample could have fathered this particular child."

As I thanked Mrs. Henderson and dismissed the case, young Timothy Collins triumphantly kissed his new girlfriend — at least I assume from the length of the kiss that she was not his sister.

And judging by the baffled yet grimly determined expression on Clea Beecham's face, I had a feeling I'd be seeing her back in court as soon as her attorney could serve papers on her other ex-lover.

They left my courtroom and a social worker came forward to petition for the termination of parental rights to two young half-brothers barely out of diapers. The mother was a seventeen-year-old crack addict who left the boys alone for hours at a time. They had been in foster care several times. The final straw for Social Services was when she left them locked in a closed car on a hot

September day and they nearly suffocated before someone noticed and broke open the door.

Several witnesses, including her own aunt, took the stand to testify as to her unfitness to care for the boys.

"I'd take 'em myself," said the aunt, as tears cut new furrows in her cheeks, " 'cepting I'm already raising one for my boy and two for my girls and I just can't do no more."

Both fathers were unknown.

The mother had not bothered to come to court.

The woman who had fostered the boys almost from birth wanted to adopt them permanently. After testifying on the sorry state of the boys' health and physical dirtiness each time they were returned to her care, she took a seat on the front row and watched me anxiously.

I went back through both case jackets and still saw nothing to indicate that the natural mother had half the maternal instincts of the average alley cat. Carrying a child in her womb for nine months doesn't automatically turn any female into a mother; and much as we'd like to think every baby's wanted and loved, wishing's never made anything so.

The foster mother had only a grade-school education, but Social Services called her a decent, caring person. God knows those boys could use some decency and caring.

I signed the termination forms and called for the next case.

Shoveling smoke.

5

Upon their arrival among their friends and countrymen in North Carolina, Highlanders are kindly received and sumptuously entertained . . .

"Scotus Americanus," *1773*

Homemade music permeated all layers of my childhood — Daddy's fiddle, Mother's piano, Aunt Sister's dulcimer, my brothers and cousins and their children, each with banjo, guitar, or mouth organ. "Sweet Hour of Prayer," "Golden Bells" and "Golden Slippers," and "Shall We Gather at the River?" Those that couldn't play could always clap and sing.

They rollicked me out of bed on Saturday mornings with "Hell Broke Loose in Georgia" and lullabyed me to sleep with

"Whispering Hope." I can never hear *Soft as the voice of an angel . . .* without getting a warm snugly feeling of peace and utter security.

Mother and Aunt Ida's daughters had high, clear soprano voices; Aunt Rachel sang alto; Daddy half-talked, half-hummed; and the boys ranged from bass to tenor.

Mother, Aunt Ida and some of the older cousins are gone now, Aunt Rachel lives with her middle daughter over near Durham, four of my brothers live out of state, nieces and nephews are scattered from Manteo to Murphy, and Daddy doesn't like to leave the farm much anymore.

Nevertheless, there are plenty of us that didn't roll far from the tree and on Wednesday nights, after choir practice or prayer meeting, anybody in the mood for more music shows up at a barbecue house halfway between Cotton Grove and Makely for a late supper and a little picking and singing with the owner, a second cousin once removed who plays a righteous fiddle. Counting spouses and kids, there're never more than fifteen or twenty of us at any one time, but we flat-out raise the roof when we all get going.

I can hold my own with a guitar and since nobody's ever thrown off on my voice, I also sing harmony or lead if we're a voice or two short.

Outside the barbecue house, the November night was cool and damp. Inside, an open fire, the first of the season, was cheerfully burning on a central glass-and-stone hearth. We had finished eating, pushed back the chairs and table to clear a space in front of the hearth, and now we were working on the second verse of "Have a Little Talk with Jesus," which is a staple whenever Herman joins us. He has trouble staying on pitch with most songs, but loves to take his deep bass all the way down to the bottom of the well. Since it looks as if his wheelchair is going to be permanent, the rest of us are happy to indulge him.

He and Annie Sue, his teenage daughter, were bouncing the chorus back and forth between them when the front door of the restaurant opened and my brother Zach held it wide while gusts of chilly November air rushed across the warm room and made the fire blaze up before us.

Zach's the assistant principal at West Colleton High where he also teaches math and science. He knows the physics of heat and cold, yet he stood in the open doorway, letting all our warm air escape into the night.

There were cries of "Shut the door, you fool!" and "Were you raised in a barn?" but Zach just stood there grinning at us till he had our attention good, then all of a sudden, he stepped aside.

And there in the doorway stood another Zach.

It took us maybe ten or twelve seconds before it registered that we really were seeing double.

"Adam?" said Will. "Well, I'll be double-damned!"

Adam and Zach are six and a half, almost seven years older than me. In our family, they're called the "little" twins to distinguish them from Herman and Haywood, the "big" twins, who are actually two inches shorter but almost eleven years older. Herman and Haywood don't look much more alike than Robert or Andrew or Ben, but Adam and Zach are almost identical. We can see their differences, of course, but teachers and casual friends were always getting them mixed up.

As you might gather from their names,

Mother and Daddy thought they were absolutely the end of the family and whenever Adam and Zach griped about the A-to-Z teasing they got at school, Mother would tell them, "Just be grateful I didn't let your daddy name you Alpha and Omega."

It'd been so long since Adam last visited that if it hadn't been for Zach's face keeping us familiar, we might not've recognized him.

There were awkward hugs and handshakes and lots of questions and exclamations: When did he get in? Why didn't he let everybody know he was coming? Had he been home to see Daddy yet? How long was he staying? And where was that good-looking wife of his?

I stayed perched on the edge of a table and watched, so I was probably the only one who saw the cloud pass over Zach's beaming face when Karen was mentioned. There was something different about Adam but I couldn't quite put my finger on what it was.

Adam was always a focused, eyes-on-the-prize kid. Family legend has it that at the age of five, when sent to the field to help pick up sweet potatoes before a sudden, and unexpectedly early, temperature plunge could freeze the exposed yams and turn them to mush, he marched up to Haywood, who was happily loading the heavy crates onto the tractor flatbed, and said, "Have I *got* to be a farmer when I grow up?"

Haywood, with his inarticulate love of plowing and planting, was puzzled. "Well, what else would you want to be?"

"Somebody who doesn't have to burn up in the summertime or freeze his poor little tail off in the winter," Adam said resolutely.

From the moment he saw his first hand-held calculator, he knew that he wanted to work in electronics. Will and Jack still say that the real reason he chose computers was because most electronic research is done in a temperature-controlled environment.

"Beats housing tobacco in July," Adam retorts.

He won all the science medals West Colleton High had to offer, graduated with a 4.0 from NCSU, then landed a teaching fellowship at Stanford. While working on his doctorate, he moonlighted part-time at NorCal Polytronics, which was where he helped design one of NorCal's first patented microchips.

That chip was almost immediately superseded by newer technological breakthroughs, but it got him the doctorate that put him on a fast track at Crystal Micronics International, one of the hottest of the hotshot companies to spring up in Silicon Valley.

Of all my brothers, Adam's the one that's prospered most materially. He's the only one with a Ph.D., and his early fascination with microelectronics has brought him a wealth of fine things — he and Karen have a big sprawling house out near Palo Alto with a pool, a gardener, his-and-her Jaguars in their four-car garage, a boat they keep berthed in a marina over on the San Francisco Bay, and, oh yes, two snotty kids in expensive prep schools who have to be bribed by their mother to come east with her every summer.

So there was a little stiffness after the first spontaneous exclamations. Some of the older boys are resentful that Adam's been home only four or five times in twenty years.

"Got the big head, didn't he?" Andrew or Robert or Herman will say. "Staying out there in California with his fancy job and fancy living?"

Envy's part of it, of course. They can't help feeling jealous that Adam is so much more richly rewarded when they work just as hard. Mostly, though, it's a suspicion that maybe Adam *has* gotten above his raising and turned his back on us.

To cover the awkwardness, Will handed his fiddle over to Adam, picked up his harmonica, and we launched into "Foggy Mountain Breakdown." Adam started out rusty, but by the time we got to the first repeat, he was right there with us. And he barely missed a lick when Will took us on over into "Leather Britches." On "Orange Blossom Special" he had built enough confidence to try some complicated variations as he and Will out-hammed each other on corny locomotive sound effects. We finished the set with a rowdy version of "Roll in My Sweet Baby's Arms."

For a moment, the old solidarity of playing together worked its magic and put us all back on equal footing again. Haywood's callused, work-stained fingers chorded his fiddle strings and maneuvered his bow just as nimbly as Adam's soft, well-kept hands. Herman's deep bass hit every note as true as

Adam's light tenor.

Sitting amid my family, awash in the music we were making together, was like being ten years old again. It was fine — so fine that, even though most of us had to work next day, we didn't break up till nearly midnight.

Out in the parking lot, Haywood helped Herman's son Reese maneuver Herman's wheelchair into the van.

"Won't the fellowshipping *good* tonight?" Haywood said, giving his twin a quick bear hug.

As the rest of us called goodnights to each other across the chilly parking lot, the men drifted over to look at the newest addition to Reese's pickup and one of my female cousins shook her head. "They come out of the womb going *Voodn-voodn-vroom* and they never get over it, do they?"

Reese had moved back home temporarily to lick his wounds after breaking up with his trashy girlfriend (Nadine's term, not mine). Angry and hurt that she'd kicked him out for someone else, Reese was now lavishing all his love and most of his money on a brand-new truck. Big wheels with a fancy diamond tread, bed liner, mud flaps, customized head- and taillights — these were only the beginning. God knows how many new extras were under the hood, and as for the outside? I didn't know they even made that much optional chrome.

"A woman may do you dirt," he told Adam sagely, "but a Ford pickup won't never let you down."

The gospel according to Saint Reese. He was preaching to the choir and it looked like Adam was sitting in the amen corner.

6

The whole expence of taking up such a run of land as I have mentioned, I mean 640 acres for a plantation to a new settler, will not exceed 10 guineas, between patent, surveyor, and the different offices . . .

"Scotus Americanus," *1773*

Next day I learned why Adam had come home just now: Dick Sutterly had made him a hefty offer for the three acres that had been sitting idle since he and Karen moved to California.

Twenty-five years ago, Adam and Zach were seniors in high school when Karen transferred into the junior class.

It was hand-held calculators all over again.

Adam came home from their second date and told Daddy and Mother that he wanted to marry her immediately after graduation. The standard arguments against a youthful marriage were advanced, but they would have had better luck arguing him out of computers.

As usual, Adam had already worked out most of the details beforehand. He would take the money he'd saved for a new car and buy a used mobile home instead. If Daddy would give him a place to put it and if Haywood, who had a backhoe, would help them dig a well and septic tank, he and Karen would live there as frugally as field mice and both would commute to their schools. It would be cheaper than paying room and board in a dorm.

"I'll work out our living expenses in the summers, she'll go to college full-time, and we'll both have our undergrad degrees in four years."

"And what if she has a baby?" Daddy asked.

Adam couldn't help grinning at that question because the younger boys always used to wonder if the reason he'd fathered eleven sons was because 1) he really wanted that many, 2) he wanted a daughter so bad he didn't care how many boys it took, or 3) he simply didn't understand the mechanics of reproduction.

"News flash, Daddy — science has discovered how babies are made."

"You getting smart with me, boy?" Daddy asked gruffly.

But by then, Mother was laughing, too, so Adam knew he'd won.

And because he himself would never have lived on land he didn't hold clear title to, Daddy had deeded Adam a three-acre site on the far edge of his holdings, big enough for a trailer and a good-sized vegetable garden.

Back then, raw farmland was going for about six to eight hundred an acre. Nowadays, such land runs three to six thousand, and a single-acre building lot can bring as much as ten or twelve if it has good road frontage.

Adam's three acres (2.9 acres, to be precise) shared an easement lane with Gray Talbert's nursery. There was barely thirty feet of road frontage and the lot was so awkwardly shaped that you really couldn't put three houses on it and meet county building regulations. So why was Dick Sutterly offering him forty-five thousand dollars? That was way more than it was worth.

* * *

"For that matter," said Seth, "how's a low-end developer like Sutterly pay that kind of money?"

"Lower your voice," said Adam. "I promised him we'd keep this quiet."

It was noon recess and Adam, Seth, and I were in the courthouse basement, in the deed book section of the Register of Deeds office, looking for the plat of Adam's land.

Not counting that first baby boy that was stillborn more than thirty-five years before my birth, Seth is Daddy's seventh son. Daddy still makes his own decisions, but being in his eighties now, he doesn't have the same zest he used to have for snaking out all the details that inform those decisions. Seth is level-headed and intelligent, and his and Minnie's farm is right next door to the homeplace, so more and more these days, Daddy relies on him to look into things like this and bring home the facts.

The last time I'd been down here to check on a deed, the place was as quiet as a library and nearly empty except for genealogists diligently sticking twigs back on their family trees by tracing land divisions from one generation to the next.

Now the room buzzed with muted questions and conversations. Almost all the counter space was taken up by paralegals doing title searches and real estate people looking for greener pastures to develop. Adam wasn't the first to get a tempting offer and Sutterly doesn't have a monopoly on bulldozers. Ever since I-40 opened, we've all had bids for bits and pieces of our land, and we've all said no thank you.

"Why are we even wasting our time here?" I asked, checking the deed book by the number on Adam's deed. "It's not like you're going to sell."

Adam lifted up the big heavy leather-bound book I'd pointed to, carried it over to a counter that had one end clear, and began turning the pages. "Page one-oh-eight, was it?"

I looked at Seth, who shrugged.

"Are you?" I asked in a sharper voice.

Adam gave an impatient twist of his shoulder. "I just want to see what's happening, okay?"

The three of us put our heads together over page 108 and got ourselves oriented.

"Possum Creek," said Seth, pointing to a wavy line that ran from northeast to southwest and is a major boundary between Knott land to the north and the Stancil farm to the south.

A hundred and thirty years ago, everything south of Possum Creek to a dirt road running roughly east to west had belonged to the Pleasant family. Leo Pleasant still owns a big chunk along the road to the west, but when the original holding was broken up, Jap Stancil's grandfather got the eastern part bounded by the creek, Old Forty-Eight and the dirt road. G. Hooks Talbert's great-grandmother got a piece back off the road, along the creek. Another Pleasant son, Merrilee Yadkin Grimes's great-grandfather, also got land along the creek, and I believe it was Merrilee's grandmother who sold it to Daddy sometime in the late forties.

So now, moving west from Old Forty-Eight along the south bank of Possum Creek, the land divisions on this plat were labeled J. Stancil, G. H. Talbert and K. Knott, with L. Pleasant lying south of Daddy. Adam's little piece formed a triangular wedge between Knott and Talbert land on the north,

Stancil to the east and Pleasant to the west.

The Talbert piece has no road frontage and Gray Talbert's nursery would be landlocked were it not for a narrow lane that runs along the western edge of the Stancil farm, right on the line beside Adam. Indeed, when their house trailer was there, Adam and Karen had used the lane as a driveway, too, rather than go to the trouble of putting in their own drive where the southern tip of their triangle touched the road. Jap Stancil still owned the lane back then and didn't mind two more people using it.

By now, the easement has existed for well over fifty years, so even if Mr. Jap or Dallas had wanted to close it, that was no longer their option. As long as Talberts want to use it, the lane has to stay open.

Land squabbles show up in district court so frequently that I know all about easement encroachments and suddenly it began to make sense that Adam was being offered that ridiculous amount.

"G. Hooks Talbert must want to develop this parcel," I said. "I saw surveyor's ribbons all along the creek. But to build houses back there, county regulations require a fifty-foot-wide road and there's only this 'cart' lane, which by definition is thirty feet wide. Your little stretch of road front, Adam, would give him all he needs to meet the requirements."

"That's crazy," Adam objected. "Why wouldn't he just get ol' Jap Stancil — he's still living, isn't he? — to sell him a wider strip?"

"Because Mr. Jap deeded all his land to Dallas years ago," I said. "Didn't Zach tell you about Dallas?"

"Oh, yeah. Shot by his wife, was it?"

"She bought the gun. Her son-in-law's the one that pulled the trigger."

"Poor old Dallas. Lived in a nest of rattlesnakes, didn't he?"

"The trials could drag out for a year or more," I said. "If Cherry Lou is found guilty, Dallas's estate will pass to Mr. Jap, but nothing can be done about establishing ownership till after the trial."

"Dick Sutterly's the one who tried to buy from Dallas," Seth mused. "Wonder if he approached Leo Pleasant, too?"

It didn't take much digging to find the book that recorded Leo Pleasant's deed, but we had to wait till someone from Ed

Whitbread's office finished using it. When we opened it to the right page, we found that it was marked by a slip of paper that held a column of three scribbled numbers that added up to the total acreage of Pleasant, Talbert and Stancil land. Almost as an afterthought, whoever had used that scrap of paper had added a fourth figure to the total: 2.9 — the precise size of Adam's triangle.

There were no subsequent conveyances in the index to indicate that it'd recently changed hands.

"Means nothing," I said. "You don't have to record a deed until you're ready for it to be public record."

"Doesn't matter," Adam said, as he studied the plat carefully. "The Pleasant farm must have a mile of road frontage, but what use is that to Sutterly if he's really bent on developing the Talbert piece? With Stancil land tied up in a murder trial, the only other way to get to it is through mine or Dad's and we all know how *he* feels abut selling."

Something in Adam's voice made me begin to wonder: Just how badly did my successful brother need forty-five thousand dollars?

I couldn't ask him then and there because Nadine and Herman were expecting him for lunch and Seth wanted to get on back to the farm. He keeps a few hogs for the family freezers and one of them was due to farrow that evening.

But when I saw Dick Sutterly heading down the hall toward the Register of Deeds, I called to him.

No reason *he* couldn't tell me what was going on.

"Adam promised me he wouldn't talk about this to anybody," Sutterly said, glancing around as if we were about to exchange plans to blow up the Kremlin.

Late thirties, early forties, Dick Sutterly has light strawberry blond hair, a round face that gets pink when he's excited and a waistline that isn't porky yet, but will be if he keeps riding around in his truck all day. I used to see him out in denims and work boots, with sawdust in his hair. Now he wears a shirt and tie under his windbreaker and split-leather brogans on his feet. No sawdust either.

We were in my chambers, a bare room with a single desk and three chairs. I was lunching on a Pepsi and a pack of Nabs from the vending machines over in the old part of the courthouse. With court due to resume in fifteen minutes, it was all the lunch I had time for.

"If word gets out, it could send land prices right through the roof," Sutterly told me.

Some big secret. As if he's the only one who's noticed the escalation of land prices in Colleton County these past few years.

Dick Sutterly's just an opportunist who happens to be in the right place at the right time. His father was an itinerant carpenter who built a Skilsaw, three nail aprons, and two jackleg helpers into a small construction company that Dick took over when the older man had a heatstroke one summer. From building modest individual houses to order, he began building two or three at a time on speculation.

Those were leveraged into ten- and fifteen-house strip plats, and these became sixty- and eighty-house subdivisions with streets and cul-de-sacs.

"Now I've got the chance for something really big," he said, his cheeks turning pink. "All I need is Adam's little scrap of land and I'm in business."

More than that he wouldn't say.

"Leo Pleasant in on this?" I asked. "G. Hooks Talbert?"

Sutterly's cheeks got pinker and pinker but my lunch break ended before I could break him.

7

Tradesmen, mechanics, and labourers of all sorts, have here an ample range before them: hither then they may repair, and no longer remain in a starving and grovelling condition at home . . .

"Scotus Americanus," *1773*

I was headed home after a mental commitment hearing in Makely late the next morning. Despite fog and rain and dreary gray skies overhead, I was cheered by the seasonal sight of holly berries ripening into bright red amidst shiny wet green leaves. Deciduous trees had finally changed color, too, but even though crepe myrtles and pecans showed skeletal limbs through rapidly thinning orange and yellow leaves, oaks and sweet gums and a lot of the other trees had barely begun to shed good. That, of course, could change overnight if we got a real cold snap.

Growth has been erratic yet steady along New Forty-Eight between Makely and Raleigh. Tucked back behind tall rolling berms that are penetrated here and there by stately brick-and-brass gateposts are the roofs of high-end subdivisions with names like Horse Run Meadows or Dogwood Ridge. More numerous though are the nameless developments, the random results of different people deciding to sell off bits of their land to builders with no overall plan in mind: no berms, no stately entrances, just cheap-to-moderate tract houses, each with its own drive giving directly onto the four-lane highway.

I swear I don't know where all these new people are coming from. Sometimes I wonder how places like Iowa or Ohio or upstate New York still have enough people to make it worthwhile keeping the lights on up there.

Doomed fields, as yet untouched by berm or bulldozer, bristled with real estate signs and surveyors' ribbons. Soybeans had been picked, tobacco and corn stalks had been cut, a few fields were even planted already in their winter crop of oats. Intermixed were stands of unharvested cotton. The plants had been sprayed with a defoliant and the coarse dark leafless stems stood in stiff contrast to the soft white fibers bursting from their bolls. A couple of days of sunshine and the cotton would be dry enough to pick.

In the meantime, November was giving us its usual annual quirks, one day cool and damp, the next day warm. The temperature had climbed back into the high seventies this morning and sent a line of thunderstorms rolling through the area, some of them so violent that I had to pull over once because I couldn't see the front end of my car.

Rain bucketed down on my sunroof and the windshield wipers were about as useful as a broom in a sandstorm. To make it even more harrowing, my lights had continued to dim in the last week and I worried that other cars, groping past me in the blinding downpour, wouldn't see my taillights till it was too late.

When the rain finally slacked off enough to drive on, I realized that I wasn't far from the cutoff to Jimmy

White's garage. Maybe he wouldn't be too busy on a rainy Friday midday to at least tell me whether it was my new battery or something worse.

Two years ago, Jimmy's single-bay garage expanded to three bays and he could probably add on another two if he could find competent mechanics willing to work as hard as he does. I doubt he's really looking though. Having enough time for his church and family seems to be more important to him than money.

Even so, whether he wanted that much extra work or not, the yard was filled with cars and I had to thread the needle to pull mine up to the side door. Warm as it was, the middle bay door was open and I could see cars up on all three lifts, but no sign of Jimmy, his son James or Woodrow, their third mechanic. I splashed across the soggy ground, opened the door and stepped into their lunchtime matinee.

Clamped in the vise on Jimmy's main workbench was a board that extended out like a short shelf. Sitting on the board was a small color television.

James had dragged up a stool, skinny little Woodrow sat cross-legged on the hood of a nearby pickup, Jimmy had swivelled his desk chair around, and two more black men I didn't recognize were sitting on a low bench they'd jury-rigged from a plank and two concrete blocks. All had take-out plates balanced on their knees, and on the floor beside them were drink cups full of iced tea from my cousin's barbecue house over on Forty-Eight. Except for their choice of china and crystal and eccentric seating arrangements, it could have been the Possum Creek Dinner Theater.

Everyone glanced over and nodded when I came in, but clearly I'd interrupted a climactic moment.

I stepped around to see what was so interesting. Another celebrity trial? Basketball previews? Highlights from the final car race of the season?

On the television, two impossibly gorgeous (and obviously naked) daytime actors were writhing together beneath tangled pink satin sheets. Talk about climactic moments — they were going at it so hot and heavy with hands and mouths and little animal noises that it's a wonder the screen didn't fog up.

So this was why I always got the answering machine if I called these men at lunchtime. Soap opera?

Jimmy tore his eyes from *The Young and the Restless* and started to put down his plate.

"Sorry," I said, "but I'm afraid something's wrong with that battery you put in last month."

"You finish eating, Jimmy," said a voice behind me. "I'll check it out for her."

I turned and there was Allen Stancil.

"Hey, thanks," said Jimmy, sinking back into his chair, his attention already focused on the TV again. "Battery tester's over there on that Mercury."

Reluctantly, I followed Allen back outside. The sky had lightened momentarily, but more thunderheads were roiling up in the west.

I popped the hood and started the engine and Allen did his thing with the battery tester. After a few minutes, he hollered for me to shut it off and he began pulling on various belts.

"Try it again."

Again, I started the engine, gave it more gas when he told me to mash down, turned my lights off and on, then switched off as he eventually closed the hood and came around to my side of the car.

"Nothing wrong with your battery or your belts, far as I can tell," he said, "but it's not charging right. Looks to me like your alternator's going to the bad. You don't get a new one pretty soon, it's gonna leave you on the side of the road somewhere."

Back inside, the soap opera had ended and the guys were clearing away. James stowed the television and its board under the desk while Woodrow and the others pushed the cinder blocks and stool out of the middle of the floor.

Allen told Jimmy his diagnosis and Jimmy shook his head and gestured to all the cars ahead of me.

"I'm sorry, Deb'rah. You know I'd do it in a minute if I could, but I'd have to send James to town for the part and the way we're so backed up — there's no way in the world we'n get to it before Monday or Tuesday. And even then . . ."

His voice trailed off into uncertainty.

"I don't mean to be butting in," said Allen, butting in. "But she sure needs to get it changed and I'm not doing much right now."

"Would you?" Relief brightened Jimmy's face. He really does hate to make me wait. "That'd be great. Y'all do know each other, don't you, Deb'rah? Dallas's cousin? Staying over yonder with Mr. Jap? He knows as much about cars as me."

Allen smiled broadly beneath his mustache. "More."

"Naw, now, I didn say that!" Jimmy laughed. "But he'll do you right."

Which was how I found myself riding over to Cotton Grove with Allen to buy a new alternator.

We left my car parked in front of the garage at Mr. Jap's place and drove to the auto parts store in Allen's old Chevy pickup. I had to slide in under the steering wheel since the door on the passenger side was held shut with a C-clamp.

"Keep forgetting to get that damn latch fixed," Allen said with a trace of embarrassment.

Didn't bother me. With him driving, I could look him over good rather than the other way around.

He'd held up rather well, all things considered. His brown hair was still thick and bushy, his belly was flat, and he didn't seem to have any teeth missing.

"When'd you grow the mustache?" I

asked, as we crossed Possum Creek and headed north toward town.

"You don't like it, darlin', I'll shave it off tomorrow morning." His voice was warm and insinuating, but there was no way I was going to step in that creek twice.

"I don't give a damn whether it stays or goes, Allen. I was just making polite conversation."

"Well, I'n talk polite, too. How come you never got married again?"

"Once was enough, thank you."

"What about that game warden? Y'all serious?"

"Oh, I always take game wardens serious," I said. "What about you? How many times you been married since me?"

"Might've put my mark on one or two." With one of those Ain't-I-a-pistol? smiles, he flashed me the black star tattooed in the palm of his left hand. "You were the last one with a preacher, though."

"Except it was a magistrate," I reminded him sharply. "Any kids?"

"They proved one on me, but that's all."

I knew that Allen had been married before I met him and I seemed to recall mention of a son. "You mean Kevin — was that his name?"

"Keith. Naw, he's grown now. Lives up in Richmond. I'm still paying for a girl that —"

He broke off so abruptly that my curiosity was piqued.

"A daughter? How old is she?"

He hesitated. "Seventeen. I got just one more year to pay on her. Wendy Nicole."

"Seventeen?"

I'm not all that good at mental math, but it doesn't take an Einstein to realize that his daughter couldn't have been in this world very long at the time we'd run off to Martinsville together. I said as much and added, "Back then, didn't you say you'd been divorced four or five years?"

"That was from Keith's mama. Sally come after her."

Rain had begun falling again and the wind was whipping wet leaves across the pavement. The pickup might be old, one door might be a different color and the other hanging on by a C-clamp, but the wipers swept the windshield cleanly and the engine purred like a happy kitten. Those two boded well for my new alternator.

"So how long had you been divorced from this Sally?"

Another hesitation. "Well, now, darlin', I don't want you to get all fussed over something that's long done and finished with."

"I'm not your 'darlin,' Allen. How long done and finished was it?"

"Actually, we only got it finalized about four years ago when Katie came up pregnant."

I sat bolt upright. "Wait just a damn minute here! You saying you were still married to this Sally when you married me?" My hand slammed down hard on the dashboard. "You committed *bigamy?*"

"See? I knew you were going to get upset."

"Upset?"

"Well, what was I supposed to do? You were the one so hot to get married that —"

This time it was my fist hit the dash and he gave me an apprehensive look.

"You ain't got a knife in that handbag, have you?"

"If I did, I'd cut your lying tongue right out of your head," I snarled. "My daddy paid you five thousand dollars not to contest the annulment and to keep your mouth shut about it and it wasn't even a legal marriage?"

"You ain't gonna tell him, are you?" Allen asked as he pulled in at the auto parts place. "I'd sure hate for you to get him mad at me all over again."

I was so outraged that I jerked at the door handle a couple of times before I remembered that it was broken. Meekly, Allen got out on his side and held the door for me, but he made sure he stayed well out of my swinging range as I stomped into the store ahead of him.

"How 'bout I don't charge you nothing for fixing your car?" he called after me.

The trouble with small-pond life is that it's awfully hard to go anywhere without bumping into a relative. When I stalked into the store, my nephew Reese was there at the counter talking to the clerk about the merits of different floor mats.

"With winter coming on, I got to do something to keep the mud off my carpet," he said with an inquiring look at Allen.

I swallowed my anger and introduced the two of them after Allen had told the clerk what we wanted. While the clerk went off to find an alternator that would fit my engine, they talked carpet cleaners and the care and feeding of vinyl interiors.

By the time the clerk came back and I'd handed over my credit card, Allen had convinced Reese he was the one to help him install his new stereo speakers in the door panels.

"You might want to see how he fixes his own doors before you turn him loose on yours," I said nastily.

Allen just smiled. "Everybody knows the shoemaker's children always go barefoot."

When we were in the truck again and heading back to Mr. Jap's, Allen looked over at me warily and said, "You ain't gonna stay mad at me, are you, darlin'?"

I knew my outraged feelings didn't really concern him. He was only worried what Daddy or some of the boys might do if I told them. Well, he could just keep on worrying.

"So who's Katie?" I asked.

"Nobody special. Just a gal I stayed with for a coupla weeks one time when Sally threw me out."

"And she had your child?"

"Won't mine. I tell you what's the truth — between paying for Keith and paying for Wendy Nicole, I quit taking my pecker out of my britches without putting on his raincoat. No way that baby was mine. She took me to court, but I got a blood test and it proved that little girl was somebody else's."

"Lucky you," I said, remembering the relief of Portland Brewer's client when the blood test let him off the hook.

"Won't luck, darlin'. It was science. You know how much I'd've had to pay if they'd proved it on me?"

"Depends on what you're making. In your case, probably a hundred dollars a week?"

"I keep forgetting you're a judge. You know all about laying child support on a man, don't you? Busting his balls?"

"Takes two to make a baby."

"So how come it's always one that has to pay?"

"Sometimes it's the mother," I said.

He snorted disdainfully. "Not very often, I bet."

"No," I agreed. "Most times it's the father that takes off."

"Hey, I paid for Keith. And I'm paying for Wendy Nicole, too. But damn if I was gonna let 'em lay a court order on me for another eighteen years just because Katie can't keep up with who she's sleeping with."

Which sounded an awful lot as if he was under a court order for ol' Wendy Nicole.

"Not behind on your payments, are you?" I needled, wondering if that had anything to do with why he was hanging around over here instead of heading back to Charlotte.

"Sally knows I'm doing the best I can. I send her money ever chance I get. Hell, I even send Katie something when I have a little extra. Poor girl never did figure out who's Tiffany's daddy."

Allen might not've fathered her child, but I was willing to bet even money that he'd left that Katie with a tiny black star on her left shoulder. And Sally, too. I knew Keith's mother had one and God knows how many women before or since. I was just young enough and dumb enough to be flattered when Allen hauled me into a tattoo shop and had the guy do me.

When we walked down the street together, my right thumb was always hooked in the back pocket of his jeans just as his left hand always rested on my left shoulder. At eighteen, that tattoo had seemed so romantic, as if the heat from his hand had magically burned through to my flesh and marked me as his woman forever.

Hard to believe I'd been so stupid. What on earth made me pick such a bad-news womanizer to go to hell with?

I was still getting used to the idea that my one fling at marriage hadn't been a marriage at all and wasn't quite sure whether this was something that would help me or hurt me if the whole shabby mess ever came out in public. One thing was certain though: the sooner Allen Stancil got out of Colleton County, the sooner I'd breathe easy again.

I decided maybe I'd give Charlotte a buzz and see if his ex-wife Sally really was as understanding about those erratic support payments as he made out. If I was lucky, maybe there'd be a nice little warrant out for his sorry hide.

8

. . . the very first year the purchaser made 11 hogsheads of brandy of the peaches and apples in his garden and some cyder . . .

"Scotus Americanus," *1773*

Annoyed as I was with Allen, though, I had to admit he was handy with a wrench.

While he wrestled my faulty alternator out of the engine and installed the new one, I stood at the front of the shabby cinderblock garage and talked with Mr. Jap, who'd come over from the house when he saw that Allen's truck was back.

I noticed that someone had painted over the purple cross on his front door and I guessed that the "Holyness Prayr Room" was out of business.

"Yeah," said Mr. Jap with a sheepish smile on his grizzled face. "Religion never does take on me, it don't. I just can't seem to stay right with the Lord. And anyway, them Mexicans has gone back to Florida, they did."

The rain began again as he came in, and the old man pulled a slat-backed chair over to the open doorway so he could sit and watch it fall. There was no wind. The heavy drops came straight down, hammered the tin roof, then sheeted off the edge of the front shed like a waterfall. Inside, cigarette smoke mingled with the smell of steel tools and machine oil and gasoline fumes — masculine smells I would always associate with my father and brothers as they endlessly tinkered on cars and tractors, tobacco harvesters and bean pickers, mowers and hayrakes.

Something's always breaking down on a farm and men are always cussing and putting it back together with duct tape and baling wire and a squirt of WD-40.

But Mr. Jap wore a contented smile as he settled deeper into the chair and watched the rain come down. Every once in a while Allen would drop a wrench or mutter and Mr. Jap would look even happier.

"Just like the old days," he said, "when Dallas or some of your brothers would come over and work on their cars. Sometimes I couldn't find a wrench for my own work because they was using them all, they was. Good as he was at driving, Dallas didn't have much feel for a engine. Your brother Frank, now —"

He cocked his head at me. "Where'd Kezzie tell me Frank is these days?"

"Southern California. San Diego."

Frank's my next to oldest brother. He spent twenty-six years in the Navy as a machinist and retired as a master chief petty officer. He and Mae come for a long visit every other year and they talk about how nice it'd be to live closer, but she's from California and their kids have married and started families of their own out there, so we don't really expect them to move back.

"That Frank, he could do anything with a motor that needed doing, he could. Many a time he'd just listen to it running and hear what was wrong before he ever lifted the hood."

He cut me a sly look. "Good at making things, too, he was. When he weren't but twelve, he made the prettiest little copper worm you ever saw. Not a kink nowhere."

A worm, of course, is the coil that runs from the cap of a still through a barrel of cool water and acts as a condenser. Some of those homemade copper stills are works of folk art and the worm is the hardest part to shape because copper tubing is so soft it'll crimp and collapse when you start to bend it. A lot of operators won't bring their coil out to the still until they're ready to start running a batch.

And even though destruction is their job, few ATF officers are so hardhearted that they can bust up a pretty copper cooker without a niggling regret when they smash the worm.

Or so they tell me.

They do the telling with sidelong glances if they know my daddy's reputation and I'm never sure whether they really do feel that way or if they think they're making Brownie points with me.

"Some of both, probably," Dwight said when I once asked him about it. A deputy sheriff hears a lot of scuttlebutt. "They're the hounds. Mr. Kezzie was a fox. A hound won't have much fun if there's no fox to chase, now will it?"

Trouble is, I'm not comfortable asking Daddy about those days and he never volunteers. I know the older boys talk about it amongst themselves once in a while, but it's almost like they're the Masons and Adam and Zach and I have never quite learned the secret handshake. Most of what I've heard about making illegal whiskey comes from ATF officers, SBI agents and occasional old-timers like Mr. Jap.

"So how'd Frank make the worm?" I asked Mr. Jap.

The old man laid his finger alongside his nose. "Don't know as I ought to be telling a judge, no I don't."

I smiled. "The statute of limitations ran out on Frank a long time ago."

"Well, I'll tell you then," he said happily. "He set right over there on that workbench with a piece of copper tubing and we saw him studying and studying on it, me and old Max Pleasant, Leo Pleasant's daddy, we did. Max says, 'What you making, young fellow?' and Frank told him."

"He did?" That surprised me. Whenever I do get my brothers to reminisce a little about those early years, they always say that they knew to be close-mouthed about whiskey making. Mr. Jap would have been safe since he'd operated a still on contract to my daddy, but Max Pleasant?

"Oh, yeah. You think because Leo's so set against that new ABC store they're building out here in the country that nobody in his family ever messed with making it? Leo's daddy took Kezzie's money same as a lot of us, yes he did. And so did Leo's mammy when Max got caught and sent away for two years. No need for Leo to act so prissy pants. Whiskey paid the taxes on his farm many a year back in the thirties and forties, yes it did."

A deep cough rattled Mr. Jap's thin chest as he lit a cigarette and took a long drag.

"Anyway, Max asked young Frank if he needed some help. 'No, sir,' says Frank, all polite. 'I reckon I can figure it out myself.' And danged if he didn't. Oh, he messed up a couple of inches when he tried to bend it around a big iron pipe after he got it soft with my blowtorch. But he just set there and studied some more and finally we seen the light bulb go off in his little head. He went out yonder to the edge of the field, he did, and got him some sand, wet it down good and rammed it in the tubing till it was packed solid. Then he hit it with the blowtorch again and that tubing near 'bout wrapped around the pipe all by itself with not a dimple in it. After that, he flushed the sand out and it was perfect. I used it for eight years, I did, before the liquor agents found it."

Since he seemed in a telling mood, I asked, "How'd you learn to make whiskey?"

"Your own daddy showed me. Didn't he never tell you about that? He used to help his daddy and after Mr. Robert died, he got me to help him, he did. He was real particular about how we made it, too, he was — clean, pure water and we never doctored it up with lye or wood alcohol. That's how come he always got top dollar for his jars. Nobody never went blind nor even got sick neither, drinking Kezzie Knott's whiskey, no they didn't."

"You ever get caught?" I asked.

"Naw." There was pride in his voice. "I never made it all that much after we growed up. Oh, I'd run me off maybe twenty or thirty gallons when Elsie needed more cash money than I could lay my hands on, but mostly I helped Kezzie with the distribution. He give me a flat wage, he did, to keep everybody's cars and trucks running. Dallas used to make him a little spending money when your daddy was short of drivers. Allen, too, if he was staying with us."

I knew some of the broad outlines of Daddy's illegal operations. My grandfather had been a poor farmer with a houseful of children and when corn dried up in a drought year or boll weevils got all the cotton, he'd run a little white whiskey for enough cash money to put shoes on their feet and clothes on their backs and maybe pay taxes on his forty-three acres of land.

There's always been a conflict between the makers of morality and the makers of whiskey, and an ABC store is still the only place you can buy hard liquor in the state. (As the saying goes, "North Carolinians will vote dry as long as they can stagger to the polls.") But there's also been a mutual dependence. The evils of alcohol are well documented and make for fiery sermons, yet the higher the sin tax, the more profitable the shot houses, those unlicensed back-country dwellings where you can buy a shot of untaxed liquor day or night and on Sunday morning, too, if the proprietor knows you. In many communities, the biggest bootlegger is also the biggest contributor to local fund-raisers, the first to reach into his pocket when a poor family suffers tragedy, the one who'll hold a note two or three times longer than any bank. A lot of people may know who's running whiskey in their community, yet they keep their mouths shut. Not out of fear, but out of gratitude for the personal help the bootlegger may have given to their families in times of stress.

When you throw in the basic anarchist nature of old-time independent farmers, it's a wonder there's not a still behind every tree in North Carolina, stills operated by conflicted, God-fearing farmers who can't see much difference between making whiskey and growing tobacco. What's all that bad, they'll ask, about sending corn to market in a jar instead of on the cob? And one or two have even been heard to wonder out loud how come the government supports tobacco, yet outlaws marijuana?

My grandfather was killed when

Daddy was still a boy. The revenuers couldn't catch his souped-up Model T, so they shot out his tires and he crashed into Possum Creek and drowned before they could get to him. Nowadays there'd be a lawsuit for wrongful death; back then it was good riddance to bad trash as far as the revenuers were concerned.

Although he hadn't even started shaving yet, Daddy took over as head of the household and whenever times were tough, he'd amble off down to the swampy part of the creek and use his father's recipe to cook up the mash. With the scrimping and saving of his first wife, he accumulated enough cash to bankroll a little country store at Pleasant's Crossroads and after that he had a loyal supplier of sugar and Mason jars. By the time he married my mother, he had put a couple of layers of insulation between himself and the production end and was directing a distribution network that some people say reached from Canada to Mexico.

That network supposedly included some of the biggest names in early stock car racing, men who bought and then juiced up their first cars with the cash they got hauling moonshine out of Colleton County. Indeed, the sport got its start in North Carolina with young daredevils who outran law officers on moonlit nights and got together on weekends along deserted dirt roads or out in isolated pastures to see whose car could go fastest. Lee Petty always downplayed or flat-out denied any whiskey connection, but Junior Johnson, Curtis Turner, Little Joe Weatherly, Wendell Scott, Buddy Arrington?

When they hit a roadblock, every one of them knew how to execute a "bootleg turn" — that quick reverse and one-eighty dig-off that throws dirt in the lawman's eyes and has you flying back down the road like it's the devil's racetrack. Before the law can get a good look at your license plate, you're going, going, gone, and all he sees are taillights fading in his rearview mirror.

Today, the Highway Patrol calls it a three-point turn and they teach a sedate version in Driver's Ed, but everybody out here knows who invented it.

And why.

"Did you know Daddy was a bootlegger when you married him?" I asked my mother that summer she was dying.

She nodded. "But like every woman

since Eve, I thought I could change him. He didn't need the money anymore. The store was doing well, he had land and sons to help him farm it and tobacco was booming. He swore he'd quit if I'd marry him. And he did quit."

Mother's smile was rueful as she reached for the old battered Zippo lighter that was always near to hand. Even though she seldom lit a cigarette anymore, she liked to hold it in her thin hands, run her fingers over the worn insignia engraved on the front, then flip open the cover and make the little flame blaze up inside the wind guard. "It's like the way I quit smoking a dozen times or more. Quitting's easy. Staying quit's a different matter. Right now it's been almost eight years for him."

She shook her head. "Or maybe I'd better say I *think* it's been eight years since he's messed with it. He could have started up again yesterday or he could start tomorrow. Whiskey's the only thing your daddy's ever lied to me about. At least, it's the only lie I ever caught him in."

And then she did laugh, a rich warm chuckle that sounded almost like her old self.

Laughter balanced so tightly on the edge of tears that summer and her voice was tremulous as she touched my face. "Oh Deborah, honey, try to marry a man you can laugh with, okay?"

"Okay," I promised, unable to keep my own voice from wobbling.

She smoothed my hair away from my eyes and said, "You reckon you've met him yet?"

"Come give 'er a try now," said the man I'd married before my mother was two months in her grave.

I went over and got inside my car and cranked it up.

Almost immediately, Allen declared the operation a success. "Your battery's charging good as new now, darlin', but your oil looks a little dirty. Better let me change it for you, long as you're here."

He didn't really wait for my consent, just started jacking up the front end so that he could squeeze underneath while lying flat on one of those rollerboard creepers.

If Mr. Jap hadn't been sitting there with a hopeful look on his face, I'd have paid Allen and left. Instead, as Allen disappeared underneath the front of my car carrying an oil pan, I went back over to the open doorway and leaned against the jamb. There was really nowhere I needed to be this afternoon and Mr. Jap clearly wanted to talk. I kept thinking of Daddy with eleven living sons and Mr. Jap's one son buried over at Sweetwater Baptist with Allen Stancil the only blood kin left to him.

Whatever Allen wanted here — money or a temporary place to hole up — I was pretty sure that when he got it, he'd be long gone and Mr. Jap would be alone again except for Merrilee and her dutiful Sunday morning check on him.

"Some folks don't even have that much," my internal preacher reminded me.

I stared out into the rain while Mr. Jap talked happily about his plans for the garage. As soon as Billy Wall paid him what was owed, he was going to get that hydraulic lift fixed and buy a bigger air compressor so that they could run an air chisel *and* a sandblaster, start blasting the rust off some of those old cars. Why, there was a doctor over in Widdington been after him for over a year for that old Stingray.

"Offered me nine hundred dollars just

as she stands, he did."

And Allen knew a dealer out in Charlotte that'd write him out a check tomorrow for ten thousand dollars if he'd give the word and let the man haul 'em out, but he and Allen were going to do the restoring themselves and make a bundle.

Allen had turned into a car-fixing genius, to hear Mr. Jap tell it. He'd bought a badly wrecked car from some guy on the other side of Raleigh and almost overnight he'd fixed it up good enough to sell.

"And that's just with my old tools, it was. Think what he'll do when we get us a new acetylene torch and a paint sprayer and maybe some of them newfangled electronic testers."

He lit another cigarette. "I know a lady over in Cotton Grove as can reupholster seats and make new head linings, she can. Real good and real cheap. Yes, ma'am! Give us another five or six years and we'll be *the* place to come for restoring old cars, yes we will."

The way he talked about stretching that corn money, he sounded like a fat man who expected to button a thirty-eight-inch waistband around a forty-two-inch beer belly. Of course, he could also be counting what he might eventually receive from Dallas's estate.

"I guess you'll be glad when the trial's over and everything's settled," I said.

Mr. Jap's lips tightened. "I don't see why it has to take 'em so long. The DA says it'll probably be June and then if she's found guilty" — he almost spit the word *she* — "he says she'll probably appeal and it could drag out for years. Well, let her, say I. In the end, she'll burn in hell, she will, for a thousand thousand years. Ain't no way she can appeal that!"

He leaned his head toward me and spoke confidentially of how John Claude Lee was handling things. "Dallas didn't have no will, so Mr. Lee says I'll get at least half of everything anyhow, but he's sharp, he is. Got her believing that if she signs the land over to me, it'll make the jury think she didn't want Dallas dead for the money. Maybe let her get off with manslaughter instead of murder."

The rain was coming down even heavier now. It thundered on the tin roof, cascaded off the eaves and flooded the rutted drive. I'd have been more concerned if I didn't know that twenty minutes after it stopped, the rain would soak right on through this sandy soil. Creeks may flood out of their banks after hard rains, but puddles don't stand for very long around here.

"Will it bother you if she gets off easy?" I asked.

"Ain't no jury that dumb," he said with conviction, "and I'll finally get my land back, I will, and then I can sell —"

He broke off with a guilty air.

"You're thinking of selling it?"

"Just a little bit, but I promised I wouldn't say nothing about it right now and you got to promise me you won't say nothing to nobody neither, 'specially not to Kezzie, you won't."

It was one thing for Dick Sutterly to be maneuvering to develop G. Hooks Talbert's relatively small acreage, if that's indeed what he had in mind. But Mr. Jap's was much bigger and alarm bells clanged in my head at the very thought.

"I'm sorry, Mr. Jap, but if you're planning to sell some land between you and Adam so Dick Sutterly can get at G. Hooks Talbert's land, don't you think my daddy has a right to know about it?"

"That ain't what I'm selling," he said hotly, "and even if it was, it ain't nobody's business but mine, no it ain't."

9

Vegetation is amazingly quick in this province; the soil, in general, will produce most things; the climate has something so kindly, that the soil, when left to itself, throws out an immense quantity of flowers and flowering shrubs.

"Scotus Americanus," *1773*

I'd planned to sleep in next morning, but the telephone beside my bed woke me at first light and it was Haywood's wife Isabel in my ear explaining why they hadn't driven over to Kinston yesterday to catch that chartered plane to Atlantic City as they'd planned.

"You know we always go on a Friday so we don't have to miss church, but the cows got out yesterday and by the time we got them back in, it was too late, so

Haywood and Anthony, they're going to walk all the fences today instead."

I listened groggily, wondering what cows and missing their gambling weekend had to do with me. The whole idea of Haywood — *Haywood,* for Pete's sake! — sitting in a casino in Atlantic City blows my mind whenever I try to picture it. For starters, he's just over six feet and weighs just under three hundred. He's most comfortable in his size 14EEE brogans, denim overalls, and an old felt porkpie hat, out on the tractors with Anthony, his black tenant. And he's usually pretty frugal with a dime.

But somehow he and Isabel got talked into trying a "free" weekend in Atlantic City a few years back and they loved it so much that every two or three months, they'll join a bunch of similar-minded folks from eastern Carolina and head for the flashing neon lights. The flight, overnight accommodations, meals and floor show are all complimentary — glamorous bait for the gullible. Sometimes the promoters sweeten the pot even further with a couple of rolls of quarters.

But unless their free charter flights are bringing in bigger gamblers than Haywood, I can't see that they're getting much return on their investment.

He gets a big kick out of playing the slot machines, pushing his quarters in, pulling the handle, and watching all the lights and symbols flicker and dance. He paces himself though and he knows to the quarter exactly how much he and Isabel can lose, usually two or three hundred dollars. Once their modest stash is gone, he quits. He figures it's worth a few hundred to get off the farm for twenty-four hours, walk on the boardwalk, enjoy the food and the entertainment. "Don't cost no more'n a weekend down at some fish camp in Salter Path," he says, "and it shore is a purty sound when all them quarters come spilling down."

Isabel doesn't care much for gambling. She plays the slots till her three or four rolls of quarters are gone, then she walks around the casino and enjoys the glitter. She people watches or holds a friend's place at a hot machine while they go to the bathroom or grab a bite to eat; and when her feet start hurting, she goes upstairs to their room, orders room service, then either watches television or naps till Haywood comes up to take her down to dinner — "Prime ribs with au jus," Haywood tells me, patting his ample waistline with remembered pleasure — and the floor show.

Some of my churchier brothers and sisters-in-law think this is all vaguely sinful, but Haywood just shrugs. "Sin is in the eye of the belittler," he says. "We gamble on the weather, we gamble on tobacco prices and the price of beef. Don't you reckon it's all mute to God?"

So I yawned and listened to Isabel's tale of those dratted cows and eventually she worked her way around to why she was calling.

"They're having a special two-night promotion because Thanksgiving's such a slow day. They're even going to give everybody fifty dollars playing money, so I was talking to Nadine and Minnie and they say it doesn't matter to them whether we get together Thanksgiving Day itself or next Saturday since Adam's planning to leave Wednesday and won't be here anyway. And Mr. Kezzie never cares if it's Thanksgiving or not, so if it's all right with you, it's all right with everybody else 'cause Amy and Will were supposed to go to her mother's on Thursday and this way, they can —"

"It's fine, Isabel," I assured her. "Whatever y'all want to do. Just tell me what to bring and where to bring it."

"Well, why don't you bring the paper plates and napkins? Nadine says she has plenty of plastic cups if we don't mind blue. Not very Thanksgiving-y, but they'll drink the same. And Minnie and me, we thought we'd have it at the home-place. We can set up sawhorse tables in the potato house and bring in some heaters if it turns off cold. It's good for the grandchildren to get together there, don't you think? Before they all get grown and scattered and Mr. Kezzie gets too old or something?"

A pang went through me at that "or something" that none of us ever want to name.

"Stevie'll still be off from school that weekend and Valerie and her family can come, too," said Isabel. "I don't know about Robert's children, but Doris said she'd ask them."

"Daddy doesn't like to give Maidie a lot of extra work on the weekend," I warned.

"She won't have to do a thing. We'll be bringing all the food and the boys'll set up the tables and bring down chairs. No dishes to wash."

I told her it sounded good to me, that

I'd try to find some plates and napkins to match Nadine's blue cups, and that if I didn't see her before then, for them to have a happy Thanksgiving in Atlantic City. Then I turned over and tried to get back to sleep, but it was no use. I was wide awake now and even with the windows open, the room was too warm for comfort.

I slipped on a light robe and stepped out on the second-story brick veranda that runs the length of the house. The rain had stopped around midnight but nothing had dried off. The bricks were still slick with water and Hambone's paws almost skidded out from under him as he came bounding up the steps to greet me with his coat damp from dew and fog. The morning air was so heavy and humid, I felt I could almost squeeze it like a sponge.

Downstairs, I poured myself a glass of juice and watched live shots of falling snow on Aunt Zell's kitchen television. Colorado had already had a blizzard or two this year and now a strip of the country from the Blue Ridge right up through northern New York was getting snow today. According to the weatherman, though, Colleton County, along with the rest of eastern North Carolina, was going to remain under the influence of this humid offshore southern breeze.

"Such unhealthy feeling weather," said Aunt Zell, as she does every November when the shorter days make us think of winter but the warm humidity of Indian summer hangs on and on.

The table held half a dozen small crystal bowls of pansies that she'd just picked from a border that lines the brick patio out back. She handed me one for my sitting room and clustered three more on the window ledge over the sink where they would catch the sun if it ever broke through the morning fog. The rest would be placed around the house for the weekend.

I sat down at the table and Hambone jumped up in my lap. Though not yet fully grown, the young beagle was almost too big to hold anymore. He laid his head on the edge of the table and stared soulfully at Aunt Zell.

"A friend told me that the French call November *le mois du mort,*" I said, scratching the dog's soft ears.

"Maybe things die back in France," she said wistfully. "Here, they all seem to be catching their second breath. I saw a gardenia bud on that bush in the back corner. My spirea's starting to bloom again and the hydrangea leaves are just as green as they were in August. Camellias are going to be blooming before the pecans finish dropping. And that reminds me."

She crushed the stem tips of yellow, pink, scarlet, and white roses and arranged the mixed bouquet in a silver vase. "If you're going out to the farm today, Kezzie said he'd send me a quart of pecans he's picked out if I wanted to start on my fruitcakes."

I'm probably one of only fifty people in the whole country who really like fruitcakes, especially Aunt Zell's. Daddy's one of the other forty-nine. Much as I wanted her to get started, too, I had plans for the weekend and they did not include a trip out to the farm. We were going to head over to Durham and do town things for a change.

"Sorry" I said, "but Kidd and I are —"

At that precise instant, the phone rang. Aunt Zell answered, smiled at me, and said, "Yes, she's right here. We were just fixing to start talking about you."

I made a face and pushed Hambone off my lap. Kidd knows I like to sleep in on

Saturday morning and he would have dialed my private number upstairs before trying Aunt Zell's. The only reason he'd be tracking me down this early was to say he was going to be late, right?

Wrong.

"I'm really sorry, Deborah, but you remember what it's like to be fourteen, don't you?"

If he hadn't sounded so torn between duty and desire, I might've told him that I certainly did remember. That, yes, fourteen's about the time when a girl figures out how to blend guilt and charm to get what she wants. And that what Amber Chapin wants is no other female in Kidd's life.

Instead, speaking as graciously as I could between clenched teeth, I assured him that I could survive the weekend without him if his daughter needed his companionship more. "It's okay. Honest."

As I hung up, Aunt Zell and Hambone both gave me an inquiring look.

"So, Hambone," I said. "How would you like to go for a ride in the country?"

His stubby little tail wagged furiously.

Nice that one of us was happy.

10

The cause, then, that could induce a people of this cast, to forsake their native lands . . . and make them seek for habitations in countries far distant and unknown, must, doubtless, be very cogent and powerful.

"Scotus Americanus," *1773*

By the time I finished running errands around Dobbs, it was after lunch before I got out to the farm.

Adam's rental car was parked out back, but Daddy's ancient red Chevy pickup was nowhere in sight. Neither of them was in the house either, so Hambone and I walked on down the lane to Maidie and Cletus's little house.

"Adam's out somewhere with the dogs and Mr. Kezzie went off this morning to get a haircut," said Maidie, who was gathering dried marigold seeds from her dooryard flower garden. "I expect he'll be back any time now."

She tried to get me to sit on her porch swing and wait for Daddy, but Hambone was going crazy with all the smells and sights, and I decided to see if we could find Adam.

"Well, he might be burning some brush over by the creek," said Maidie. "Seems like I smelled smoke coming from that way. Don't know who else it'd be less'n that Gray Talbert's burning off his weeds again."

She chuckled at her own joke and her gold tooth flashed in the weak sunshine that was trying to break through the gray clouds.

Maidie came to the farm as a teenager to help Mother when I was just a child. It was supposed to be a temporary thing till the woman we called Aunt Essie came back from attending the birth of her first grandchild up in Philadelphia. But a loving-natured Aunt Essie met a widowed Philadelphia policeman with two motherless teenage girls and Maidie met Cletus Holt, one of Daddy's best tenants, and both of them decided they'd landed in greener pastures.

Even though IRS irregularities were what had sent Daddy to prison before I was born, his farm workers preferred cash under the table and no Social Security deductions. Mother wouldn't play those games with the people she hired, and she was always meticulous about paying into Social Security and a pension plan, too, for Maidie and Cletus. Maidie made him keep it up after Mother died.

I suppose if I were more politically correct, I'd bemoan this surviving remnant of old-time mutual dependence — white landowner, black domestic. Instead, I was grateful for the continuity.

"Where's that good-looking man of yours?" Maidie asked me now. "Not run off with some pretty young thing, has he?"

"As a matter of fact, he has," I said ruefully.

Instantly, her teasing smile faded into concern, but before she could offer me sympathy and start heaping scorn on Kidd, I quickly explained that the pretty young thing in question was his daughter. Maidie wasn't completely mollified.

"She's living right there in New Bern, ain't she? How come they can't see enough of each other through the week?"

I shrugged. "I don't know. Maybe it's her birthday or something."

Maidie gave me a shrewd look. "Onliest child your boyfriend's got and you don't know when her birthday is? 'Pears to me you don't like her much, do you, honey?"

"She's the one doesn't like *me*," I protested.

"Which one of you's the grown-up?" Maidie said, as she went back to gathering flower seeds.

I may have a law degree and I may be a judge, but seems like I never win an argument with her.

It was a good half-mile to where Maidie thought Adam was and when I got there, I saw a smoldering bed of embers, all that remained of a pile of brush. There were dog tracks and the imprints of a boot that could be Adam's, but no other immediate sign of him.

I whistled and Blue and Ladybelle came loping up the cut that leads down to the homemade bridge across Possum Creek. Hambone gave one sharp excited bark when he saw them, then hurried over to me for protection, knowing he was the interloper in their territory.

The two older dogs approached in measured dignity. I assured Hambone that they were friendly and he took me at my word, frisking around the taller dogs, inviting them to romp. Ladybelle was too polite to raise her eyebrows at Blue, and both of them patiently endured the youngster's enthusiasm, but their manner clearly questioned my judgment in requiring them to put up with such an unruly visitor without a nip to teach him some manners.

The four of us walked to the head of the cut. Across the bridge, at the opening into the far field, I saw Adam and another man standing beside a white pickup. At first I thought it was Reese, but as the dogs and I started across the bridge, the second man got into the truck. When he slammed the door and drove away, I saw a familiar logo on the door: Sutterly Homes.

"Was that Dick Sutterly?" I asked curiously as Adam met us halfway across the bridge. "Why'd he take off like that?"

"We were finished talking for now," Adam said.

We got to the end of the bridge and

Adam squatted down by the water's edge to dip his left hand in the creek. I saw that his handkerchief was tied around it like a bandage.

"You hurt?" I asked. "What happened?"

"Burned myself," he grunted. "Nothing serious."

Nevertheless, he held his hand in the water another minute or two before pulling it out with the handkerchief dripping wet. I could see red around the edges on the palm of his hand, but he wouldn't untie it to let me see just how bad it was.

"I told you. It only stings a little, okay?"

"Fine. So what were you and Sutterly talking about?" I asked, still suspicious of Sutterly's motives and Adam's meeting with him.

"Hey, back up there," he said sharply. "This isn't one of your courtrooms."

The boots he wore were probably his, but the jeans were probably Zach's. Certainly the maroon-and-green rugby shirt was Zach's because I'd given it to him two Christmases ago. Makes cross-country packing easy if, at the other end, you can borrow from your twin's wardrobe.

My brothers from Daddy's first marriage tend to be big-boned and solid, and they top out between five ten and six one. Like Will and Zach, Adam stands about six three with the hard lean build of the men on Mother's Stephenson side of the family. Unfortunately, I got the worst of the genetic blend: Daddy's bones but the same volatile Stephenson temper as Mother and my three youngest brothers. We're quick to anger, quick to tears, quick to forgive.

"Sorry," I said. "It's just that Dick Sutterly makes me nervous the way he wants to slap a house on every square inch at this end of the county."

But Adam wouldn't let me off that easily. "What difference does it make to you? You live over in Dobbs. Not out here."

"And because I don't live here, I'm not supposed to care? Because you live in California, it doesn't matter if you help wreck it for the others?"

"Get off my case," he said angrily, striding away so abruptly that the dogs were torn between staying with me and trailing after him.

I almost had to run to keep up with his long legs. "What's going on here, Adam? You're the richest one of us all. How much money do you need, for God's sake, that you'd sell Daddy out to Dick Sutterly and G. Hooks Talbert for a measly forty-five thousand?"

"Rich?" He turned on me with a snarl. "You people are sitting over here on seven million dollars' worth of property in one of the most economically sound areas in the country and you call me rich?"

"Seven *million?*" I was stunned. "Who's got seven million?"

"Doesn't anybody ever do the simple arithmetic?" He shook his head in exasperation. "How many acres do you and Daddy and the boys own all together?"

"I don't know. Two thousand? Maybe twenty-five hundred?"

"Be conservative. Say two thousand. And what's it going for these days? Rock-bottom prices?"

"Thirty-five hundred an acre," I hazarded.

I broke off a twig, stooped down, and did the multiplication in the dirt. The zeroes that lined up behind the seven astounded me. Adam was right. It had never occurred to me to do the math.

Daddy and most of the boys are farmers.

If you're a farmer, you may cycle a lot of cash from one growing season to another. You go into debt to buy heavy equipment and you pay for expensive repairs. You buy fertilizer, pesticides, and disease-resistant seeds. Then you have to hire extra labor to plant and harvest. Money comes in, money goes out, but it's hard to ever feel rich because so little of that money seems to cycle into your own pocket to stay. No sooner is the crop sold and your debt paid off than it's time to borrow more and start all over again.

But if you're a Knott and there's a little extra cash lying around at the end of the year, you buy land. You don't sell it. Except to each other, as Adam had sold to Zach and me what he'd inherited from Mother years ago before the prices started to soar.

I stood up and erased the numbers with my sneaker. It unsettled me just to think about it. Seven million dollars?

"Minimum," said Adam. "So if you want to cough up that *measly* forty-five thousand, I'll deed you my measly three acres and you can keep on being dewy-eyed and romantic about The Land as if it were a mystical entity and not negotiable property."

"But why?" I asked again. "You and Karen aren't having problems, are you?"

"Ever hear of downsizing?" he asked grimly.

I looked at him blankly. "You lost your job?"

Adam wouldn't meet my eyes and suddenly I realized what had seemed different about him when he arrived Wednesday night. The surface sheen was still there, but underneath he was no longer the cocksure golden boy.

"What happened?"

"Same old same old. Crystal Micronics got bought out by Global V.I. last winter and since my seniority entitled me to a bigger benefits package than my G.V.I. counterpart, I was the one the bottom-liners cut loose in February."

"You've been out of work since February? But with your skills and your experience —"

"Silicon Valley's full of forty-year-old men with my skills and my experience. We've sold the boat and the Jags, let the maid and gardener go, and put the kids in public school this year. If it weren't for Karen's job, we'd have had to dump the house instead of selling it last week for a break-even price."

"You sold your house?" Now I *was* distressed. I knew how much Karen loved that house. "Adam, why didn't you tell us? Let us help?"

"And listen to Haywood and Robert and Andrew brag about bailing their uppity little brother out of his troubles? No, thanks. And don't you go blabbing to them either, you hear?"

"They wouldn't brag," I said defensively.

"You know what I mean."

We had reached the burned spot and I helped him kick wet sand onto the last smoldering coals.

"Hey, don't look so gloomy. It's going to be all right. Eventually. With what the house brought and with what I have left from my severance package, I've got almost enough to form a partnership with two other guys in my position. All three of us had been wanting to go out on our own for years, but the corporations made it too comfortable to leave. Now we're going to start our own company. Dick Sutterly's so hot for that three acres that I'm betting he'll go sixty thousand. That would put me just over what I need for my third. Hell, if it works out,

I could be back in a few years to buy you all out."

The return of his arrogance infuriated me. "And in the meantime, Dick Sutterly sticks one of his cheap housing developments right there across the creek, but you don't give a damn because you'll be out in California while Daddy's back here with his heart breaking. Street lamps lighting up his night sky, horns blowing, kids trashing his creek. The boys are right. You did get uppity and big-headed and you've turned your back on your own family."

We were back to glaring at each other over the dogs' heads.

"You ever give two thoughts about what this family's like from where I stood?" said Adam. "Number ten son in a gang of eleven boys? But at least Zach and I were special because we were twins and we were the babies, right? And then seven years later, along came the darlin' baby girl the family'd been praying for, for all those years, so suddenly Zach and I were just two more little interchangeable Knott boys."

Quick tears flooded my eyes. "I didn't realize you hated me."

Ladybelle came to me instinctively and

nuzzled my fingers.

"Oh hell, Deborah, I didn't hate you. I'm just trying to make you understand why I had to get away, find some individuality. And now that I've got this chance for real independence, I'm not going to lose it. I don't care what you or Karen or any of the boys think. One way or another, I'm going back to California next Wednesday with sixty thousand dollars in my pocket, okay?"

I probably would have called Hambone to heel and headed straight back to Dobbs right then if Ladybelle and Blue hadn't suddenly perked up their ears and started racing for the cut.

Adam and I had been so riled up that neither of us had heard Daddy's truck coming hell-for-leather through the field on the other side of the creek. He rattled across the log-and-board bridge and roared up the rise and the dogs had to scatter to keep from being hit.

The dogs? Hell, Adam and me, too.

At the very last instant, Daddy saw us and skidded to a stop that threw up an arc of dirt. He leaned across the seat and flung open the door and yelled, "Get in! We got to go call Dwight. Somebody's done and killed Jap!"

11

The simple truth shall be told, and let facts be judged of as they really are.

"Scotus Americanus," *1773*

Since I knew Dwight's number by heart, I was the one who actually called the Sheriff's Department over in Dobbs. Dwight wasn't there, of course, but the dispatcher promised to get a team underway while she ran him down.

I gave her the directions to Jasper Stancil's garage and told her we'd meet the officers there. Then we headed back in Daddy's truck, this time by way of the hardtop public road, which was marginally quicker.

"I was coming home from getting my hair cut," Daddy said, "and thought I'd stop by and speak with him a minute."

The community barber shop was a

little one-room, one-chair affair at Pleasant's Crossroads about four miles from home. Beneath the brim of his white straw planter's hat, a narrow ring of pale skin divided Daddy's white hair from the back of his sunburned neck.

"Got my ears lowered," he used to joke after each fresh haircut.

There was no joking today as we crossed the bridge and sped toward Jap Stancil's place.

"Jap's truck was out at the garage, so I pulled up beside it and honked my horn. Them double doors was closed, and when he didn't step out, I went in at the side door to see if he was there. And that's when I seen him — laying there in his own blood and a tire iron right beside him."

In Daddy's Colleton County accent, words like "tire iron" come out "tar arn," but neither Adam nor I needed to think twice about his meaning.

Nor did it occur to us that Jap Stancil might not be dead or that his death was accidental. Daddy's seen a lot of violence over the years. He'd know.

He wasn't real happy that I'd insisted on coming back with him and Adam. Even though he brought me up on a working farm that routinely slaughters hogs and cows and chickens for the freezer, even though he helped me get a job that routinely brings the dregs of the county before me, even though he hasn't seen me in ruffles and Mary Janes since I was old enough to routinely reach for jeans and sneakers, in my daddy's heart I'll probably always be his dainty little baby girl who needs protection and shielding from the harsh realities of life.

And death.

Squashed in between the two men, my knee in danger of getting banged every time Daddy shifted gears, I couldn't keep the images of what we were soon going to see at that garage from being colored by Adam's earlier jibes.

As a child, I was never terrorized on the school bus like so many other kids. The bullies soon learned that messing with me meant they were messing with Adam and Zach. And if the little twins couldn't handle it, there was always Will, who kept an eye out for all three of us. My biggest battle was making them let me take care of my own problems and I seldom won it till after all the boys were grown and out of the house.

Now I had to wonder if protecting me was something the boys had wanted to do, out of family solidarity, or because they knew what Daddy would say if they didn't.

If I ever fell out of a tree, got stung by yellow jackets, was chased by a dog or ran into a barbed wire fence, sooner or later, when Mother was patching me up, Daddy would ask her who was supposed to be watching me? Where was {Zach}{Adam}{Will}{Jack}{Seth}? Pick one, any one. Hell, pick two or three if I were seriously hurt.

"Oh, Kezzie, hush," Mother would say. "They're not responsible for her and anyhow, hardheaded as this one is, you're never going to keep her wrapped in cotton."

Nevertheless, he would pick me up and pet me till I'd stopped crying. Being wrapped in cotton didn't sound like much fun the way Mother said it, but sitting on his lap, leaning against his strong chest, diverted by the inner workings of his big gold pocket watch while Mother applied bright orange Mercurochrome to my scrapes or cuts, made me feel cherished and safe.

"How much petting you reckon he gave

the boys?" asked the preacher. "Or Adam?"

By the time I was old enough to notice, Zach and Adam were almost too big for lap-sitting, but I seem to remember all three of us squooshed in together like a lapful of puppies to watch television or listen to Mother read, with Will and Jack and Seth and even Ben sprawled on the rug or couch next to us. And the way my brothers still hug each other, going and coming?

"And didn't your daddy go right off and find some burn salve for Adam's blistered hand while you were talking to the dispatcher?" asked the pragmatist.

If Adam feels shortchanged, maybe it's his fault, not mine or Daddy's.

As we approached Mr. Jap's place, I said, "You might want to put your tires exactly where you had them before, if you can."

But Daddy'd already had the same thoughts. "I'm not gonna mess up Dwight's trail," he assured me, and carefully drove off into the weeds where it was clear no other tires had passed since the rain stopped last night.

"Mind where you put your feet," he

warned Adam and me as he stepped across the overlapping tire tracks.

Dwight's tracking skills were going to be put to the test if he tried to sort them all out. It was clear that at least three or four different vehicles had been past today.

The dirt drive that enters beside the old garage continues across an expanse of fallow ground too weedy and unkempt to be called a lawn, circles on around behind Jap's house, then exits onto the road on the other side of the house. But the drive forks in a couple of places along the way. One fork leads over to Dallas's house and storage barn. Another joins the lane Kidd and I had used a few weeks earlier. It was the one Dick Sutterly took after he finished talking to Adam, the same one that Daddy had used just now to cross the creek when he met Adam and me.

Mr. Jap was never territorial about Daddy and the boys or their tenants crossing his land. We've all used it as a shortcut to the stores at Pleasant's Crossroads. Nor has Gray Talbert ever complained, not even when he had good reason to keep strangers from poking around his place. Not that actual strangers would know much about the back lanes since the woods on both sides of the creek are posted with those phony Possum Creek Hunt Club signs. A lane can look well traveled and still dead-end at an irrigation pond.

Seeing poor Mr. Jap was as bad as I expected, but by no means as bad as it could have been. Sprawled face-down on the damp cement floor halfway across the shop, he looked a little larger in death than he had in life.

Adam seemed uneasy with this close view of violent death and murmured, "Who would have thought the old man to have had so much blood in him?"

Along with the Bible, Dickens and *One Hundred and One Famous Poems*, Mother had read Shakespeare aloud to us of a winter's evening, and we three younger ones can glibly quote from her favorite plays.

Daddy gave me an odd look. I shrugged and we both turned our attention to the condition of the shop. At the far rear corner stood a massive iron safe so old that its original green paint and gold lettering were nearly undiscernible beneath the layers of dirt and grease. According to Daddy, this was where Mr. Jap had kept the few papers he considered valuable: his farm deed before he signed it over to Dallas, his marriage certificate, Dallas's birth certificate, Miss Elsie's death certificate, Social Security papers, promissory notes, insurance policies and the like.

The acetylene torch lay atop the safe door, which had been burned off its hinges, and papers were scattered all around.

Adam started to walk over there, but Daddy pulled him back. "Better not mess with anything till Dwight gets here," he said and we stayed clustered just inside the doorway.

"Why was he killed?" I asked.

Daddy pushed his white straw hat back on the crown of his head and said, "Don't know, shug. He sure won't worried about dying when I seen him down at the crossroads this morning."

He gestured to Mr. Jap's truck parked just beyond the door and we could see some conical bushel baskets sticking up above the tailgate. "He brought some of that fancy corn, a few squash and pumpkins and a dozen bags of turnip greens down to the flea market to sell. I told him I was going to eat a sandwich at the store when I finished getting my haircut. Asked if he was going to be there, but he said he had to come on back. Said there was somebody he was expecting."

"Who?" Adam wondered.

"He didn't say, but I expect it was the Wall boy. He was supposed to come sometime this weekend and settle up with Jap about the corn."

"Did you know Mr. Jap was thinking about selling some of his land?" I asked.

Daddy gave me a hard look. "Who told you that?"

"He did. Sort of."

"How could he do that?" Adam protested. "You said it was going to be tied up in court till after the murder trial on Dallas's wife."

"He said John Claude had about talked Cherry Lou into renouncing any of her rights to the land. She thinks it would take away her motive, maybe get her a lighter sentence."

"When'd he tell you all that?" asked Daddy.

"Yesterday." I felt my face flush as I added, "Jimmy White was too busy to look at my car, so Allen Stancil changed the alternator for me here. Mr. Jap was here, too."

I wasn't sure if Adam remembered my involvement with Allen or even knew about it in the first place since he was off in California then, but certainly Daddy did. Neither of them said anything, although Adam looked around as if wondering for the first time where Allen was. "I never knew him too well, but didn't he used to be even rougher than Dallas when he was growing up?"

Daddy shrugged. "Elsie did what she could for both of 'em. Dallas got hisself straightened out a long time ago. I don't know about Allen. Jap didn't talk much on him."

And with good reason, as Daddy and I both knew.

We heard the patrol cars first as they made the turn off New Forty-Eight, then we saw the flashing blue lights come over the rise.

"Well, now," said Daddy, and Adam and I automatically snapped to attention. "I don't believe we ought to say nothing to Dwight — not right yet anyhow — that Jap was talking about maybe gonna sell some of his land."

12

I venture this brief account under the eye of the public and as it may be supported by the concurring testimony of many gentlemen of repute and credit who have been among our settlers in North Carolina . . .

"Scotus Americanus," *1773*

Dwight Bryant hung around our house so much when he was growing up, he could have been another of my brothers, fitting in somewhere between Will and the little twins. He has a football build now, but back then it'd been one-on-one basketball down at the barn and baseball out in the pasture. Whatever ball was in season, he'd be out there with the boys when they were free to play even if it meant he first had to help with their chores after he'd finished his own chores at home. Dwight's father was killed in a tractor accident when he was young and his strong-minded mother never remarried, so I guess Daddy is the closest thing he has to a father figure; and Daddy's always been partial to him, too.

That doesn't mean though that Dwight didn't cross-question us three ways to Sunday after the crime scene unit got there and he could give us his full attention. As Detective Chief of the Colleton County Sheriff's Department, he would never stint his duty; but at least he didn't start right in lecturing me for getting myself mixed up in another murder, not with Daddy sitting there on the tailgate of his old pickup.

Adam said he hadn't seen anyone while he was burning trash back near the creek. Nor had he noticed the sound of a truck or car passing on the far side. Both of us had forgotten to wear a watch, so we didn't know when it was that Dick Sutterly drove off toward Mr. Jap's place, but Adam said they'd been talking about ten minutes when I got there. We both agreed that it was probably close to twenty minutes from the time he left till the time Daddy arrived.

"According to my piece, when I got back in my truck after finding Jap, it was exactly twenty-two minutes after one."

Daddy pulled on the slender gold chain that was linked to a belt loop and his pocket watch slid into view. He flipped back the lid and compared the old-fashioned dial with Dwight's digital wristwatch. They were less than a minute apart.

"And no," he said, before Dwight could ask him, "I didn't see Sutterly nor his truck neither when I turned in here." He paused, remembering. "Did see Dallas's wife when I passed. Least I reckon it was her, raking up leaves in her backyard. She might've noticed something."

There were too many trees between the two houses for a clean view even if all the leaves had fallen, but it was true that she might have noticed if someone left by the far drive or if someone circled around by the back lanes.

Dwight made a note of it. "Now, you say you saw him at the flea market this morning. Did he seem any different?"

Daddy shook his head. "Nope. He was just Jap. This close to Thanksgiving, he reckoned it was the last time he could put out his corn and pumpkins before folks started wanting holly and mistletoe. He was thinking of shooting some down for next week. I thought it was a little early myself, but then I seen Christmas trees shining in some windows already, so maybe he was right."

Mistletoe is an evergreen parasite on hardwoods. The seeds ripen inside waxy white berries and many cling to a bird's beak while it's eating. When the bird next lands in an oak or pecan tree, it cleans its beak on the nearest twig and the sticky seeds are glued to the spot. If conditions are just right, the seeds will sprout and send feeder roots down through the bark and soon there's a bushy green ball of mistletoe putting out more white berries. Since the bird usually does its beak cleaning out on the tips of a tree's branches, twenty or thirty feet off the ground, this does not make for simple gathering. Nevertheless, with a .22 rifle, a good marksman can prune you off enough mistletoe to kiss half the county.

"Jap did say he needed to come on back before dinner," Daddy told Dwight. "Said he was expecting somebody."

"He didn't say who?"

Daddy shook his head. I wasn't surprised that he didn't speculate about the Wall boy. He wouldn't put suspicion on somebody unless he knew it was true.

"What about Allen Stancil?" asked Dwight. "Any of y'all see him today?"

We told him no.

Even though Dwight had met Allen back when he and my brothers were messing around with their first cars, he was in the army and stationed in Germany at the time Mother died and I started college. There was no reason for him to've heard about my running off to Martinsville with Allen and I didn't see any point in bringing him up to speed on it at this late date. I just hoped nobody else would either.

J.V. Pruitt, who's acted as the county's coroner most of my lifetime, stepped out of the garage. He's an undertaker, not a doctor, but he's seldom second-guessed by the ME over in Chapel Hill.

I have never seen Pruitt when he wasn't dressed in a three-piece suit, white shirt and dark tie, and a plain felt hat — tan in the summertime, dark gray in the winter. He tipped his winter hat to me and nodded to Daddy, who always contributes to his campaign and hangs his poster in the crossroads store.

"Just what it looks like, Dwight," he said now. "A single blow to the back of his head with that tire iron. Wouldn't take much strength, just determination."

"When?" asked Dwight.

"Now, Dwight, you been doing this long enough to know we can only approximate. When was he last seen?"

Dwight glanced at Daddy, who said, "Well, I seen him down at the crossroads around ten-thirty and I found him at one twenty-two."

"Well, there you are," said Pruitt, straightening his already straight tie. "Death occurred sometime between ten-thirty and one twenty-two. Chapel Hill won't get it any tighter than that."

The garage was a good hundred feet off the road, but a hundred feet back wasn't enough to deter the curious. Cars were starting to clog up both lanes as people slowed to a crawl and craned their necks to see what had brought the blue-lights out to Jap Stancil's. A highway patrolman arrived and began directing traffic in an effort to keep things moving.

As we stood out there talking, the crime scene unit had strung yellow tape across the drive to preserve the tracks. Their photographer finished up inside and came out to take close-ups of the separate tread marks, carefully laying a foot rule beside each one so as to have an accurate scale if and when the tires were found.

Unfortunately, that yellow tape only covered the entrance to the drive. Before anyone realized what was happening, a white Subaru sedan circled around behind Jap Stancil's house and came jouncing down the lane toward the photographer, who hastily stood and tried to wave it back.

Merrilee Grimes ignored him till she was less than four feet from hitting him where he stood. Then she slammed on the brakes, slipped out from behind the wheel, and came running toward us. "What happened? Where's Uncle Jap?"

Slender and small-boned, Merrilee probably gets all her clothes from the Petite Lady, while her husband Pete is limited to Big 'n Tall. It's not that he's fat, just really, really solid with lots of shaggy brown hair on his head and hairy arms and legs. He pried himself loose from the passenger side and lumbered after her. "Now, Merrilee, honey —"

I couldn't help noticing Merrilee's dainty black velvet slippers. They were almost instantly caked in damp sand. Not many women would wear velvet shoes outdoors in the country, but maybe she hadn't planned on taking a hike. Pete was marginally better in his suede ripple treads. Both wore black slacks and casual white windbreakers over oxford shirts. Merrilee had knotted a silk scarf around her neck and its gold and orange design was flecked with reddish brown rings that echoed her auburn hair and her close-set brown eyes. Papa Bear and Mama Bear off on a Saturday afternoon outing, but from the way they were dressed, their original destination had probably been Crabtree or North Hills Mall, not Possum Creek.

Merrilee didn't seem to recognize Dwight or Adam. Instead, she looked from me to Daddy. "What's happened to Uncle Jap, Mr. Kezzie? That yellow ribbon says crime scene. Did somebody try to rob him? Is he hurt? Did they take him to a hospital?"

Daddy stood up awkwardly. "I'm real sorry, Merrilee, but somebody seems to've hit him purty hard. Mr. Pruitt here don't think he ever knowed what happened, it was probably so quick."

Tears filled her eyes as his words sank in. "He's gone? Just like that? Who hit him? Deborah?"

"We don't know yet," I said and put out my arms to her just as Pete caught up and engulfed the two of us.

We stood in that unwieldy bear hug until I managed to detach myself, still patting her slender back and murmuring sympathetic noises.

For a moment, there were only the sounds of traffic and her muffled sobs on the mild November air, then she sniffled and her hand groped for Pete's pants pocket. Without asking what she wanted, Pete automatically pulled out a large white handkerchief. Even after she blew her nose, tears continued to spill from her eyes. She remained in the protective circle of Pete's arms, but we could almost see her spine stiffen.

"Where is he?" she said. "I want to see him."

"Now, Miz Grimes," said Dwight.

"Aw, now, honey," said her husband, "you don't want to go in there and remember him like that."

She pulled away and headed toward the open side door.

Young Jack Jamison, one of the sheriff's deputies, looked inquiringly at Dwight, who shrugged and followed.

Jamison stepped aside and Merrilee and Pete entered with the rest of us close behind.

"Poor Uncle Jap," she whispered and knelt on the dirty concrete floor to hold his hand for a moment as her eyes closed in silent prayer.

When she opened them again, Pete held out his big hairy paw to her and she came to her feet as gracefully as swansdown.

"You could look that delicate and graceful, too, if you always had a two-ton Mack truck around to hoist you up," the pragmatist whispered snidely into my ear.

"For shame!" scolded the preacher.

Merrilee's eyes fell on the wrecked safe. "So he *was* robbed! Did they take all his money?"

"We didn't find any cash," said Dwight. "Did he keep much on hand?"

"Just what he got from Social Security and from selling vegetables at the flea market."

"If that's the only money he had, it doesn't seem worth going to all that trouble cutting the safe open with the torch," said Dwight. "What about papers? Could you tell if anything's missing?"

She shook her head. "He never opened it for me. I'd forgotten it was even out here. Dallas may've kept his deeds in it, but except for that, I never knew him to have anything worth taking." She looked around the shabby garage hopelessly and her eyes came sadly back to the body still sprawled on the concrete floor.

"When did you last talk to your uncle?" asked Dwight.

"Wednesday night," she answered promptly. "Pete and I come by every Sunday morning and I call him every Wednesday night to see if he's all right. We live just below where Forty-Eight and Old Forty-Eight join up, and sometimes we drop by on our way in and out from work, but Sunday and Wednesday, regular as church bells, he knows — *knew* — he could count on me."

"Did he sound normal Wednesday night?"

"Well, actually —" After all that bragging, she seemed a shade embarrassed to admit that maybe it was Pete that talked to Mr. Jap that night, not her. "I got home late and then had to get ready for prayer meeting."

"How'd he sound to you?" Dwight asked her husband.

"Same as ever," said Pete. "Allen answered the phone and put Uncle Jap on and —"

"Allen!" shrieked Merrilee. "That's what's missing — Allen Stancil!"

Dwight looked around at the rest of us, but no one had seen Allen that day.

Daddy didn't remember seeing Allen's pickup when he came through the lane on his way to the crossroads. " 'Course, I won't looking for it, but I believe I'd've noticed if it was there."

Adam said he hadn't seen anyone except Dick Sutterly come through the back lanes while he was out by the creek, and I'd come Old Forty-Eight by way of Cotton Grove from the north, which meant I hadn't passed the Stancil place on the way to Daddy's.

"I'll bet he did this," Merrilee insisted. "I bet he and Uncle Jap had a falling-out and he hit Uncle Jap and took his corn money and ran."

"Corn money?" asked Dwight.

"He raises ornamental corn," said Merrilee.

It was clear that Dwight didn't think this amounted to much, so I briefly described my encounter with Mr. Jap and Billy Wall a few weeks ago. "The Wall boy was supposed to sell the last of it this past week. I think they expected to net about ten or twelve thousand."

Merrilee was sure this was all the motive a user and taker like Allen Stancil needed and she insisted that Dwight put out an arrest call on him.

Dwight doesn't jump to conclusions, but he agreed that it probably wouldn't hurt to have a talk with Allen.

"Prob'ly wouldn't hurt neither to find out if Billy Wall ever actually paid Jap," Daddy told Dwight reluctantly.

As we walked back outside, we saw Blue and Ladybelle trotting down the lane toward us.

Daddy seldom gets as flustered as he was at that moment. He hollered at the dogs, gave a sweeping motion of his hand, and they instantly veered off and went and jumped up in the bed of his pickup.

"Dwight, I'm plumb ashamed of them," he apologized.

Dwight gave a rueful laugh. "Don't worry about it, sir. Everybody else has been up and down this lane. Couple of dogs can't do much more damage."

"Wonder what they did with Hambone?" I said. Aunt Zell wasn't going to be too happy with me if I lost her beagle pup. "If you're finished with me for right now, Dwight, maybe I'll walk back and see if I can find him."

"Just try to walk in the middle of the lane and stay off any tire tracks," he said.

He had a few more questions for Daddy, so Adam said he'd wait and ride back in the truck.

I gave Merrilee my condolences again, then skirted the yellow tape and struck off down the lane. Almost immediately, I noticed something that I hoped Dwight wouldn't: the dogs had been around the garage sometime after the rain stopped last night and when they arrived just now.

They could have wandered over in the early morning hours, of course. Blue and Ladybelle are never chained up at night. On the other hand, at their age, they don't usually roam far from the house unless they're with one of the family. I thought back to my earlier conversation with Adam. He never actually *said* that he only briefly crossed the creek to talk to Dick Sutterly. I kept looking for boot tracks, but if he'd walked this far, his tracks could have been covered up by those laid down by Sutterly and Daddy.

Daddy's zigzag treads were the only ones I could recognize and they overlay most of the marks. Occasionally, though, different drivers had veered from his straight path and I saw a crisp wide diamond tread, an equally crisp hexagonal pattern that reminded me of chicken wire, and one tire that must have been completely bald since the tread mark was smooth and patternless.

The lane soon entered the first patch of trees, then crossed alongside Mr. Jap's pumpkin patch. The vines were browning off after all the rain and a wonderful funky smell rose up from the earth itself — damp sand, dead weeds and grass, decaying leaves. Every gust of the wind winnowed down more leaves from the trees around me.

For that matter, the wind was out of the north and had picked up enough to blow my hair, push away the gray clouds above, and open up large patches of blue that let the sun shine through. Despite the sun, though, the temperature was dropping perceptively minute by minute. For the first time since last March I thought seriously of sweaters and jackets and wool skirts. Maybe we were finally going to get some colder weather for Thanksgiving.

As I stepped from bright sunlight into the last stretch of thick woods before the creek, I heard the scuffle of leaves, as if a larger animal were passing somewhere to my left. I quickly slipped behind a large oak tree and waited.

Deer have been coming back into these woods, working their way west along the Neuse and then down along Possum Creek. Andrew's son A.K. had taken a nice little six-point stag last year and most of his male cousins, especially Reese, were determined to best him before the season ended in January. I've seen lots of tracks these past few years, but only twice have I seen the deer themselves.

The woods had gone suddenly silent. Uneasily, I noted that even the mindless chirp of sparrows and chickadees was missing and the busy scratching of towhees had stopped as well. My flesh crawled as I sensed that someone else was there in the woods, watching.

Behind me?

I whirled and saw nothing at first. Then there was movement and a young man in full camouflage materialized in the underbrush. He held a .22 rifle loosely in his hands.

The barrel was pointed just as loosely in the direction of my heart.

Behind me, from the other side of the lane, a cold hard voice said, "I do believe you're trespassing, Judge Knott."

13

I have seen the inhabitants hunting foxes, bears, and deer, through the woods . . .

"Scotus Americanus," *1773*

I turned and made my voice as cool as his. "Mr. Talbert, I presume?"

We had never formally met, but I've seen him on Channel 5 and in the *News and Observer* enough times over the years. Discussing plans of a new merger, standing behind various governors as they announce the successful luring of yet another rustbelt industry to North Carolina, beaming widely on election night as Jesse Helms or others of his conservative cronies squeak into office, G. Hooks Talbert moves in much more rarefied circles than a district court judge does.

Nevertheless, if he hadn't pushed my name with the Republican governor who appointed me to replace a judge who died in office, I'd still be practicing law from the attorney's side of the bench.

Not that supporting me was his choice, of course. Normally, a man of his standing would never waste political pull on a minor local judgeship and certainly not for a Democrat, but he was caught in a Mexican standoff. Behind my back, Daddy had sent him word that if I didn't get the appointment, Channel 5 would be getting a videotape of the vigorous crop of marijuana which Grayson Hooks Talbert Junior was growing in his greenhouses at the time. I'd been ambivalent when Daddy told me what he'd done, but I couldn't blame him for savoring his revenge — not after he'd been so roundly snubbed when he offered to buy the Talbert property years ago. (Back then, word was sent to *him* that, quote, "Mr. Talbert doesn't care to have any dealings with a known bootlegger," end quote.)

G. Hooks must have hated having to ask a moderate like Governor Hardison for a personal favor almost as much as I hated getting on the bench that way, so we may not have met, but as we warily faced each other there in the underbrush, yes, each knew who the other was.

He held his squirrel rifle cradled in the crook of his arm with the barrel pointed skyward. Walking toward us around the bend in the lane was a third hunter whose own .22 was slung across one shoulder.

Like G. Hooks Talbert, this man was expensively togged out in brown coveralls and fluorescent orange hunting cap. He had the same well-barbered steel gray hair and moved with the same I-own-the-world aura of self-entitlement as G. Hooks. Another Triangle mover and shaker, no doubt, but I couldn't put a name to him.

"Well, Hooks, she's certainly bright-eyed and bushy-tailed, but is she in season?" he asked, with a warm, crinkly-eyed smile at me to show that he was just kidding.

I gave him a cool nod and didn't smile back.

Nor did Talbert.

"This is Judge Deborah Knott," he said.

"Judge?"

His disbelief was probably conditioned

reflex. After all, most of the judges in his Old Raleigh circle would be male. They would wear Brooks Brothers suits, play gentlemanly rounds of golf, and sport distinguished touches of gray at their neatly trimmed temples. Although my sky blue sweatshirt is from the Bull's Head over in Chapel Hill, my jeans and sneakers are both off-brands. My hair, rougher than a haystack at that moment, is almost shoulder length and shows no immediate signs of going gray. (And never will if Ethelene down at the Cut 'n' Curl has her way about it.)

"District Eleven-C," said Talbert. "Judge Knott is one of the few with a D after her name to ride in unopposed last election."

I had been appointed in the summer and my place on that ballot was mostly pro forma. Because local Republicans hadn't sensed the potential for such widespread bloodletting, they didn't bother to run anybody against me for the rest of Perry Byrd's term. I can only hope the pendulum swings back a little before I have to run again.

"I don't believe I caught your name, Mr. — ?"

His eyes briefly met Talbert's. "Just call me Tom."

The wind shook loose another cloud of yellow leaves from the branches above us and he gave an exaggerated shiver. "Hooks, I think I'll head on back to the car. Reckon there's any hot coffee left in the thermoses, Bob?"

"Yes, sir," the younger man answered smartly, which made me think he was either a very junior member of the man's firm or maybe his chauffeur.

"Coming, Hooks?"

"I'll be along in a minute."

"Nice meeting you, Judge," he said, and then they were gone.

"You didn't happen to see a half-grown beagle pup, did you?" I asked, ready to keep walking myself.

Talbert's eyes narrowed suspiciously. "That's why you're poking around out here? Looking for a lost dog?"

I almost asked him if there was anything here he didn't want me to see, like maybe plants that deviated from the USDA's list of recommended nursery stock? Somehow, I managed to control my tongue. "I was afraid he might've tried to follow me."

"Over to Stancil's place? Something

going on over there? We heard sirens and horns before."

"Jasper Stancil's been killed," I said. "They're treating it like a homicide."

Briefly I described events and it was almost like speaking to a computer. His face didn't change expression. He didn't frown or exclaim, but I could sense a realignment of facts and a new set of calculations going on behind his pale blue eyes.

Okay, so the bloodlines were a little attenuated. G. Hooks and Mr. Jap were probably only third cousins twice removed and it wasn't like the two of them had anything in common beyond some land boundaries. Even so, three generations back, those land divisions were the result of a very real family connection and for him to treat Mr. Jap's death like a problem in binary logic suddenly made me forget all my self-administered lectures on discipline and discretion.

I heard myself say, "I guess this complicates your plans?"

"Plans?"

"To buy a strip of road frontage from Jasper Stancil."

It was almost enough to ruffle his composure.

Almost, but not quite. Of course, he's been practicing control at least twenty years longer than me.

He gave a polite nod, said, "Hope you find your dog," and turned to follow the others.

Just before he disappeared into the underbrush, he glanced back at me. "You're up for election again when? Next year, is it?"

14

. . . Their behavior at home is consistent with their appearance abroad.

"Scotus Americanus," *1773*

I'd asked for it, of course, but I didn't like the implications of Talbert's question. I hadn't had to spend much money on campaigning before. If he decided to take a personal interest in my next election, he could channel enough money to an opponent to more than swamp me. Even down here at the bottom of the political food chain, money makes a difference.

Even less did I like the corollary thought to the question I'd asked G. Hooks. Mr. Jap's death might complicate *his* plans, but suddenly things were rosier for Daddy and the brothers who still live and farm along Possum Creek.

If we could keep Adam from selling, there would be no access to the Talbert land. No access meant no immediate development, no change to our way of life here on the north side of Possum Creek. For a little while longer, we could fish and hunt or just revel in the sheer luxury of space.

Adam's right: we may not all live here — I'm a judge in Dobbs, Frank's retired out in San Diego, Will's an auctioneer in Cotton Grove, Herman's an electrician in Dobbs — yet, except for Adam, our roots go down deep in these sandy fields and scruffy woods. Even the grandchildren, who are starting to scatter out across the state, look to this part of Colleton County as a fixed anchor. My brothers aren't much for putting emotion into words, but Haywood once said it for them: "When you step out on your own back porch and everything is Knott land for as far as you can see, why boys, don't y'all's spirit just fill up in a plenteous amplitude?"

I crossed the creek in a bittersweet mood that echoed the falling leaves and I wondered how much longer such plenteous amplitude could endure.

Adam accused me of romanticizing

our land. If by that he means I know the spiritual value of what we have and don't want to see it disappear beneath a grid-work of named streets with manicured grass and biscuit-cutter houses, he's right. Guilty as charged.

As I came up the slope, Hambone rushed down to meet me, whimpering in his relief at finally seeing someone he could attach himself to. Almost immediately, his confidence was restored enough that he dashed into the edge of the woods and began to bark at something. His little beagle tail wagged happily and he kept running back and forth as if wanting to share something wonderful with me.

"Whatcha found, boy?" I asked.

The leaves and grasses had been smoothed down into a narrow trail that led into the undergrowth, and sure enough, there by the trail sat one of Andrew's homemade wooden rabbit gums. He and Daddy raise and train rabbit dogs, and rabbits are integral to that training.

Out back of his house, Andrew has fenced in a quarter-acre circle with shoulder-high chicken wire. The yard itself is overgrown with weedy grass and shaggy bushes, and Andrew's hauled in tree limbs, a few logs, and several lengths of hollow plastic pipes, six to ten inches in diameter. He traps rabbits and releases them into the training yard, then turns the pups in. The rabbits bounce around the yard and the puppies yip and tumble after them till the rabbits get tired and go hide in the hollow pipes.

The object of the exercise isn't to have the dogs catch the rabbits. It's to get them familiar with the rabbit's scent and to learn to break off the hunt when called.

Like Daddy, most of my brothers hardly ever take a gun with them when they go out to the woods to run the dogs. Mainly they just like to be outdoors, listening to the song the dogs sing when they catch the scent.

The trap door had fallen shut on the rabbit gum Hambone had found and when I hefted one end of the thing, I felt the telltale slither as the animal inside scrabbled to maintain its balance. Rabbit, possum or coon? From the lively scratching, it was probably a rabbit, but sometimes other young animals will go in after the fruit bait and trip the door.

Hambone was beside himself with excitement as I set the box down and I couldn't resist. I grabbed him by the collar and held it tightly with one hand while lifting the trap door with the other.

Instantly, a rabbit tumbled onto the ground, blinked once in the afternoon sunlight, and lit out across the bean field. I gave him about a ten-foot head start, then let go of Hambone's collar. He lunged after the rabbit, yipping and singing as if he'd been doing it all his life. I knew there was no chance in the world that he'd ever catch up, but he'd have a blissful twenty minutes thinking he might.

Smiling to myself, I carefully returned the box to the same place Andrew had left it, reset the trap door, then took a handful of leafy twigs and brushed away most of our tracks so maybe Andrew wouldn't notice that we'd freed one of his rabbits.

For just a moment, I had managed to forget the sight of poor Mr. Jap lying there on that cold concrete floor.

By the time Hambone conceded he was never going to catch his first rabbit and we got back to the homeplace, Daddy's old red Chevy was just pulling into the yard. Blue and Ladybelle jumped out of the back and the three dogs touched noses and smelled bottoms. From the reproachful look the older two gave me, I almost could swear that Hambone had told them of his adventure and what they'd missed.

The wind was blowing steadily from the north now, the temperature had dropped at least five degrees, and Adam was shivering in Zach's cotton knit shirt. Daddy slammed the truck door and held the fronts of his thin denim jacket together as he headed for the house.

"Time to put a match to the fire," he said.

Adam and I followed him inside and found the kitchen already warm and cozy. Maidie and Cletus were waiting for us and had lit the old wood heater and put a fresh pot of coffee on. Vegetable soup simmered on the range and an iron skillet waited till it was time to cook cornbread nice and crusty for supper. Daddy never expects Maidie to cook on the weekends, but Adam was spending a couple of nights out here and whenever there's company, she feels obliged to step in.

Now she took Daddy's jacket and handed him a thick wool cardigan that Seth and Minnie's children gave him two Christmases ago. There was a time when he would have scorned wearing an extra layer indoors, and sorrow brushed my heart as I realized that the cold bothered him more than it used to.

"Time was," whispered the preacher. "Time is."

And time will BE! I thought defiantly.

The pragmatist nodded. "And time will be," he said quietly. It was neither promise nor threat, only simple acknowledgment.

The five of us sat with warm mugs of coffee in our hands while Daddy and Adam and I took turns telling Maidie and Cletus what had happened.

Cletus never says much, especially when Maidie's there to do the talking, but when he does speak, he always goes straight to the point. "Reckon that shiftless Allen Stancil's gonna be a rich man now."

"Maybe," I said. "Depends on whether or not Cherry Lou signed her interest in the farm back over to Mr. Jap this week."

Adam shrugged. "I don't see why that makes any real difference. If she didn't do it yet, he just has to wait till the trial's over. He *is* Mr. Jap's only kin, isn't he?"

"There's Miss Elsie's niece," said Maidie. "She's Dallas's first cousin."

"But no real blood kin to Mr. Jap," I said. "The Yadkins and the Stancils both come down from a common Pleasant ancestor — G. Hooks Talbert does too, for that matter — but that's too far back to count. No, the laws of inheritance are pretty clear. When Dallas died without children or a will, half of his real property — the land — automatically went to his surviving parent and the other half to his wife. Cherry Lou. But since she can't benefit under the Slayer Statute, and, assuming a jury convicts her, her half of Dallas's estate would automatically pass to his closest next of kin, which was his father. Now that Mr. Jap's dead, it goes to *his* blood kin, and that's Allen Stancil."

"But Cherry Lou's not been tried yet," Maidie argued, "and if Mr. Jap died 'fore he could get it, seems like to me it'll have to start all over again back with Dallas, and Miss Merrilee and Allen will share and share alike since they're both first cousins to Dallas."

Daddy agreed. "Sounds like the fairest way to me."

"What's fair and what's legal are two different things," said Adam.

He spoke with such bitterness that Maidie immediately gave him a worried look.

" 'Get out of the way of Justice. She's blind,' " I quoted lightly.

"Then maybe we better get that lady a white walking stick," Cletus chuckled.

"What happens if Allen's the one that did it?" asked Maidie.

"It would be up to the Clerk of the Court," I said. "Ellis Glover might decide Merrilee has a legitimate claim after all. On the other hand, Allen does have a couple of children and they'd be within the five degrees of consanguinity required by North Carolina law, which has to be closer than Merrilee."

Daddy frowned. "Con-sang-*what?*"

"Consanguinity — blood kinship. You count the degrees by counting generations up to the common ancestor and then back down to the related person." I ticked them off on my fingers. "One up to Mr. Jap's father, one down to his brother, another to his brother's son — Allen, and then down to Allen's children. That's four degrees. If somebody related to you dies without a will or any immediate heirs, you can put in a claim if you're within five degrees of blood kin."

Another thought occurred to me. "On the other hand, if Allen *is* involved, Merrilee could argue that the Slayer Statute blocks his kids from inheriting. It'd be a pretty little legal battle."

Daddy dismissed consanguinity as irrelevant legalistic gobbledegook since he couldn't see that Allen had any call to hurt Mr. Jap.

"Jap was ready to give him everything he had to get him a real car shop. Y'all know how he always liked messing with cars better'n working the land. Land ain't never meant nothing to Jap Stancil except a place to stay, something to take money out of, never put none back in. He's clear-cut his woods twice and never planted a single tree. Why, Billy Wall's been a better steward of that land than he ever thought to be."

Proximity since childhood might have made Daddy and Mr. Jap friends and cohorts, but I realized now that Jap

Stancil had never shared Daddy's values.

"Ever since the government closed down his shop, Jap's been wanting to get another one," he said. "That's why he kept all them old cars setting around when they was fools out in Charlotte or down in Wilmington that'd give him three times what they was worth. 'Money in my pocket, Kezzie,' he told me. Bad as he hated losing Dallas, he was happy to get Allen. Only this time, he won't going to fix people's transmissions and carburetors. Him and Allen was going into pure restoration big-time, he said. Going to take them old heaps and make 'em look like they just rolled off the assembly line in Detroit."

"Using what to buy their tools and equipment?" I asked, hoping to goad him into telling what he knew about Jap's plans to sell land. "Billy Wall's corn money?"

"It was a start," he said mildly and shifted over to reminiscences of his and Jap's boyhood days along Possum Creek. He told us again about Mr. Jap's courtship of Elsie Yadkin, him a braggedy, drinking, cussing roughneck, her a timid little churchgoing lady half engaged to a deacon's son, and how he'd made the deacon's son back off and leave the field to him. "And Jap might not've quit all his bragging and drinking and cussing out in the shop, but he always remembered that Elsie was a lady and he never brought it indoors nor let Dallas bring it in the house neither. Merrilee's a lot like her Aunt Elsie, the way she's settled that Grimes boy."

"It's a wonder they never got caught driving drunk, what with all the drinking they did," Adam said provocatively.

But if he was hoping to get Daddy to talk about the bootlegging days, he didn't have any more luck than I had with Mr. Jap selling land. Daddy just sat there in front of the wood heater with his hands around his coffee mug and his long legs stretched out to the warmth and a sad smile on his lips as he remembered whatever he remembered.

Eventually, and over their protests, I stood to go back to Dobbs.

"The soup smells wonderful," I said as Daddy pressed me to stay to supper and Maidie promised there was plenty for everybody, "but Aunt Zell was going to start on her fruitcakes this evening and she'll be waiting for the pecans."

Maidie took a gallon bag of shelled nuts from the freezer and put them in a paper bag for me.

"And, Cletus, would you get her a bottle of that — gin, is it?" Daddy asked slyly. "Wouldn't be Zell's fruitcake without some gin."

The bottle Cletus took from beneath the sink had a Gilbey's label and a broken tax seal, but if I took a sniff, I would not expect to smell juniper berries. A faint aroma of apples or peaches, maybe, but not juniper berries.

Maidie and I rolled our eyes at each other, but Aunt Zell would be disappointed if her fruitcakes had to do without their usual drenching of homemade brandy.

I asked Adam if he wanted to catch a movie somewhere, but he yawned and said all this fresh air was getting to him. "I think I'll make it an early evening since I promised Herman and Nadine that I'd go to their church with them tomorrow morning."

"Better you than me," I said cattily. "Their minister's a chauvinistic born-again who gets so tangled up in his own rhetoric that it's sometimes hard to tell if he's proved his point or the devil's."

"Deborah Knott, you be ashamed of yourself!" Maidie scolded. A preacher is a preacher is a preacher to her, but Cletus gave me a wink and a grin.

Daddy walked out to my car with me to remind me that North Carolina law requires that open containers of alcoholic beverages be transported in the trunk. (He's an authority on those laws.)

Once the bottle was properly stowed next to my toolbox, he whistled up the dogs. They came running through the late afternoon sunshine, Hambone trotting along after them. I opened the car door and the pup hopped right up on the front seat. As I stood on tiptoe to kiss Daddy's leathery, wind-chilled cheek, he gave me a hug.

"You take care of yourself, now."

"I will," I promised, sliding in after Hambone. "You, too."

He gave me an ironic smile that said he knew how we were starting to worry about him. And then, just as he used to say when I was a very little girl, "Don't you fret yourself, shug. I ain't gonna die till you're an old, old lady."

Now, as then, the words still made me smile. Never mind that when I was very little, thirty-six seemed old, old.

I started to switch on the engine when Daddy rapped at my window.

"Almost forgot to tell you," he said. "Dwight said for you to call him when you get back to Dobbs."

There was a sheepish look on his face that I couldn't quite interpret.

15

Whether others shall follow my example or whether matters shall strike them in the same light, is what I know not, nor am I much solicitous about . . .

"Scotus Americanus," *1773*

I drove back to Dobbs with a zillion questions tumbling through my mind.

Like (1): was G. Hooks that good a poker face or did he have alternative options?

Like (2): was Adam really tired or was he just not anxious for more questions about his two-point-nine acres of road frontage?

Like (3): were (1) and (2) linked?

And then there were (4), (5), (6), and (7): what was Daddy up to? Where was Allen? What did Dwight want? And who *did* kill Jap Stancil? And why?

"That's eight," the pragmatist said pedantically.

"Mind your own business," I told him.

The cold orange rays of the setting sun were nearly horizontal to the earth as I approached the edge of town. When I was a child, the town was more compact and tobacco farms began two blocks after the last stoplight. Now, with cars and the need for spaces to park them, every major road was strip-malled for two miles out with gas stations, convenience stores, video rental shops, fast food drive-throughs and grocery stores. Many of the stores were already boarded up and derelict. It reminds me of the slash-and-burn practices we so deplore in the Amazon rain forests: build a big ugly chain store, suck out all the quick money you can, then abandon that store and go build another where the action's hotter.

"Queens Boulevard with longleaf pines," laments a Yankee friend who says she moved down here to get away from that sort of car-centered urban blight.

She should have gone to Oregon where

they have sensible growth plans, not North Carolina where we try to throw up a six-lane bypass around any town with a population of more than eighty-three people.

I parked at the back of the drive and carried Hambone, Daddy's "gin" and the pecans in through the side door of the big white brick house.

The warmth inside Aunt Zell's kitchen lifted my chilled spirits a little. Every counter was covered with bowls of chopped and floured fruits, loaf pans lined with waxed paper, and canisters of flour and sugar. She was only waiting for the shelled nuts to start mixing in earnest. The Gilbey's gin bottle got stashed in the pantry. It wouldn't be needed till she was ready to wrap the cooled cakes in cheesecloth.

"Soon as I take them out of the oven, Ash and I are going over to the fish house for some shrimp. Don't you want to come, honey?"

"Thanks, but maybe I'll just fix a sandwich later."

She hadn't heard about Mr. Jap, so I gave her the condensed version, then went upstairs to call Dwight, who said,

"If you don't have anything on for tonight, why don't you come over to the office and let's talk some and then maybe go back to my place and watch a video."

"Which one?"

"Audrey Hepburn and Albert Finney," he said, knowing my fondness for old movies. *"Two for the Road."*

"I'll bring my two-for-one pizza coupon," I told him.

There's absolutely nothing romantic between Dwight and me, but that didn't stop me from peeling off my jeans and sweatshirt and heading for the shower to wash away the smell of wood smoke and dogs from my hair and body.

For the last few weeks, I'd been cutting back in anticipation of Thanksgiving and Aunt Zell's fruitcake and I was pleased to discover that I no longer had to suck in my breath to button my black twill slacks. Emboldened, I slipped on my favorite fall jacket. The lines were vaguely oriental — black silk appliquéd with strips of brown and gold velvet that can do nice things for my sandy brown hair if the stars are in the right alignment. For once, it didn't make me look like an overstuffed teddy bear.

Gold earrings, low black heels, a dash of lipstick and I was ready to go when I finally remembered another phone call I wanted to make.

In addition to being my former law partner, John Claude Lee is also my second cousin, once removed; so when I can't prevail upon him as a colleague, I can always fall back upon the claims of kinship.

I caught him just as he and Julia were getting ready to leave for a panel discussion on ethics that he'd been asked to moderate over at Campbell University, so he didn't have too much time to debate the proprieties with me.

He'd already heard from Cherry Lou's attorney and from Dwight Bryant, too, which saved having to rehash Mr. Jap's death. "Just tell me one thing, John Claude, and then I'll let you go. Yesterday, Jap Stancil told me that Cherry Lou was going to sign her half of the farm back over to him."

"That was injudicious of him," my cousin said disapprovingly.

"But — ?"

"Injudicious *and* premature. As you may know, Avery Brewer is her court-appointed attorney. We finished drawing up the papers yesterday afternoon and she was to sign them on Monday."

"What happens to those papers now?"

"Obviously their usefulness has been negated."

"She wouldn't go ahead and sign it over to Allen Stancil instead?"

I could almost hear his raised eyebrows over the phone line.

"Really, Deborah," he said frostily, clearly remembering with distaste his previous encounter with Allen. I wasn't about to tell him that he'd gotten me an annulment for a bigamous marriage. "I should think that you of all people would see the unsuitability of that when there's a strong possibility that he's involved in his uncle's death."

"But what if he isn't?"

"Then it will all come to him in due time without Mrs. Stancil's gesture."

So either way, Allen gained nothing he didn't already have in his pocket. Even so, "I'm surprised you let a client die without a will." I was thinking out loud, not really expecting an answer, but John Claude chose to think I was questioning his professional standards.

"I had drafted one that he was to sign

on Monday as well. A simple instrument. It divided his estate equally between Stancil and Merrilee Grimes, with Stancil getting the house, garage, equipment and all the cars and Mrs. Grimes to receive an equal value in land."

And an unsigned will is worth less than the paper it's written on. But assuming either had been a motive, which piece of paper had Mr. Jap been killed to prevent? The will or the deed?

And what if Cherry Lou or her children weren't really all that eager to throw in the cards?

"Is there any chance that Cherry Lou Stancil could be acquitted?" I asked.

"With a jury, there's always a chance," he replied dryly. "But if I were Avery Brewer, I shouldn't aspire to be a Johnnie Cochran."

"Which is why they picked you to moderate an ethics discussion," I told him. "Break a leg, hear?"

16

That these accounts are genuine and true, we hope, will appear from the following general description of the province in question, in which all that is intended, is to lay before my countrymen things most essential for them to know . . .

"Scotus Americanus," *1773*

All was quiet when I arrived at the Colleton County Sheriff's Department in the basement of the courthouse. Indeed, the duty officer at the front desk was absorbed in a paperback romance and she barely acknowledged my wave as I passed. Saturday night, yes, but much too early for any bloody knife-fighters, spaced-out deadheads, wife beaters, drunk drivers or other violators and disturbers of the peace who would be showing up — stitched, sober and sorry — in my courtroom next week.

As I approached Dwight's office, I heard the low rumble of male voices, then a raucous laugh that could belong to no one except Special Agent Terry Wilson, State Bureau of Investigation.

Dwight's always been like another brother, but Terry and I came awfully close to making it legal once. Fortunately, we had the good sense to back off, and then we had the even better sense to stay friends.

That didn't stop him from giving me an exaggerated leer when I came in. "Damn, but that Kidd Chapin's a cocky bastard."

"Why, Mr. Wilson, whatever do you mean?" I asked in my best Scarlett O'Hara drawl.

"Letting a good-looking woman like you out alone on a Saturday night? If he's not cocky, then he's sure 'nuff crazy."

We talked trash a few minutes longer, till I asked him about Stanton and he came crashing back to reality with a frustrated groan. Stanton's his son by his first marriage, sixteen years old and climbing Fool's Hill, to hear Terry tell it.

"He's a mess! You know how I wasn't going to let him have a car till he could pay for the upkeep and insurance?"

"Yeah, and even when you were laying down that law last year, I told you it wasn't going to last much past the candles on his birthday cake."

"I'd've stuck to it, hadn't been for his mama. All those after-school activities? She didn't like him hitching rides with any kid who's got a driver's license, so we bought him a good used car and he got a weekend job. Only now he needs to work more hours to pay for the upkeep so he's cut out a lot of the after-school stuff. He's even talking about not going out for baseball next spring."

"I've heard my nieces and nephews sing the whole five stanzas," I said. "They need a car to get work, but the main reason they have to work is to support the damn car. If they schedule their study halls for the end of the day, the schools will even give them early release so they can work longer hours to buy newer cars. Between school and work, they're putting in ten- and twelve-hour days. When do they have time to study?"

"They don't," Terry said grimly. "Stanton's grade average has dropped a whole letter. He keeps this up, he'll be lucky to get into Wake Tech."

"You sure you don't want to hang around tonight, split a pizza with me and Deb'rah?" asked Dwight. "She's buying."

"Wish I could, but I'd better get on back to Raleigh. Unlike you two, I've got a *real* date tonight."

"Yeah? Anybody we know?"

He gave a sheepish grin. "Stanton's algebra teacher. We're chaperoning their Thanksgiving dance tonight."

"Well, good luck to you," said Dwight, "and we sure 'preciate your help on that drug evidence."

"No problem. Just let me know how it turns out, okay?"

He gave me a hug and then he was gone and I turned to find Dwight giving me an odd look.

"What?" I asked.

"Allen Stancil. I ran a background check on him. Criminal and civil. Want to see what I came up with?"

"Not unless there's a warrant out on him," I said warily. "Is there?"

"Not at the moment. But if we don't hear from him by tomorrow, I may put an apprehend on the network."

He pushed a bunch of printout sheets across his desk anyhow and I leafed through them. Allen had certainly led a busy life, beginning all the way back to his teenage years when he was caught hauling a load of bootleg whiskey through Greensboro before he was old enough to get a valid driver's license. I knew that Mr. Jap had recruited him and Dallas both to transport moonshine occasionally, but trust a fourteen-year-old to keep cool with all that power under the hood? Of course, Daddy had been head of a household before he was fourteen, so maybe it didn't seem as outrageous back then as it does now. Allen's age was all that saved him on that one.

Most of the recorded violations were minor and had been punished by fines and a scattering of light jail sentences that ranged from overnight to thirty days. No moral pillar of the community but no wife beater or serial killer either. He did seem to get questioned an awful lot about stolen cars, though.

"Guy I talked to out in Charlotte says they just busted up a big chop shop operation — one of those places that steal cars to order and then chop them up for parts."

I hate it when Dwight patronizes me. "They can dismantle a car in seven minutes flat, then sell the parts for more than the original car's worth. I do know what a chop shop is, thank you very much."

"Sorry. Anyhow, the guy says Stancil was one of the known associates and that probably the only reason he didn't get hauled in, too, was because he's been out of the area the last month when they were doing their heaviest surveillance. They don't have any actual evidence against him."

"Guilt by association?" I said dryly.

Dwight had been leaning back in his swivel chair, one foot lazily propped on an open desk drawer. Now he came upright with both feet on the floor.

"Oh, come on, Deb'rah. You're holding his rap sheets. You think he came over to Colleton County and got religion? He was just getting out of Dodge City before the bullets started flying. You can't really believe the guy's clean?"

I thought back to yesterday — was it really only yesterday and not weeks ago? — when Mr. Jap was bragging on Allen's automotive skills and prowess: "He bought a old wrecker from some man out from Raleigh, he did, and in just two days, he got it fixed up good enough to sell, yes, he did."

Now that I considered how fast he'd "fixed it up," there was a better than fifty-fifty chance that Allen had probably bought a wreck and immediately transferred its vehicle ID number plate to a stolen car of the same make and model. He could then register the stolen car as rebuilt and sell it legitimately.

"No," I said slowly, "he's —" I broke off as the implication of something on Allen's printout suddenly leaped out at me.

"What the hell is this?" I asked, pointing at the dateline on every sheet.

Last Monday's date.

"You started checking up on him before Mr. Jap was killed. Why?"

The guilty look on his face was the mirror image of the look on Daddy's face when he said Dwight wanted to see me.

Exasperation jetted through me. "I don't believe this!"

"Now, Deb'rah —"

"Don't go 'Now Deb'ring' me, you egg-sucking hound! Daddy told you about

Allen and me, didn't he? And the two of you thought you'd take care of him. Just run him on out of the county before he got dug in too deep at Mr. Jap's."

"It's not my fault if Mr. Kezzie wants to protect you," Dwight said stiffly.

"It's your fault that you keep indulging him," I snapped. "If you and the boys don't quit sticking your noses in my affairs —"

"You're going to get out your trusty butcher knife and chop 'em off?"

The trouble with trying to stay mad at Dwight is that he can usually make me laugh. And once my anger was diffused, I had to admit — to myself if not to Dwight — that getting Allen Stancil out of Colleton County had been high on my list of priorities, too.

"No warrants on him, hmm? I was hoping maybe he was behind in his child support payments or something."

"Support payments? According to the records, he stayed in hot water over them, but that kid's way past twenty-one now."

"No, there's a minor girl, too. Wendy Nicole." I riffled through the civil judgments against Allen, but there was nothing about a Wendy Nicole Stancil or her mother Sally. "Probably sweet-talked her into keeping it out of Child Support Enforcement," I muttered. "Probably told her that he'd pay her what he could when he could and 'You can't git blood outn a turnip, darlin'.' "

"I thought I read that the little girl's name was Tiffany and that the paternity case against him was dismissed," said Dwight.

"Tiffany came later. A lot later." In amongst the sheaf of papers Dwight had managed to accumulate on Allen, I found a summation of the case and read, " 'Tiffany Jane Morgan, daughter of Katherine J. Morgan.' She'll be four years old in January. According to Allen, Tiffany's mother didn't know *who* the father was so she picked him as the nearest warm body. Wendy Nicole is his, though. By his second wife. She's seventeen, which means he still has a year to pay on her."

Dwight was more interested in Allen's present than in his past.

"Everybody seems to know that Billy Wall was coming with all that money," he mused. "Allen had to know, too."

"You talked to Wall?"

Dwight nodded. "Said he came by

around eleven-thirty. Jap was out in the garage alone. Said he paid him his share of the produce money in cash — forty-nine hundred in hundred-dollar bills — and Jap took his notes out of that old safe, put the money in, and spun the lock on it."

"Was Allen there?"

"Billy said his truck was gone and he didn't see him. He didn't hang around, he said. Just counted out the money, talked a couple of minutes about Jap's plans for the garage and then left."

"So now you're looking at a time of death between eleven-thirty and one-thirty. Did you talk to Cherry Lou?"

"Yeah, but she's real hostile. Says good riddance to all Stancils and she saw nothing."

"What about Dick Sutterly?"

"Pretty much the same thing. Says he came in through Gray Talbert's lane and went out by Jap's. But I may have to talk to him again because he was real curious about the time frame and who was where, you know? And he was driving around that whole section from Adam's land to Gray Talbert's nursery and on back out past Jap's around one o'clock."

He paused a second, then assumed an offhand air. "Says Adam and the dogs were on Talbert's side of the creek when he came up on them around twelve-thirty."

"Oh?"

"And somebody's dogs were around the garage after the rain stopped."

"Lot of dogs still run free," I observed. "See any footprints?"

"Just yours going back. And the dogs, of course. And I had somebody walk that lane all the way to the creek."

"It wasn't Adam," I said.

"Never said it was. I'm just thinking that somebody was mighty lucky with that many people all around the place that morning — Adam, Mr. Kezzie, Cherry Lou, Dick Sutterly."

"For what it's worth, G. Hooks Talbert and a couple of his friends were out there, too. Hunting." I gave him an edited version of that meeting. "They could've seen someone."

Dwight smiled, knowing that Knotts and Talberts are polar opposites. "You'd love it if G. Hooks was involved, wouldn't you?"

"Wouldn't break my heart."

"Whoever did it probably didn't go

there planning to," Dwight said thoughtfully. "Say somebody dropped in on Jap and maybe he bragged about how much money his corn brought. The killer might've just acted on the spur of the moment."

"Carpe diem," I said. It was the motto on a coffee mug Dwight had given me when I first filed for judge.

"Exactly," he said. "Seize the damn day. Smash an old man over the head and burn open his safe and take his money. So what do you think, Deb'rah? Was it Allen?"

"If it was, it's the second dumbest thing he ever did in his life. Mr. Jap planned to spend all that money on him, Cherry Lou Stancil was going to sign her half of the farm back over on Monday, and what I bet John Claude didn't tell you was that he was also supposed to sign a will on Monday."

"Huh?"

When I told him the terms, Dwight frowned. "If he dies before the will's signed, Allen gets it all?"

"*If* Cherry Lou's convicted."

He waved aside the possibility that she might not be. "So with a will, Allen gets half; without one, he scoops the lot. How much you reckon we're talking about?"

I shrugged. "Ninety acres of land with good frontage, say five thousand an acre and that's on the low side. Say another fifty thousand for the house, garage and equipment — that's half a million right there. Then all those old classic cars sitting around under the sheds and shelters? Everybody says they're worth thousands in mint condition, but I couldn't begin to say what they're worth as is."

Evidently Dwight hadn't done the math in a while either. "Raw Colleton County farmland's going for five thou an acre?" he shook his head in amazement. "I don't think Mom and Dad paid more than three hundred when they bought their place."

"Welcome to the twenty-first century," I said.

By the time we left to pick up our pizzas, Dwight and I had sketched out a rough list of possible killers.

He wanted to put Allen at the head, I opted for Cherry Lou's two kids.

"After all, they connived at Dallas's death. Who's to say they really understand inheritance laws? Or maybe they do, but think Avery Brewer's going to get their mother off."

"After they've cut a deal with the DA to testify against her?"

"They haven't testified yet," I said. "Put 'em down."

With an exaggerated sigh, he wrote down Ashley Wentworth and Bradley Fletcher. "But if they go on the list, so does Merrilee Grimes."

"Waste of time," I told him. "She gains only if the will's signed."

"But she gains if he dies before Cherry Lou gives the farm back because she's no kin to Jap."

"Merrilee wasn't one real drop of kin to him before." I was getting a little tired of explaining how the laws of inheritance work. "All you people keep thinking it goes back to Dallas and starts again with Dallas's heirs. It doesn't. We're still looking at Mr. Jap's heirs — Allen or Allen's children."

"Yeah?" There was a mulish look of disbelief on Dwight's big homely face.

"I'm a judge," I told him. "I know the law."

"Then maybe I ought to list Allen's children, too."

"Makes as much sense as having Merrilee there."

"And to be strictly fair, I've got to list Adam." Before I could protest again, he said, "Good as Adam's doing in California, I grant you he's the most unlikely one of the bunch, but he *was* out there alone during the relevant time."

No way could Adam kill somebody, I thought, but that still didn't mean I was going to tell Dwight about my brother's current financial problems.

"Who else could we make a motive for?" Dwight mused.

I hesitated. Daddy had asked Adam and me not to mention Mr. Jap's plans to sell, and even though he seemed to think it was okay to confide *my* secrets to Dwight, I couldn't bring myself to go against him completely.

"Well, Dick Sutterly's been trying to get Adam or Mr. Jap to sell. Maybe he thought he'd have better luck picking up the Stancil farm from Mr. Jap's heirs than from Mr. Jap?"

Dwight looked dubious, but he added Sutterly's name to the list all the same. At the very bottom, he wrote down Billy Wall's name. "He says Jap Stancil was alive when he left, but unless someone else saw Stancil alive later, I'll have to keep him in mind."

There didn't seem to be anyone else with an immediate motive. He stuck the list in the case jacket and stood up to go with a mischievous look on his face. "So if killing Mr. Jap would be the second dumbest thing Allen Stancil ever did, what was the first dumbest?"

For once, I did not rise to Dwight's bait.

Daddy always says a catfish would never get caught if it'd just learn to keep its mouth shut.

17

All modes of Christian worship, not detrimental to society, are here tolerated . . .

"Scotus Americanus," *1773*

Sunday morning dawned clear and sunny. There was a decided nip in the air as I left the house at 10:54. Dwight and I had wound up talking about my problems with Kidd's daughter and his problems with his ex-wife before we put the video on, so it was nearly one before I got home and close to two before I fell into bed.

Aunt Zell and Uncle Ash had left in plenty of time for Sunday school at ten, but I'm doing good to make eleven o'clock preaching services. I'll always consider Sweetwater my home church, but I moved my membership when I joined my cousins' law practice because I hate to get up early on the weekends. And proximity really was my original motivator for choosing First Baptist Church of Dobbs.

Honest.

"That's still an admission of sloth," the preacher had said, disdainful that I couldn't spring out of bed on Sunday mornings and drive twenty miles to Sweetwater.

"Never hurts a newly qualified attorney to share hymn books and amens with some of the most prominent citizens of the county," the pragmatist had reminded him.

"Opportunism in church is worse than sloth and furthermore —"

It was such an old argument that I pushed them both to the back of my head and hurried into the sanctuary just as the first hymn was announced. Portland and Avery Brewer moved down to make room for me at the end of a pew near the door and my voice joined with theirs as we sang hymn number one-ninety, "Come, Thou Fount of Every Blessing."

Because it was the Sunday before Thanksgiving, the young and earnest minister exhorted us to count our many blessings and give thanks to the Lord. Obediently, I fixed my eyes upon my favorite stained-glass window, a pastoral scene where sheep grazed calmly while an improbable lion lay down amongst them with sleepily benevolent eyes. Instead of the upcoming national holiday, I thought back to the earliest November I could remember.

Now that I considered it, that was probably about the time our simple little country church was changing over from its old-fashioned Harvest Day.

Harvest Day at Sweetwater Baptist was usually a Saturday in late October or early November. There would be a morning praise service in gratitude for bountiful crops, then lunch on the grounds with hot dogs stuck on straightened-out coat hangers and roasted over an open fire, followed by marshmallows toasted on the same wire hangers. When I pulled mine out of the fire, they were always black on the outside and melted ambrosia inside.

After the weenie roast, there would be an auction to raise money for the church. Men donated cords of wood, bales of cotton, carved cedar walking sticks, fresh apple cider, and ten-pound bags of pecans, walnuts or peanuts. Women gave crocheted tablecloths, embroidered aprons, colorful patchwork quilts, fancy cakes, or quart jars of canned fruits, the peaches and cherries glowing like jewels in that crisp autumn sunlight.

Will got his start as an auctioneer at one of the Sweetwater Harvest sales.

Daddy wasn't a churchgoer, but he always came to the sale and donated a hundred-weight of cured tobacco and bid on a quilt or some cakes. Growing boys always needed covering or feeding.

Relatively speaking, Southerners — especially those out in the country — have only recently taken to Thanksgiving. Certainly it was never a major holiday when I was very young. Oh, we colored pumpkins and turkeys in kindergarten and put on assembly plays in Pilgrim costumes of buckled shoes and hats and gray clothes with wide white collars. And we'd get Thursday and Friday off and the mail wouldn't run on that Thursday, but otherwise, it was just an ordinary day of the week. Like as not, Daddy and the boys would harvest beans or cut stalks that day while Mother and Maidie and I went about our usual chores.

It wasn't till I was in middle school and after some of the boys had married town-bred girls who celebrated Thanksgiving like the rest of the country that Mother started cooking a turkey and making a special holiday meal.

Daddy still thought it was a made-up holiday imposed on us by the North. As a boy, he could remember when Thanksgiving depended on annual presidential proclamations and was vaguely mistrusted as a remnant of Yankee puritanism. "They tried to outlaw our Christmas, so we never much bothered with their Thanksgiving," he says, harkening back to lore handed down from before the Civil War.

Mother was a girl but old enough to remember when President Roosevelt stabilized Thanksgiving in 1939 and made it the fourth Thursday in November instead of the last Thursday, a distinction with a difference. "And not for the glory of God," she would say dryly, "but for Mammon. November had five Thursdays that year and Mr. Roosevelt thought it would help stores get out of the Depression quicker if the country had an extra week of Christmas shopping days."

Which is why Haywood and Isabel would feel no qualms about flying off to Atlantic City next Thursday instead of staying home to eat a big meal. As long as we get together sometime toward the end of the week, our family still has no fixation on any particular day.

My Thanksgiving reverie was suddenly interrupted by a sharp nudge in the ribs by Portland Brewer. Everyone else had their heads bowed for the prayer that closed the minister's sermon. Once again, I'd missed it entirely.

Oh, well.

We stood for the singing of a final hymn — "Bringing in the Sheaves" — a last benediction, then we left the shadowy sanctuary and passed into the bright sunshine where red, gold and brown leaves lay thickly on the sidewalk and swirled along the gutters. Last night's chilly wind had finished stripping the crepe myrtles and maples. The oaks alone still held their brown leaves.

As Cherry Lou Stancil's court-appointed attorney, Avery Brewer wanted to hear my account of Mr. Jap's death.

"Too bad she didn't get to sign the farm back over to him," I said. "That leaves her going to trial with her primary motive still intact."

"You never know," Avery said gamely. "Juries have acquitted with a lot more evidence than a Kmart sales slip for the weapon."

"Right. And I suppose Millard King's going to argue accidental discharge of said weapon and have Tig Wentworth plead to involuntary manslaughter?"

Portland grinned at her husband. "Now there's a thought, honey. She *said* the shotgun was a present. Maybe her little ol' son-in-law tripped on a mole run as he was going out to give it to him."

Avery was not amused and went on ahead to warm up their car.

As the rest of the congregation streamed through the broad oak doors, then clumped for snatches of Sunday morning conversation along the steps and sidewalk, Portland touched my sleeve and drew me aside.

"Can I speak to you a minute, Deborah? Off the record?"

"Sure, Por. What's up?"

Portland was a Smith before she married Avery Brewer and is Uncle Ash's brother's daughter, which makes us courtesy cousins. Not that the courtesy is needed. We've been good friends since we got thrown out of the Junior Girls' class in Sunday school for teasing prissy Caroline Atherton. Indeed, Portland's one of the reasons I stuck with law. After nearly messing up my life, I looked around to see what my friends were doing with theirs and Portland seemed to be having the most fun.

She and I were still the same height and approximate build, only on her, it looked better. She had short wiry black hair that curled all over her head as if a mad beautician had styled a Persian lamb, and her brown eyes were worried as she drew me even further away from the crowd.

"You remember that contested paternity suit I argued before you a couple of weeks ago?"

"Vaguely. Refresh my memory."

"Beecham versus Collins? Single mom and cute little girl? I represented the alleged father."

"Oh, yeah. The one where blood tests proved he couldn't have fathered the child?"

"That's the one."

"So?"

"So day before yesterday — Friday? I got a call from one of Collins' friends. He's facing a paternity suit, too, and Collins recommended me."

"What's wrong with that? You won the case, why wouldn't he recommend you?"

"Because I wasn't Collins' only recommendation," Portland said grimly. "This friend tried to be subtle about it, but he asked me to make certain that we used Jamerson Labs and that it'd sure be nice if Mrs. Diana Henderson could be the technician who actually draws the blood and runs the test since she did such a good job for ol' Tim there, wink-wink, nudge-nudge."

"What?"

She nodded unhappily.

"He *bribed* her?"

"Maybe."

As the implications sank in, I said, "You're talking perjury here. And subornation of perjury, too. Or conspiracy. And that's just for starters. Who approached whom?"

If possible, Portland looked even more unhappy. The ethical ground she was walking over at the moment was shakier than Jell-O.

"I don't know, Deborah. Swear to God. And maybe I'm jumping to conclusions."

"Do you honestly think so?" I asked her squarely.

Her eyes met mine. "No."

"Who was the opposing attorney? Ambrose Daughtridge? I want your client and Mrs. Henderson in my courtroom first thing tomorrow morning."

"*Ex*-client," Portland said hastily.

"Whichever."

"We'll be there." She gave my arm a squeeze, then with her wiry dark curls bouncing in the sunlight, she hurried over to the curb where Avery waited in their car.

As I started to cross the street to my own car, a white pickup stopped in the crosswalk in front of me and my nephew Reese leaned over and pushed open the passenger door.

"Want to buy me a cup of coffee?" he asked.

With those oversized tires, I had to hike my Sunday skirt to make that long step up to the cab, but one glance at the diamond-patterned treads made me think that it might well be worth the price of a cup of coffee to hear what Reese had to say about yesterday morning.

18

As in every rising colony, so in this, tradesmen are much wanted; and the demand for them must increase in proportion to the number of settlers that resort to it.

"Scotus Americanus," *1773*

As the youngest of my father's twelve children, I have nieces and nephews who range in age from four years older than me, right down to high school.

Reese, the second of Herman and Nadine's four, had to be at least twenty-six, but going on for sixteen if the love and money he was lavishing on this juked-up truck meant anything.

The white exterior was waxed to a diamond sheen that dazzled my eyes, and the heavy chrome bumpers were even shinier.

The interior was lushly upholstered in a supple honey-brown vinyl that made everything — from the adjustable seat to the doors to the dashboard and even the steering wheel itself — feel buttery soft. Besides the standard accessories, the dashboard had a built-in CD player with extra speakers concealed in the doors, and the lid of the padded armrest not only had a place to hold drink cups, it flipped back to reveal a cellular phone. The golden oak gun rack across the rear window and the stock of the Winchester hanging in the rack both matched the light caramel tones of the upholstery.

"Done much hunting this season?" I asked as I buckled myself in.

"Naw. Don't have time. Got a few doves back in September, but we been so busy wiring that new subdivision south of town lately, I'm doing good to get away by dinnertime on Saturday. Now that daylight savings is over, sunset comes mighty early."

"What about sunrise?" I asked snidely.

He snorted and took the turn on the truck lane a hair too sharply so that we bumped up over the curb. "You sound just like Ma."

"Bite your tongue, boy!"

Nadine's a good woman, but she can be awfully rigid about the morality of early rising and hard work and going to church three times a week.

Reese laughed. "Yeah, I'm thinking of getting me a doublewide and putting it out near the long pond. Dad said he'd cut me off an acre or two if I wanted it. I shouldn't never have moved back home again. If I stay out late on a Saturday night and then try to sleep in, they act like I'm going straight to the devil. I tell you what's the truth — I'm getting too old to have to be up and out on Sunday mornings before they get back from church."

We pulled into the drive-through at Bojangles and I told him I'd spring for a sausage biscuit as well, if they were still serving breakfast. "I got up too late to eat, myself," I admitted.

The truck windows operated electronically. Reese pushed the button to lower his and yelled down into the staticky speaker, "Two sausage biscuits and two large coffees. No cream. No sugar. You do take your coffee black, don't you, Deb'rah?"

"Uh-huh."

"Good. Coffee stains'll sponge right up

if you spill it on the carpet, but that creamer stuff's hell to get out."

He sounded like Hints from Heloise.

When we drove around to the serving window, those oversized tires put us up so high that Reese had to lean out and reach down to take our order. "And could we have some extra napkins?"

"Don't you trust me not to smear sausage grease on your seats," I teased.

"Never hurts to be safe," he said mildly.

That was so unlike the old devil-may-care Reese that I took a good long look at him as he reseated his ball cap so that his light brown hair lay smooth before he pulled out of the Bojangles driveway into the Sunday church traffic that clogged the main commercial street through town.

He has the clear, forget-me-not blue eyes of all our clan and the solid regular features of most of his cousins. None of my brothers are movie-star gorgeous and neither are their children, but nobody in our family's ever stopped a clock either. Reese has always had girlfriends — "trashy girlfriends," according to Nadine, but she'd say that about any woman he moved in with if there wasn't a gold band on his finger first.

He's been working for Herman and Nadine since high school and has never shown too much energy or ambition. All he seems to want is to put in his forty hours, then spend the weekends hunting and fishing and maybe a quick roll in the hay between football games. His younger sister Annie Sue is the only one of Herman's kids with a real feel for the electrical business.

But ever since Herman's brush with death left him in a wheelchair, we haven't heard much grumbling either from or about Reese. He wasn't slacking either. A couple of knuckles on his hands were scraped raw where he'd banged them when he was pulling wire across ceiling rafters or while he was trying to bore holes though hard-to-reach floor joists. For a moment, I almost wondered if the real reason he broke up with his last girlfriend and moved back home was so he could be there to help out as Herman adjusted to his loss of mobility.

"Even hedonists can rise to the occasion," whispered my idealistic preacher.

"Get real," said the cynical pragmatist. "This is Reese, for God's sake."

I took another look around the interior

of his truck and decided I was probably imagining things.

Nevertheless, I took his sausage biscuit out of the greasy paper it'd come wrapped in and carefully tucked a fresh napkin around the bottom so he could eat while he drove without strewing crumbs.

A third of the sandwich disappeared in a single bite and his mouth was full as he said, "I could eat a horse."

I broke off a small piece of my sausage and biscuit, barely enough to take the edge off my own appetite, and passed the rest over to him. He grunted his thanks and wolfed it down, too.

Yeah, this was Reese all right.

With the rich smell of sausage and coffee filling the cab, we drove aimlessly in a wide looping circle around Dobbs, enjoying the drive. Not going anywhere, just going.

"Dwight Bryant call you yet?" I asked.

"Nope. What about?"

"About what time you drove past Jap Stancil's garage yesterday?"

"Who says I did?" His voice was wary.

"Saw your tracks."

"Must've been from last week sometime. No, wait a minute, I remember now. I did cut through last Tuesday to see if I could fit a trailer between those willows near the long pond."

"Oh, come on, Reese. It rained hard all day Friday. Didn't stop till after midnight. Your tracks were laid down sometime yesterday morning. New crisp diamonds in a wide tread. You're not going to tell me any of the other boys have tires like yours."

"Okay, so it was me," he said grumpily. "You don't have to go telling the whole county, do you?"

"Why not?"

" 'Cause I was suppose to be working. Finishing up a house there on Forty-Eight. But dammit all, Deb'rah! Dad and Ma don't want me to work on Sunday, the state don't allow Sunday hunting and I've not taken a full Saturday off in two months. Ruth and Jessica were riding their horses along the creek in the new ground Thursday evening and Jess told me she saw some pretty big deer tracks."

Ruth is Andrew's younger daughter by his second wife and Jessica is Seth and Minnie's middle child. Both are still in high school.

"Well, you know how A.K. keeps bragging about that head he's got mounted? I thought it'd sure be fun if I took a little drive through, maybe bag a big buck myself if I got lucky."

"And did you?"

He shook his head. "Nope. Saw the tracks though and man, they're *humongous,* but that's all I saw."

"What time was this?"

He shrugged. "I don't know. I wasn't paying much attention to the clock. I knocked off around ten-fifteen, ten-thirty, and drove straight on over. I was maybe ten minutes away. Say ten-thirty, maybe ten forty-five?"

"See anything of Mr. Jap when you drove past the garage?"

"Nope, not a soul. I would've stopped to ask Allen about a sticky valve, but his truck wasn't there neither. You don't think Dwight's really going to come asking me stuff, do you?"

"If someone tells him those are your tire tracks, he will. You ought to go ahead and tell him yourself 'cause that could help narrow down the time range. Dwight's got no reason to mention it to your dad, especially if you ask him not to."

But Reese was getting a look on his face like a right-sided mule hitched up to left-sided traces. No way was he going to pull that load.

"Granddaddy already said he saw Mr. Jap at the crossroads around ten-thirty. I'm telling you I didn't see anybody when I drove in or when I drove out, and I don't see why I've got to get involved."

He drained the last of his coffee, crushed the foam cup in his hand, and turned down the street that would bring us back to my car. I sipped my own coffee and tried to figure out why he was so reluctant to speak to Dwight.

There was a sour feeling between us when he pulled up beside the church.

"Thanks for breakfast," he said stiffly.

As I opened the door to climb down, a gust of cold wind caught my hair and tangled it in the bolt action of the Winchester behind me.

Awkwardly, Reese reached over to untangle me and I said, "You *do* have a deer license, don't you?"

He shook his head and looked at me sadly. "What do you think I am, stupid or something?"

Anger I might've believed. Ironic

laughter I might've believed. But all that innocence shining in his bright blue eyes?

I held out my hand and wiggled my fingers. "Come on, Reese. Show me."

He slammed his hand down hard on the seat between us. "Okay, so I don't have a fucking deer license. You satisfied? When've I had the time to buy one? Will you tell me that? And now I suppose you'll tell your boyfriend and I won't be able to turn around without a game warden breathing over my shoulder."

"Get a license," I told him, sliding down to the street without breaking the heel on my shoe. "And leave your gun home till you do."

I slammed the door and was walking away when I heard both windows power down.

"You know something, Deb'rah?" Reese shouted angrily. "You used to be a damn sight more fun before you got to be a judge."

Before I could answer, he screeched off from the curb, ran a red light at the intersection and tore off down the street in utter disregard of the thirty-five miles per hour speed limit.

"Thank goodness it's Sunday and the streets are deserted," the pragmatist said piously.

The preacher was too dismayed to comment.

19

This is a great spur to their diligence, and an ample reward for their toil, which is far from severe . . .

"Scotus Americanus," *1773*

I was in the shower next morning when my phone rang and by the time I was dried off enough to pick up, Portland Brewer was well launched into a complicated message for my machine.

"— so there's just no way we can —"

"Sorry, Por, I was in the shower. Want to start again?"

"Not really," she said ruefully. "Not if you're going to be horsey about what I've got to tell you."

I took the towel off my head and began finger-combing my wet hair. "You couldn't reach the blood tech or your ex-client yesterday, right?"

"He's somewhere between here and Baltimore, according to his girlfriend, and she doesn't expect him back till tonight. I've left messages with her and with his office."

"What about the technician?"

"Unlisted home phone. And Jamerson Labs doesn't open till nine this morning. I'll try again then, okay?"

"Fine," I said. No point riding my high horse over Portland. She knew the seriousness of this without any lectures or exhortations from me. "Just let me know when you've got them rounded up so we can tell Ambrose."

Portland might not have been waiting for me in chambers, but Merrilee and Pete Grimes were. After handling the details of Dallas's funeral for Mr. Jap, Merrilee considered herself an old hand at dealing with the Medical Examiner's office over in Chapel Hill. To her frustration though, she wasn't being allowed to deal.

Anything that upsets Merrilee upsets Pete, and both of them wanted me to do something.

"They're ready to release Uncle Jap's body, but Duck Aldcroft says he can't send a hearse for it because Allen's Uncle Jap's next of kin and nobody's seen him since Friday."

"Did you speak to Dwight?" I asked, fiddling with the zipper of my robe. Judge Carly Jernigan's widow had given me this robe and its old-fashioned metal teeth had caught a fold of my blouse. I was hoping to work it loose without marking the white silk.

"He says he's got the Highway Patrol keeping an eye out for Allen's truck, but if you ask me, that doesn't sound too urgent."

Pete gave a supportive rumble. "If he smashed poor old Jap and took off with the money, he could be halfway to California by now."

Merrilee nodded vigorously. "And Uncle Jap could just lie over there in Chapel Hill and — and — and *rot* for all he cares!"

Pete hitched his chair closer to hers and embraced her protectively. He was such a man mountain and she was so small and dainty that images of King Kong and Faye Wray flashed through my head as Merrilee automatically leaned into his arm.

An attorney stuck his head in the door

waving a show-cause order I'd promised to sign and I was conscious that it was time to head for the courtroom even though I still hadn't called over to Social Services as I'd planned. The zipper chose that moment to release my blouse and yes, it left an ugly metallic mark right at my bustline.

"Look, Merrilee, Pete," I said, "John Claude Lee was acting as Mr. Jap's attorney. Why don't you go speak to him, see what he can do about the situation? After all, you'd have been one of the —"

I abruptly caught myself, but Merrilee's narrow little Yadkin eyes sharpened alertly.

"I'd've been one of what?"

I shrugged, annoyed that I'd let myself be distracted into speaking indiscreetly and even more annoyed because I knew Merrilee would never leave until I satisfied the curiosity I'd unleashed.

"One of what, Deborah?" she asked again when I'd signed the show cause and the attorney was gone.

I stood and finished zipping my robe. "I spoke out of turn, but it doesn't really matter, I guess. Mr. Jap was planning to sign a will today that would have split his estate equally between you and Allen. You would have been co-beneficiary. Now, of course, it'll probably all go to Allen. I'm sorry, Merrilee."

Pete was frowning as he worked it out in his head, but Merrilee was suddenly transformed. Tears streamed from her eyes, but her smile was radiant.

"Oh, Deborah! Was he really going to leave me half?"

I'd never seen anyone react quite like this to hearing they're not going to inherit a penny. "The will doesn't count, Merrilee, because he didn't —"

She brushed that aside. "I don't care about his money. Don't you see? All these years, ever since Aunt Elsie died, I've been looking in on Uncle Jap, making sure he was all right, doing the sort of woman things Dallas couldn't and Cherry Lou wouldn't. And then when Allen came — Uncle Jap was never one for thanking people, not that I wanted to be thanked. Jesus says, 'As you do it for the least of these, you do it for me,' and that's what I tried to do, but even so, it was hard to watch Allen taking and taking and Uncle Jap acting like he hung the moon. And now you tell me that he was going to will me half of what he had?"

She jumped up and gave me a hug. "Thank you for telling me, Deb'rah. Now I know that he *did* appreciate that I loved him and that he loved me back."

"Aw, honey," said Pete, looking as if he could eat her with a spoon. "Of course he loved you. Everybody loves you."

Remembering how enthusiastically Mr. Jap had planned Allen's future with a well-equipped garage, even if it meant selling off some of his land to get the cash, I had to wonder whether the equitable division in his will sprang from love and gratitude or was the result of John Claude's power of persuasion and sense of fair play. John Claude would surely have pointed out to the old man that Elsie's niece was just as deserving as his nephew.

"You go talk to John Claude," I told Pete and Merrilee. "If he can't help you with the ME's office, come on back and I'll issue you a writ or something."

I convened court almost on time, but as soon as I decently could, I declared a fifteen-minute recess and phoned Birdie McElveen.

Birdie is a chain-smoking, hard-nosed supervisor of Colleton County's Child

Support Enforcement. More to the point, she's a close friend of Aunt Zell's and thinks I'm cuter than a speckled pup.

I didn't have to explain to her why I wanted to know the financial situation between one Allen Stancil and his ex-wife Sally Stancil regarding their minor daughter Wendy Nicole, currently of 1212 East Lever Drive in Charlotte, the address I'd memorized from the dossier Dwight had compiled on Allen. It was enough for Birdie that I wanted the information and she was sure she could have it for me by mid-afternoon.

She was better than that. When we broke for lunch, a clerk arrived with a message to call her.

"There *is* a support order on record," Birdie told me, "and the caseworker thinks he's behind by about forty-five hundred dollars, but you know how it is — if the mother doesn't holler, no one automatically goes hunting for the father. Besides, the caseworker says that he's paid the support directly to the mother more than once. It's supposed to be monitored and it messes up the paperwork if they don't do it by the book, but the caseworker thinks he's probably been giving her some of the money right along since she's not screaming for help."

Birdie paused and I could hear her lighting another cigarette.

"So then?" I prompted.

"So then I called Mrs. Stancil at her work. Said I was a supervisor in Child Support Enforcement, which I am."

"Only not in Mecklenburg County."

"I didn't tell and she didn't ask. Just said yes, ma'am, he did get a little behind, but he's been making payments regularly. In fact, he came by this weekend and —"

"What?"

"That's what she said. He was there, left this morning right after breakfast, but he gave her two thousand in cash and that caught him up with everything he owed her."

"She didn't happen to say when he got there, did she?"

"Sorry. I thought you wanted information on the father's fiscal situation, not his physical whereabouts. If I'd realized —"

"That's okay, Birdie. I didn't realize it either. Thanks, though. I owe you one."

"You owe me more than one," she said

with tart affection. "I'll put it on your account."

As I took off my robe and put on my jacket to go out for lunch, I wondered if Pete and Merrilee could be right. I hadn't considered Allen a serious suspect and I didn't think Dwight did either, but he'd acted broke when he fixed my alternator on Friday. Where did he get two thousand in cash to give his ex-wife this weekend?

My appetite gone, I headed down to Dwight's office in the basement. He would have to be told.

But when I entered Dwight's office, there sat Allen in his black leather jacket and scuffed cowboy boots, with a mournful look on his face.

"Hello, darlin'," he said. "Ain't this one hell of a note about Uncle Jap?"

20

None of either sex or profession need fear the want of employment, or an ample reward and encouragement in their different occupations and callings.

"Scotus Americanus," *1773*

"What's going on here?" I asked inanely.

"Stancil's helping us with our inquiries," Dwight said in a deadpan parody of a cliché-ridden British mystery we'd watched together a few weeks ago.

Allen didn't quite catch the reference, but he understood the game. "Dwight here don't know whether to tell me he's sorry about Uncle Jap or read me my rights. You're still a lawyer, ain't you, darlin'? Reckon I could hire you?"

"Using what for money?" I asked. "I

thought you were broke."

"Oh, I always keep a little jingle in my jeans," he said with an easy smile.

"You may not need an attorney, but you can't blame Dwight for wondering how come you ran off like that."

"Hey, I didn't 'run off.' Uncle Jap knew where I was. If I'd of thought for one minute he was going to get hisself killed —"

"So where were you?"

"Greensboro. Like I told Dwight, I had to go look at a car."

Greensboro's about ninety minutes to the west of us, give or take ten minutes, depending on road conditions and how heavy you're willing to push the speed limit. It's also only a little more than halfway to Charlotte and I didn't understand why Allen was lying. Seems like he'd want to document as much distance as possible between himself and the murder scene.

He must have seen the disbelief on my face because he started shoring up.

"One of my old buddies asked me to take a look under the hood of a car he's thinking to buy. I give you his number, Dwight. You don't believe me, just call him."

Dwight looked at the crumpled piece of paper that held a scrawled phone number. "What's his name again?"

"Raiford Hollyfield. His wife's Jan."

"Anybody else see you there?"

"His sister stays with 'em. I forget her name. But I got there around ten o'clock Saturday morning and we went right over to see that car. A nice little Cutlass Supreme. They'll tell you." He turned back to me. "All I've heard is that somebody's killed poor old Uncle Jap. Not when, not how. Come on, Deb'rah. Don't I have the right to know?"

"You'll get all the details soon as I confirm your story," Dwight said sternly. He raised his voice and called, "Hey, Jack! You out there?"

A slightly pudgy, baby-faced officer came to the open doorway. "Yes, Major?"

"How 'bout you take Mr. Stancil here into the squad room? Get him a cup of coffee, maybe a sandwich?"

"And a newspaper?" Allen said slyly.

"Sure," said Dwight. "Give him the latest *Ledger*, Jack."

The *Ledger* is Dobb's biweekly. It comes out on Tuesdays and Fridays. Today being Monday, it wouldn't help Allen much.

"He's probably already read about the murder," I said, taking the seat Allen had vacated.

"I doubt it," said Dwight. "Even if it made the Greensboro paper, they wouldn't have as much on it as the *News and Observer* and you know what that was."

A bare paragraph on an inside page of the Metro section: "Man Killed in Colleton County."

"Not to say he couldn't have talked to somebody down here an hour after Mr. Kezzie found the body. Phone lines were still working, so far as I've heard."

He punched in the numbers on his own phone. The connection between Dobbs and Greensboro was extraordinarily clear for I could hear the rings from where I sat, then a woman's staccato "Hello?"

"Mrs. Hollyfield?"

"Just a minute. Jan?" Jan Hollyfield's voice was too soft for me to make out more than a murmur.

Dwight identified himself, then explained that he was trying to confirm Allen Stancil's whereabouts this past weekend. Could Mrs. Hollyfield help him? Had she seen him? She had? When?

"No, ma'am, he's not in any trouble. Not if you can tell me when you saw him . . . Yes, ma'am, he does know I'm calling you. That's how I have your name and number, ma'am."

Whoever Jan Hollyfield was, she was certainly cautious about divulging anything to a police officer she didn't know.

"Yes, ma'am. I understand." He slowly spelled his name and rank and gave her the Sheriff's Department's number, then hung up.

"She's going to have her husband call me back."

"Through the switchboard? Cagy lady."

"Does make you wonder why, don't it?" He pushed a button on his keypad and spoke into the receiver. "Faye? Could you call Detective Harry Smithwick over in Charlotte? Remind him that I talked to him last week about that chop shop they broke up a month or so ago. Ask him if he's got anything on a Raiford or Jan Hollyfield, now living in Greensboro, okay?"

Dwight pushed the phone away and gave me an inquiring look. "You come downstairs because you heard we'd picked up Stancil?"

I shook my head. “Actually, the main reason was to ask if you’ve put names to all the tire treads past Mr. Jap’s that morning.”

He shuffled through the folders on his desk and came up with a set of black-and-white photographs. “This one’s your dad’s, this one’s Dick Sutterly’s, the bald one’s Billy Wall’s, and we don’t have a match to these diamond treads yet, why?”

“They’re Reese’s. Herman’s boy?” I paused and took a closer look at the tracks left by Billy Wall’s truck. “I thought he said he bought new tires a few weeks ago.”

Dwight wasn’t interested in Billy’s tires, he was more concerned about Reese.

“You can talk to him,” I said. “Just try not to do it around Herman or Nadine. He was supposed to be working that morning, but he took off to see if he could get a shot at a deer back along the creek. He says he went past the shop around ten forty-five and didn’t see any sign of anybody going or coming.”

“What time did he leave?”

“I don’t believe he said, but I got the impression that he probably wasn’t in there more than thirty or forty minutes."

Dwight made a note of it. "Okay. And thanks. This'll save us a little running around. Maybe narrow things down even more."

"One other thing," I said. "And it's probably not important."

"But?"

I shrugged. "I don't know why Allen's trying to make you think he spent the whole weekend in Greensboro, but Birdie McElveen talked to his ex-wife in Charlotte about an hour ago. He stayed at her place last night and left from there this morning after giving her two thousand in cash."

"Yeah?" He pulled the phone back closer — it was starting to wear a rut in his desktop — and said, "Faye? If you do get hold of Smithwick, I think maybe I better talk to him myself."

As I stood to go, Dwight said, "How did Birdie McElveen happen to be talking to Stancil's ex-wife this morning?"

I gave him my blandest shrug.

"And why'd she call you with that information?"

"Well, you said there weren't any warrants out on him. I might've wondered out loud to Birdie if he was evading his responsibilities," I admitted. "She's in Child Support Enforcement and you know how dedicated she is to her work."

"Yeah? Now listen, Deb'rah —"

"Oh, my Lord, look at the time! I'm supposed to be back in the courtroom in twenty minutes and I haven't had a bite of lunch. See you," I said and got out of there before he could start lecturing me to mind my own business and stay out of his investigation.

No sign of Allen or Jack Jamison as I hurried through the halls. He'd probably conned the deputy into buying him a real lunch.

More than I was going to have. It looked like Nabs and a Diet Pepsi from the vending machines over in the old courthouse basement again.

By late afternoon, all the routine crimes and misdemeanors of the day had been disposed of and I was left with a civil matter: Stevens vs. Johnson. Desecration of a family graveyard.

Five minutes into the case, I knew I was watching the latest episode in a long-running family soap opera.

The combatants were two cousins. Geraldine Stevens and Annice Johnson.

Mid-thirties, blond, so similar in appearance they could have been sisters. When the women married, their mutual grandfather had deeded each of them adjoining building lots. Proximity had only worsened their feud.

Geraldine's two acres made a fairly neat rectangle, slightly deeper than it was wide, with sufficient road frontage for an ample semicircular drive.

Annice's drive was barely wide enough to let a Geo through. Her two acres looked a little like the outline of the United States if you cut off California, Oregon and Washington and squared off Texas. "Florida" was an eight-foot-wide strip that touched the road. That eight feet was Annice's only bit of road frontage because an old family graveyard occupied a tenth of an acre where Texas and the Gulf of Mexico should have touched the road bank.

No matter who holds a title to the land where it sits, a graveyard itself is an encumbrance protected by the law in perpetuity. It may not be desecrated, moved nor adversely disturbed without a court order and the consent of the nearest kin.

According to Annice, who brought

along before-and-after photographs, the graveyard had fallen into shocking condition these last eight years. Their grandfather had tended it until poor health forced him to put down his rake and hoe and pruning shears. Nobody else ever picked them up.

Once there had been only a single magnolia tree in the center. After years of neglect, volunteer pines and cedars and wild cherries had sprung up out of the very graves themselves. Honeysuckle and poison oak had overgrown the stones so badly that the men in the family had to go with bush knives and chainsaws to clear a way for the gravediggers when it was time to lay the grandfather to rest last spring.

"She was scared to do anything while Grampy was alive," said Geraldine, "but the minute he was buried, look what she did."

Geraldine's suit asked for no money damages, merely that her cousin be forced to remove the new driveway that now encroached upon the cemetery.

"First she wanted me to sell her a strip of my yard and when I wouldn't, she asked Grampy to let her take part of the graveyard. But he said no because his

Aunt Sally and Uncle George were buried right there at the edge. They didn't have a bought stone, just some rocks for a marker. Marker rocks that *she* moved."

I repressed a sigh. It seems that growth doesn't affect lifestyles alone. It governs death styles, too.

Home burials have become increasingly rare and many of the little private graveyards have been abandoned as the descendants die off or move away or are simply too distantly descended to care any longer. If they even remember.

That overgrown square sitting out in the middle of a field can get real tiresome to a farmer who's had to keep plowing around it. "Nobody ever visits it," he rationalizes to himself and the day comes when he simply plows right through it. The stones make good doorsteps or garden benches.

Bulldozers dispose of gravestones even more efficiently.

Every time new crowds up against old, old is what gives way.

A few years earlier, the cousins' grandfather had drawn a diagram of the different plots, each rectangle neatly labeled in his old-fashioned wavery handwriting.

I was shown this drawing along with a copy that had all the property lines drawn in to scale. In that one, the rectangles labeled "George Patterson — d. 1894" and "Sally Patterson — d. 1913" appeared to be approximately ten feet from Geraldine Stevens's property line.

"Here's how it is right now, Your Honor," said her attorney, one Brandon Frazier, who was so young that you could almost hear his shiny new law degree crackling in his back pocket. "These two little piles of rocks right there have been moved so that they're now almost twenty feet from my client's property line."

Fifteen of those feet had been paved over in August.

"She's driving back and forth right over her own great-great-aunt and -uncle!" Geraldine said tearfully. "And it's wrong!"

"Tell me, Mrs. Stevens," said Edward ("My friends call me Big Ed") Whitbread as he rose ponderously to his feet. Ed Whitbread is not my favorite attorney. He's pompous and dull-witted and he opposed me in the primary when I first ran for judge. "How old was your grandfather when he drew this diagram?"

"I don't know. Seventy-five or eighty maybc."

"And was he a professional draftsman?"

"No, he was a farmer."

"A farmer," Whitbread said portentously. "I see. Yet you claim he made an accurate drawing, to scale, with no formal training, when well past seventy?"

"My Grampy was sharp as a tack right up to the month before he died, and he certainly knew where his Aunt Sally was buried. He was eleven years old and he remembered going to her funeral."

"I'm sure he *thought* he remembered," Whitbread said genially.

As the questioning continued, Allen entered the back of the room and slid into a rear bench. He was alone and didn't appear to be fleeing, so I had to assume that his alibi stood up to a cursory check and that Dwight had turned him loose.

But why was he here?

And why was I worrying about Allen when young Mr. Frazier was summing up for the plaintiff?

With little else to fall back on, he cited the drawing as ample proof that his client's cousin had willfully changed the dimensions of the cemetery, thereby showing great disrespect for the dead who had a right to lie undisturbed.

"No respect for her ancestors?" Ed Whitbread snorted at the very idea. "Your Honor, you've seen the photographs of how disgracefully overgrown that cemetery looked before my client took it in hand. And you've seen the photographs of how it looks today."

I might disdain Whitbread, but he had a point. In the earlier snapshots it was hard to even see the headstones. Now the trash trees were gone, a single magnolia's lower limbs had been pruned so that a concrete bench sat in its shade, and the well-mowed grass made the plot look almost like a small park. Azalea bushes neatly bordered the wide new driveway. Very pretty.

"Mrs. Stevens," I said. "In the years preceding your grandfather's death, did you ever help your cousin clean off that graveyard?"

"She never cleaned it off," said Geraldine. "I would've helped if everybody else did. But after Grampy quit doing it, nobody else ever offered."

(What Allen thought of her answer could be read on his face. He was following the testimony like a play and her words made him roll his eyes at me. One thing — maybe the only thing — that could be said in Allen Stancil's favor: I never saw him shy away from hard or dirty work.)

My options were clear. If I believed Geraldine and dear old Grampy's diagram, which I was inclined to do, then opportunistic Annice had indeed moved the rocks and, in defiance of the laws of North Carolina, was now driving over the remains of her great-great-aunt and uncle. Not that much could be remaining after nearly a century.

No matter how I ruled, the animosity and hard feelings between these two cousins would no doubt continue. If I found for Geraldine and ordered Annice to remove the paving and restore her drive to its previous narrow width, the cemetery would probably fall back into a neglected state. Clearly Geraldine cared nothing about old Grampy's final resting place. It wasn't in *her* front yard. The important thing was to give her cousin grief by making Annice tear up that new driveway.

If I found Geraldine's suit without merit — and except for a freehand diagram drawn by an old man, she had shown me no overwhelming proof to support her accusation — the graveyard would probably be kept in immaculate condition from here on out. *Not*, however, because Annice gave a true goddamn about the place. She reminded me of Adam, only instead of a business in California, her goal was a driveway wide enough to accommodate a Cadillac. One thing about it, though: from now on, Annice would be forced to prove to a watching world (i.e., her neighbors and the rest of the family) that she had more respect for her ancestors than anyone could ever ask.

"The law is the law," the preacher said sternly. "You can't overlook the desecration of two graves just because a half-abandoned site is now prettied up."

I thought of our own family graveyard, bordered in old-fashioned roses and kept in loving repair. My mother is there. So is Daddy's first wife. They lie amid my grandparents and great-grandparents and children that died of diphtheria and croup a hundred years ago. Daddy and some of the older boys want to be buried there, but will any of the grandchildren?

"The law is the law," the preacher repeated inexorably.

"The letter of the law is not always the spirit of the law," the pragmatist pointed out.

I remembered *Roots* and the Bicentennial and how they inspired amateur genealogists to go out and inventory all the little graveyards in the state, and I knew that this law had been expressly written to keep them from quietly disappearing beneath a farmer's plow or a developer's bulldozer.

"I'm sorry, Mr. Frazier," I said, "but your client has failed to provide meaningful proof of her claim that this graveyard has been desecrated. I find her suit without merit. Case dismissed."

Allen Stancil caught up with me as I was pushing open the rear door to head for my chamber.

"Just what I'd of done, darlin'. If you're finished now, could you give me a lift home?"

21

I would therefore offer them a caution, and recommend temperance and abstemiousness to them for the first season, till by degrees, they are inured to the place . . .

"Scotus Americanus," *1773*

One of Dwight's deputies had picked Allen up and one of them could have taken him home, but there was such a hangdog look on his face that I felt sorry for him. Besides, I was still curious about where he'd been all weekend and why he'd been evasive with Dwight about it.

But we had driven out from Dobbs with less than a half-dozen sentences between us. Every conversational remark went nowhere, so I quit trying and concentrated on the road west from Dobbs.

Night was coming on clear and cold. The sun slid below the chilled horizon and bare-twigged trees were silhouetted against the vivid red-orange sky like gothic stone tracery against a stained-glass window. Venus hung like a solitary jewel at the precise point where the vermilion of sunset met the deep blue of night.

Allen seemed so sunk in thought that we were almost to the Old Forty-Eight cutoff before he finally roused himself enough to say, "I could sure go for a piece of catfish. How 'bout we swing past Jerry's for some takeout? I'm buying."

"I don't think so," I said.

"Aw, come on, Deb'rah," he wheedled. "For old time's sake? I pure hate to eat by myself and the thought of going back to Uncle Jap's house with him not there no more —"

For once, there was no double meaning, no suggestive randiness in his voice. It was just starting to sink in that the old man was really dead, and it seemed to be hitting him hard.

Reluctantly, I turned off Forty-Eight onto the two-lane hardtop that leads to Jerry's.

Jerry's Steak & Catfish is a head-shaking phenomenon to the old-timers around here, our first homegrown example of "If you build it, they will come."

When Jerry Upchurch's father died a few years back, Jerry was determined to keep the land in the family, so even though he had a secure job managing a restaurant in Raleigh, he bought out his two sisters and set about looking for a way to make the place pay. He knew he didn't want to farm tobacco — he'd had his fill of that growing up — but he had a son who thought catfish might flourish in the irrigation pond, both his sisters and his wife knew a thing or two about cooking, and there were teenagers in the family who could wait and bus tables. There were also several displaced farmworkers in the neighborhood who were willing to skin and fillet catfish or wash dishes for good steady wages.

Before anybody could turn around three times, a rough-hewn restaurant rose up in the pasture overlooking the pond.

Cracker-barrel sages laughed at the Upchurches behind their backs. A catfish place out in the middle of nowhere? Half a mile off the main road? When we already had a barbecue house that served lunch and supper, not to mention service stations at every main crossroads with their soft-drink boxes and snack-food racks? How was Jerry going to find enough customers in a county where housewives still make biscuits from scratch every night?

Cracker-barrel sages hadn't noticed that full-time, biscuit-making housewives were getting sort of scarce on the ground, or that most of those new houses held outlanders with different eating habits. They hadn't paid attention to how many of their own sons and daughters, never mind all the new people, were driving home every evening from jobs in Raleigh instead of walking in from the fields. Nor did they realize how happy it made working wives not to have to cook and wash up a pile of dishes every single night.

The Upchurches have since trebled their dining room and dug two more catfish ponds.

"They got 'em a license to print money," those cracker-barrel sages tell each other now, as if they knew it all along.

Jerry admits that the money's nice, but he's just happy he got to stay on Upchurch land and build something for the next generation.

While Allen went inside, I waited in the car overlooking the fishponds and watched aerators jet water ten feet up into the night sky. Each jet spray is illuminated by a different-colored spotlight as if they were ornamental fountains instead of a simple way to oxygenate the crowded waters. We were early enough that only a few people had arrived ahead of us, and Allen soon returned with a big brown paper sack that filled my car with the smell of hot fish and cornbread.

Jap Stancil's house was less than five minutes away, and a cold cheerless place it was to walk into. Allen set our food on the kitchen table and lit all four bricks of the wall-hung gas heater while I rummaged in cupboards and drawers for glasses and silverware.

The kitchen was clean and tidy, not a spoon or mug out of place; but like most rooms inhabited by old widowed men, it held the spare and faded grayness of a house long without a woman: no curtains or tablecloths, no African violets blooming on the windowsill over the sink, no colorful potholders hanging by the stove, no cheerful rag rugs. No bright grace notes of any description. No softness. All was well-worn spartan utility.

I transferred our food from the compartmentalized foam trays onto chipped stoneware plates and Allen took two beers from the refrigerator.

"Here's to Uncle Jap, then," he said, lifting his can with a smile that tried to be sardonic and failed miserably.

"To Mr. Jap."

I touched my glass to his can and we began to eat.

Maybe it was the friendly clink of knife and fork against our plates, the hot hushpuppies, or the rapidly warming air. Or maybe it was only the beer that unlocked Allen's tongue and set him talking about Mr. Jap and Miss Elsie and Dallas.

I knew that Allen had been born in Charlotte and that his father was killed in a stock car pileup before he was eight, but I didn't know that his mother had been the neighborhood punchboard, good-hearted and lazy and never too particular about who supported her. I didn't know that he used to run away to down here whenever his latest "uncle" got too free with belt or strap.

"Mama always made them send me back, but sometimes I got to stay for three or four weeks till she could get the money together for my bus ticket. Aunt Elsie was real good to me. That woman made the best lard biscuits in the world, big as bear claws, and she never grudged me a bite. She'd give me clothes that Dallas had outgrowed and take me to town for new tennis shoes 'cause mine always had holes in 'em. And Uncle Jap treated me like I was his." Allen gave me a crooked smile. "I used to really wish I was, you know?"

Clean hand-me-downs, new sneakers, all the hot biscuits and molasses a growing boy could eat, plus a male relative who wasn't a mean drunk. Who would think that this old clapboard farmhouse had once been Eden?

Allen took another big swallow of his beer.

"Even after I was grown and Aunt Elsie was dead, Uncle Jap never turned me away from his door."

"Home is the place where, when you have to go there, they have to take you in," I said softly.

"Yeah," said Allen, who might not know the poem but had lived its meaning. "This is the only real home I ever had after my daddy died."

I could have needled him about making — or not making — homes with any of the women he'd married or fathered children with over the years, but that seemed like pettiness tonight.

"Uncle Jap and Dallas taught me how to drive before I was big enough to see over the steering wheel. Had to look through it to tell where I was going. I'll never forget the first load of 'shine I ran with Dallas. He was seventeen, I was twelve. That old Hudson out yonder under the shed? They hollowed out the back seat so we could hide the jars. Four cases of 'em. It wasn't much of a run, just from the crossroads over to a shot house on the other side of Holly Springs, forty, forty-five miles roundtrip. I was a little nervous going, but everything was cool till coming back through Varina, this town cop pulled up beside us and motioned for Dallas to pull over. Which he did. Only he waited till the cop got out of his patrol car and started walking toward us and then he gunned it. We must've been doing sixty-five by the time we got to the railroad crossing there at Forty-Two 'cause I know for sure all four wheels left the ground.

"That ol' cop was pretty good though. He hung right with us all the way down to Harnett County. Dallas finally lost him on them dirt roads around Panther Lake. When we got home and told Uncle Jap about it, the onliest thing he asked us was did we remember to muddy up the license plate? We said yes and he laughed and told Dallas not to get too cocky 'cause next time he might not be so lucky."

Allen crushed the flimsy aluminum can in his big fist and went back to the refrigerator. "Another one for you?"

I shook my head. "You ever bring your kids down here?"

"Yep. Keith and Wendy Nicole, both." He popped the top on a fresh beer. The foam bubbled up and wet his mustache. He brushed it away with the back of his hand. "Hell, I even brought Tiffany and her mama by one day and Tiffany's not even my young'un. But none of 'em ever really took to Uncle Jap. Guess he was too old then."

"Or they were too young?"

"Maybe."

"Did you see them this weekend?"

"See who?" he asked, suddenly wary.

"Wendy Nicole or Tiffany."

"I told you. I went to Greensboro."

"To see about a car, yeah, I know. But you also went to Charlotte."

"Dwight tell you everything he hears?"

"Enough," I lied.

"I swear to God my ass is a blue banana if they hear about it."

"If who hear about it?"

"Sally and Katie, of course."

I took a final bite of my flaky catfish fillet while I worked it out. If he'd spent last night with ex-wife Sally in Charlotte and didn't want her to know he'd been in Greensboro on Saturday, that must mean that Katie — ?

"That man you went to see about a car. Hollyfield?"

"Raiford? What about him?"

"Is Katie Morgan his sister? The one whose name you couldn't remember this morning?"

"I thought you said Dwight told you all that."

"No, *you* said he did."

"Shit."

"And you're in it up to your neck, aren't you?"

"No more'n usual, darlin'," he sighed. "No more'n usual."

Once again I wondered how on earth I could have been so young, so recklessly naive to run off with such a shiftless womanizer. In the harsh overhead light, he looked every year of the knockabout life he'd led, like a car that had just rolled 200,000 on its odometer.

"Dwight ask you where you got the money to give your harem?"

He preened a little at the term, then gave a self-deprecating shrug. "Won't none of his business long as I could prove I won't here when Uncle Jap's got stolen."

Shaking my head, I got up and stacked our dishes in the sink and put on my jacket.

He followed me outside to the car. His voice was husky and a little embarrassed as he asked if I'd walk over to the garage with him and show him where it'd happened.

"I just pulled into the driveway good this morning and that deputy was setting here waiting for me. Dwight says Mr. Kezzie found him?"

"Yes."

We made our way down the sandy drive by the dim glow of a bare bulb on the back porch to the garage two hundred feet away. Yellow crime scene ribbons lay around on the ground, but I knew Dwight had finished with the building. Mr. Jap's rattletrap truck loomed up before us, still parked where he'd left it Saturday morning. Allen touched the fender as we passed, almost like someone comforting an old horse that had lost its master.

He fumbled with the garage lock in the darkness, then opened the side door and flicked on the lights.

"He was lying there," I said.

In the fluorescent light, Mr. Jap's dried blood looked like only another grease spot on the stained concrete.

The old-fashioned iron safe still stood agape and the door lay on the floor in front of it. Gray fingerprint powder covered the acetylene torch which had been used to burn off the hinges. Someone — Dwight or one of his detectives, probably — had gathered up the strewn papers and piled them neatly inside the safe since I was here.

Allen began to look through them. "Dwight said they took Uncle Jap's corn money. You reckon that was all?"

"Did he have anything else?"

Allen shrugged. "Not that I know of.

Just his marker chits where people owed him money. Far as I know, Billy Wall's the only one he was holding paper on these days."

His lips quirked in a rueful smile beneath his bushy mustache. "He always wanted to be a big shot, like your daddy. 'Kezzie Knott holds paper on half the county,' he'd say. If he didn't have but two dimes to rub together, he'd try and lend you one of 'em just so you'd owe him. Before Merrilee settled him down, Petey Grimes and me, we'd get Uncle Jap to bankroll us to cars and stuff just to make him feel good. Soon as we'd pay him back, he'd be wanting to lend us some more. Hey, here's his bankbook."

He opened the small green passbook and riffled the pages. "Look at this. Not but three hundred dollars in it. Pitiful. Eighty-one years old and he barely got enough Social Security to live on."

"Hard to get a lot from something you never paid into," I said tartly. "He always worked for cash, didn't he? Tried his best not to let himself show up on anybody's books was what I always heard."

Allen had to smile at that. "No, he was a catbird, all right."

He lifted a yellowed envelope that had

the logo of Duck Aldcroft's funeral home as a return address. "Here's his burial insurance. All paid up so nobody'd be burdened when his time came."

"I think Merrilee's handling arrangements," I said. "Since you weren't here."

It didn't seem to occur to him that he should take offense at Merrilee's preempting his next-of-kin duties.

"Then she might ought to have this."

As he pulled the policy from the envelope, another paper fell to the floor.

He picked it up and gave it a puzzled scan before handing it over to me. "Is this a deed?"

It appeared to be a photocopy of a one-page notarized document signed by both Mr. Jap and Dick Sutterly. Hedged in therefores and whereases and dated just last week, it said that in consideration for a cash sum of one thousand dollars, Jasper Stancil promised to sell Richard Sutterly all but ten acres of his farm within ninety days of acquiring clear title to it, at a price guaranteed to be five percent above the high bid of any other would-be purchaser.

"You didn't know about this?"

"He never said a word. What's it mean?

Does it give this Sutterly guy a lien on the land?"

"Don't worry about it. This paper would never hold up in court," I said. "Even if Mr. Jap were still alive, almost any lawyer could get it set aside if he changed his mind and wanted to back out."

He took it from me and ran his rough fingers over the photocopied notary seal. "Sure *looks* legal."

To a shade-tree mechanic like Jap Stancil, it had probably felt pretty legal, too.

"Dwight ought to see this," I said. "It could mean that the killer got this thousand, too."

"*If* Sutterly paid him right then." Allen turned this new development over in his mind. "Well, I can't keep you from telling Dwight, but I believe I'll hang on to this paper for right now."

"I'm telling you, Allen, it's not worth the ink it's written in. Especially with Mr. Jap gone. Dick Sutterly couldn't use it to force a sale."

"But couldn't I use it to make him buy? Five percent above the highest bid. Isn't that what it says?"

"Lot of ifs standing between you and

this place. Cherry Lou's not come to trial yet and Merrilee could probably fight you for half if she wanted to."

"Naw, she couldn't. Uncle Jap won't really her uncle."

"But Dallas owned it last and she's as much his cousin as you were."

After spending most of the weekend educating my family and Merrilee about consanguinity, it amused me to play devil's advocate and argue the opposing viewpoint. "Ellis Glover might see it your way —"

"Who?"

"Clerk of the Court. That's who'd make the first disposition. But if Merrilee wanted to contest his decision, I bet any jury in the county would split it between you, given how much she's done for Mr. Jap over the last few years."

But Allen had stopped listening. He was standing with his back to me, his big, grease-stained hands on the slat-backed, cane-bottomed chair that Mr. Jap always sat in. When he turned, his eyes glistened with unshed tears.

"He was just a pigheaded, big-talking old man that never did no real harm to nobody. How could anybody hurt *him*, Deb'rah? He couldn't have stopped a flea from taking that money. Why'd they have to kill him, too?"

"I don't know," I said helplessly. "I don't know."

We both sighed for the wasteful sadness of it and as we went outside, he switched off the light and snapped the hasp on the lock.

The night was cold and still. Even with a jacket, I was chilly. No moon, but stars blazed overhead and the air was so crystalline that the Milky Way was a gauzy cloud that twined through the autumn constellations. I could see every star of the normally fuzzy Pleiades.

"Makes a man feel mighty small, don't it?" Allen said softly.

He put his arm around my shoulder in a friendly gesture and I found myself leaning into it for warmth as we gazed up into the glittering sky.

"You forget how big it is," he said. "Over in Charlotte, there's too many lights on the ground to let you see any but the biggest stars. But, my sweet Lord! Just look at them all up there."

I settled myself more comfortably on his shoulder and looked up, up, up into the celestial depths, bedazzled as always, and mesmerized by the eternal, unending splendor of worlds without end. By the time it fully registered that his fingers had begun — almost imperceptibly — to caress my ear in gentle stroking exploration, I was dizzied by both the visual and sensual input and breathing more heavily than I realized.

He gently turned my face to his and his mustache brushed my cheek. Our lips met sweetly, sweetly, with a growing intensity. The stars swirled overhead and I was falling into them, drowning in milky nebulae and — oh my God!

I wrenched myself away. "You bastard! Here I was feeling sorry for you, and *you* — all you want — !"

I stumbled across the rutted drive toward the porch light and my car.

From the darkness behind me, Allen called, "You want it, too, darlin'."

My internal preacher yammered at me all the way back to Dobbs, but as I lay wide awake in bed that night, the pragmatist said, *"You were wondering what you ever saw in him? Well, now you remember, don't you?"*

22

Many of the old residenters in the inland counties of this province . . . have, in general, little inclination to mingle with the new-comers, who now arrive in such crowds . . .

"Scotus Americanus," *1773*

I went to sleep Monday night firmly resolved to mind my own business and stay out of things.

Tuesday morning I showered, dressed in a simple, long-sleeved black knit turtleneck dress with black tights and Cuban heels, and snagged a cup of coffee on my way through the kitchen.

"At least let me toast you a bagel," said Aunt Zell.

(She was so pleased when Winn-Dixie added bagels to their in-house bakery. I myself still find it hard to believe that there are enough people in Dobbs who even know what a bagel is to make stocking them economically feasible for Winn-Dixie.)

"No time," I said. "I have an early court date with Portland."

Uncle Ash smeared a dab of cream cheese on half of his blueberry bagel and held it out to me. "If you don't eat, your aunt worries. Portland can wait."

I dropped a kiss on his white head, took a bite of his bagel, and left the rest for him.

"Just because she's your niece doesn't mean you can fritter away her time," I said, and hurried on out to my car.

Driving over to the courthouse, I kept thinking about Daddy and Adam and the pawprints Blue and Ladybelle had left outside the garage door where Jap Stancil was struck down.

After the rain. Sometime between midnight and when I found them with Adam.

And thinking of Adam, did he burn his hand on a brush fire? Or was it an acetylene torch?

I convened court fifteen minutes earlier than usual.

A grim-faced Portland was seated at the defendant's table. She wore an authoritative, don't-mess-with-me coat-dress of power red. Beside her sat two very apprehensive people, Timothy Collins and Diana Henderson.

Ambrose Daughtridge, who had represented Clea Beecham and her small daughter, sat at the opposing table. Mid-fifties, silver-haired, soft-spoken and courtly, he looks as if he should be cataloging books in a library at some small elite college.

I fixed the two miscreants with what I hoped was a steely eye and said, "It has come to my attention that there may have been some irregularities in the paternity testing procedure done by you, Mrs. Henderson, resulting in some false testimony in the trial. I'm going to give you and Mr. Collins each an opportunity now to correct any testimony you may have given during the trial. I warn you that perjury and subornation of perjury are both felonies that carry serious penalties. Now, before I refer this matter to the DA for investigation of these charges, do either of you have anything to say?"

Collins wanted to stonewall, but Mrs.

Henderson started crying almost immediately.

It was a shabby story that unfolded in the next few minutes. Each blamed the other for initiating the lie, but the end disclosure was that Collins paid her five hundred dollars in return for testimony that would let him weasel out of giving any support to his daughter.

I thought of Dwight, who paid above and beyond for his son Cal.

I thought of all the time and money Kidd devoted to his daughter Amber.

Hell, even Allen, scoundrel that he was, not only paid for his daughter Wendy Nicole (admittedly not always on time), he was actually helping his girlfriend out with *her* daughter, little Tiffany Jane.

But Timothy Collins, white-collar civil engineer, was ready to walk away from two-year-old Brittany, a baby he helped make, as if she were nothing more than a kitten or puppy that could be returned to the pet store for all he cared just so long as the monthly payments didn't show up on *his* charge card statements.

Dwight and Kidd and Allen were —

I lost the rest of that thought because something niggled at the perimeter of my mind. Something not only niggled, it danced up and down and yelled, "Hey! Over here! Pay attention!"

Diana Henderson? I checked back through the records. Jamerson Labs is headquartered in Burlington, only a stone's throw from Greensboro.

As I'd noticed before, her eyes were her best facial feature, but they were red and tear-drenched now. Her long nose was also red and her recessive chin quivered with suppressed sobs as I set about trying to undo the damage they'd done.

I asked my recording clerk to prepare a transcript of this morning's session and to deliver it to the DA, who would probably initiate an investigation of Mrs. Henderson's previous court appearances. I told Mrs. Henderson that she could expect him to notify the appropriate agencies as well.

"And, Mr. Daughtridge? If you wish to file a motion to set aside my earlier verdict, along with a motion for a new trial, I will allow it."

"Thank you, Your Honor."

I ended the session by calling for a ten-minute recess before getting into the day's calendar. As everyone stood for me to leave the courtroom, Timothy Collins glanced at Portland. “Guess you want me to find another attorney?”

“Yes, Mr. Collins, I certainly do,” she answered crisply.

I poured myself a cup of coffee from the communal urn in the hallway and went on into my chamber, not realizing that Diana Henderson had followed.

She stood in my doorway and fumbled with her coat. Early forties, ash blond hair and not a pretty face, but her voice still had that lovely timbre as she said, “May I speak to you a minute, Your Honor?”

When I nodded, she came in and closed the door and headed for the chair by my desk. I kept trying to look at her from a male viewpoint. The dark green knit dress she wore demurely flattered a nicely proportioned body, accenting slender hips and full rounded breasts.

“What’s going to happen to me?” she asked fearfully.

“I can’t say,” I replied, “but I suggest that you retain an attorney as soon as possible.”

Another flood of tears.

She seemed to have reduced all her tissues to damp shreds, so I went into the lavatory off my office and brought her some paper towels and toilet tissue.

"Thank you." She blew her nose and looked up at me. I was still standing beside her chair.

"Oh, God! Why did I ever let him talk me into this?" she sobbed.

I would have felt sorrier for her had not a strong conviction been growing inside me with every sob.

Her green knit dress had a loose cowl neckline.

"May I?" I asked. Without waiting for an answer, I pulled it down over her left shoulder.

There, where Allen's hand would have rested when they walked arm in arm, was a small black star. The day she had testified, it was not a mole I had noticed under her semi-sheer white blouse. It was another one of those damn tattoos.

"How much did Allen Stancil pay you to lie for *him?*" I asked her. "Or did you take it out in trade?"

My court calendar was longer than usual as the DA tried to schedule as many cases as possible in light of the Thanksgiving holiday coming up.

Despite all that I had on my mind, I

applied myself just as diligently as Cyl DeGraffenried, the ADA who was prosecuting that day. I kept our mid-session recesses to ten minutes and allowed only forty-five minutes for lunch. We got through everything except a small handful of defendants represented by Zack Young, who seemed to have disappeared even though he'd been in and out of my court all afternoon. I sent the bailiff out to look for him and asked my clerk to call his office, but I knew as well as Cyl that both would come back empty. When Zack doesn't want to be found, nobody's seen him.

"On behalf of the court, I apologize," I told his waiting clients, "but because Mr. Young can't be found, you'll have to come back another day. I'm here, Ms. DeGraffenried is here, you're here. But your attorney isn't and we can't proceed without him. Come on up after I adjourn and she'll reschedule your appearance. If this is an inconvenience, if you're mad because you've wasted the whole day sitting here, don't blame the court, blame Mr. Young. This court is adjourned."

"Oyez, oyez, oyez," said the bailiff.

Out of curiosity, I left the door of my

chamber open. It wasn't two minutes before Zack Young sauntered past.

He nodded to me, pokerfaced. "Judge."

"Mr. Young." I play poker, too.

He continued on down to the courtroom to oversee the rescheduling of his clients, and it was hard for me not to chortle out loud.

Zack's probably the best criminal lawyer in the state. If I ever get charged with anything serious, he's the one I'll retain in a heartbeat.

He had entered Not Guilty pleas for every one of those clients left waiting at the end of the day, but he clearly didn't want to argue their cases before me.

It was the first time he'd ever gone judge-shopping when I was the one scheduled to hear his cases.

Hot damn!

I went by Dwight's office to tell him about the promissory note between Mr. Jap and Dick Sutterly which Allen and I had found in Mr. Jap's burial papers. He wasn't there so I scribbled the details on his scratch pad and left it on his desk.

It was still chilly when I left the courthouse and headed for my car, but warmer weather was predicted by tomorrow morning. In the car just exiting from the parking lot, I saw a familiar face, but he didn't seem to see me even though I waved.

Adam.

And there getting into his own car was Dick Sutterly. He must have thought I was waving at him for he waved back and waited, beaming, till I came up to him.

"Was that my brother who just left?"

"Oh, yes indeed, Judge!" He grabbed my hand and shook it enthusiastically. "And let me say how pleased I am. You know, when we were talking the other day, I got the impression that you opposed my plans, but Adam — Mr. Knott — said I must have misunderstood. I really do appreciate y'all's cooperation."

In his euphoria, his cheeks were pinker than I'd ever seen and his eyes glowed with visions of the future. "I know people throw off on some of the places I've built, but this is going to change their minds. This is going to be my Carolina Trace! My Fearrington Village! A self-contained clustered village with lake and shops and —" He suddenly seemed to realize that his tongue was running away with him and he looked around warily. "But not a word to that Allen Stancil or Merrilee Grimes, okay? We don't want any talk of Phase One to get out before we can get a lock on the land for Phase Two."

It was as if the ground had begun to open up beneath my feet. Somehow I managed to keep my face friendly and my voice normal. "So you and Adam were able to come to terms?"

"He drives a mighty hard bargain," Sutterly said ruefully, "but I won't register this deed either, till after disposition of the Stancil land. We're still hoping not to have to pay top dollar, so not a word now!"

"My lips are sealed," I told him.

My car was an icebox and I sat there a long moment chilling out and trying to put all the pieces together.

A clustered village? Shops? Something as upscale as those two developments Sutterly had mentioned?

After watching Jerry Upchurch's restaurant take off, I wasn't about to predict what could succeed and what would fail out here in the country, but unless Dick Sutterly was blowing soap bubbles, this could be a multimillion-dollar operation. So who was the "we" with the big bankroll? G. Hooks Talbert and his hunting partner, the well-barbered Tom?

"I won't register this deed either," Sutterly had said, which implied more than the single deed to Adam's land. Phase One must be Leo Pleasant's farm and Talbert Nursery, with Adam's 2.9 acres as the crucial connector. Right there was enough land to make a huge start.

If Phase Two were the Stancil farm . . . ?

Mr. Jap had let slip last Friday that he was planning to sell some of his land as soon as he had title to it, a plan confirmed by that promissory note he'd signed to Dick Sutterly.

What if Mr. Jap's murder wasn't about stolen corn money or unsigned wills? What if it was really about selling land that bordered Daddy's along Possum Creek? Mr. Jap had told me not to tell Daddy, but why did Daddy himself tell Adam and me to keep quiet about any land deals? Did he suspect Adam was selling us out?

I should have broken my word to Adam. I should have warned Daddy and rallied my brothers to buy Adam's land for whatever it took, instead of letting Dick Sutterly buy it.

Sixty thousand — the going value of a mess of pottage these days.

23

The worst growth of Indian corn in good land is 200 bushels for every bushel sown, the best betwixt 4 and 500 for one.

"Scotus Americanus," *1773*

As I drove through Dobbs, maintenance workers were maneuvering the town's cherry picker along Main Street, putting up Christmas decorations in preparation for the Santa Claus parade on Saturday.

After three years and four separate hearings on the matter, the town Board of Commissioners had finally agreed to throw out our ratty old red-and-white candy canes and buy new green tinsel wreaths with big red plastic bows. Each four-foot wreath held a fat red tinsel candle with what looked like a yellow light for the candle flame. One was being attached to each lamppost and it looked as if the commissioners had even sprung for green tinsel swags to loop across the street.

Out at the Kmart, shopping carts were loaded with the schizophrenia of late November: bags of sale-priced Halloween candy were wedged in beside Thanksgiving Pilgrim candles and Christmas lights and wrapping paper. Carols were playing over the intercom and most of the store clerks were wearing red Santa Claus hats.

I ran into three people from church before I was even inside good. Reese and his sister Annie Sue were buying Pepsis at the snack bar by the door.

Reese gave me a sheepish smile that meant he was willing to bury the hatchet if I was. "Ma says we're getting together out at Granddaddy's this Saturday?"

"Yeah. You don't happen to know what shade her blue cups are, do you? I'm supposed to get plates and napkins."

Reese looked blank but Annie Sue thought they were royal. "More like Duke blue than Carolina."

When I got to the paper goods aisle, Pete Grimes was there eyeing paper snack plates like a big brown bear who couldn't decide between acorns or honey.

"We're having some folks over to watch football Thursday," he said. "You reckon I ought to get these with the NFL teams or the Thanksgiving ones?"

"Merrilee would probably rather have Thanksgiving ones, don't you think?"

"Yeah, you're right." His big paw scooped up a couple of packs and put them in his cart next to several bags of chips and liter bottles of soft drinks.

"Were you and Merrilee able to make arrangements for Mr. Jap?"

"Yeah. She was talking with Allen this morning. They decided to just have a graveside service. Tomorrow at three. Out at Sweetwater. They're going to lay him between Aunt Elsie and Dallas."

"It's a sad time for Merrilee, losing Dallas and now Mr. Jap."

"Well, it is," he agreed, but a rumbly growl escaped him. "I don't know why he couldn't have told her while he was alive that he appreciated her. She was always so good to him and he always acted like she didn't have nothing better to do. It would've meant so much to her."

"Sometimes old men don't think."

"Well, I just wish he had've. And I been

wanting to thank you for telling her about that will he didn't get to sign. It sure means the world to Merrilee and I don't believe Mr. Lee would've said anything if we didn't tell him you already told us."

Uh-oh. I'd be hearing about that slip of the tongue from John Claude.

Pete added some yellow napkins to his cart. As he trundled away, he said, "Visitation's tonight at Aldcroft's. Seven till nine."

Kidd and I were going to spend Thanksgiving together and since I hoped to be halfway to New Bern before this time tomorrow, I told Pete I'd try to make it that night.

I found some blue plaid plates and matching napkins and got enough for fifty people, just to be on the safe side. There were only about thirty-five of us in the area, but some of the kids might bring friends.

Paper plates and napkins were all I was obligated for, but we were going to be eating in the potato house and it wouldn't matter where the shells flew, so I picked up a ten-pound bag of peanuts roasted in the shell. Herman loves them.

Over the store intercom, announcements of a blue-light special on Halloween costumes ("Stock up for next year at sixty percent off!") competed with "Joy to the World." I pushed my cart through aisles crowded with goods and people, adding hairspray, a rawhide chew bone for Hambone, and some other odds and ends until I arrived at the checkout counter with too many items for the express lane.

I cruised the other lanes looking for the shortest line, and nearly ran over Jack Jamison, who seemed to be lurking instead of shopping. The rookie detective gave me an embarrassed smile and melted back into the crowd of shoppers. Eventually I wheeled my cart into line behind a very pregnant young woman with short brown curls whom I recognized a split second before she remembered me.

"Judge Knott, is it?"

I smiled and nodded. "And you're Mrs. Wall?"

"Yes, ma'am. Jenny Wall."

It's no big deal to be called ma'am by receptionists, salesclerks, and men of all ages, but it always comes as a fresh shock when a younger woman does it to me automatically, meaning only respect. (At one time or another, we've all done it with bitchy intent to slightly older women.) Makes me feel ancient. On the other hand, if I'd gotten married at sixteen as some of my classmates had, it was quite possible that I could be the mother of an eighteen-year-old like Jenny Wall and nine months on my way to being a grandmother.

Grandmothers expect to be ma'am'd.

"You look like you're about done with your Christmas shopping," I said, realizing that the reason this line was shorter than the others was because she had two carts piled high and nobody likes to be behind that much stuff.

One cart was full of newborn-baby goods, the other held toaster oven, microwave, food processor, VCR, a set of dishes and other household items.

"No, ma'am, not really. This is stuff for the baby and for the house that we're just now able to get. We don't use credit cards any more since we got out of debt and this is the first chance I've had to come shopping since Billy finished selling his corn."

I'm always amazed by how much some people will tell total strangers. But then

I realized she probably felt I was already involved in their personal lives since Billy had aired their financial difficulties in my court.

"I hope Billy took care of Mr. Thornton's bill?"

"Oh, yes, ma'am. First thing Saturday morning, before he went to see Mr. Stancil. And wasn't it just awful about that poor man? Billy hates it so bad. He won't even talk about it. It's like he feels it's part his fault Mr. Stancil got killed. Because of the money and all. Have you heard when the funeral's going to be?"

"I just ran into his nephew. He says the visitation's tonight and burial tomorrow afternoon at Sweetwater Baptist."

"Poor man," she said again.

She was carrying the baby so far out in front that I stepped around and helped unload her two carts onto the moving counter.

"When's the baby due?"

"Middle of December's what the doctor says, but Mama thinks it'll be sooner than that. I sure hope it's before Christmas. I'm getting awfully tired of being pregnant."

I couldn't imagine someone that swollen lasting another month and gave her an encouraging smile.

Her total came to over six hundred dollars and she counted out seven bills from a thick wad in her purse.

"Have a nice Thanksgiving," she said shyly before hurrying after the bag boy who was rolling her carts toward the front entrance.

"Ma'am," called the checkout clerk, waving a register tape at least two feet long. "You forgot your receipt."

"I'll give it to her," said Jack Jamison, who'd suddenly reappeared at the end of the counter.

It seemed to me that he gave the grand total a good hard look before he caught up to little Jenny Wall.

On my way out of the store, I was stopped first by one of Aunt Zell's friends who had a message for her, then by a clerk from the Register of Deeds office who wanted me to admire her new baby.

When I finally got outside, I was surprised to see Jenny Wall still standing on the curb.

"Is everything all right?" I asked.

"Yes, ma'am. Billy's getting tires and shocks on the truck and they told him it'd be ready by —" She brightened.

"Yonder he comes now."

This Kmart was one of the superstores that encompassed a tire and auto repair shop, too. As we watched, Billy's shabby old truck came rumbling out of the near bay, sporting a glossy black set of brand-new tires.

I smiled at him as he pulled up to the curb and came around to open the door for his wife. "Baby's got new shoes, hmm?"

"Yes, ma'am." He seemed uncomfortable meeting my eyes, not an unusual reaction from someone who's had to stand up and be judged by me.

I didn't prolong his discomfort, just wished them both a happy Thanksgiving and merry Christmas and went on out to my car.

But after I put my packages in the trunk and drove briskly away from my parking space, I didn't go very far. Just circled past several rows of parked cars until I was up near the entrance of the crowded parking lot where I slid in beside a dark blue van.

A few minutes later, Billy Wall's truck lumbered up to the stop sign, then pulled out into the late afternoon traffic.

Detective Jack Jamison was two car lengths behind it.

With heavy heart, I drove back over to the courthouse.

Dwight was still in his office.

"You fixing to pick up Billy Wall?" I asked.

"Now how the hell did you know that?"

"I saw Jamison following Billy and his wife over at the Kmart just now."

"You don't miss a damn thing, do you?" He pursed his lips in exasperation, then gave one of his oh-what-the-hell? shrugs. "Doesn't matter, I guess. It'll be all over the county by tomorrow morning. Yeah, we shut down Curtis Thornton's gambling operation this afternoon. Wall's one of the ones that was in to him pretty heavy. He's not a bad kid. We're hoping if we lean on him a little, maybe we can get him to testify against Thornton."

"*What?* Curtis Thornton runs a gambling operation?"

Now it was Dwight's turn to look surprised. "You didn't know?" He cocked his head at me. "Then why'd you think we were after Billy?"

Dwight's a smart detective. He connected my dots in half a second. It took me about three seconds longer to do his.

"Well, that bastard!" I said. "Using the courts to collect his gambling debts."

"Huh?"

"That's what Thornton's IOU chits are, aren't they? He makes the losers sign bad checks for nonexistent goods or services he's supposed to have provided as the operator of a tire and service business, right?"

"Whoa now, we didn't get that far."

But I was on my high horse and riding. "And then if the losers don't make good before he puts their checks through, he comes to court when they bounce to get us to put the pressure on. Talk about brass balls!"

"Billy," he reminded me.

That brought me down in a hurry.

"C'mon, Deb'rah. What do you know?"

"Billy Wall was in my court two or three weeks ago," I said reluctantly. "Curtis Thornton brought charges against him for bouncing checks. About fifteen hundred dollars, if I remember right. They said it was for new tires and some engine work on Billy's two-ton truck. I knew Billy was going to be selling Mr. Jap's ornamental corn for several thousand and I told Thornton he could wait till then. He's always taking bad checks and running to us and I thought maybe he'd start being more careful if I made him wait a little longer for his money. It never occurred to me that those so-called rubber checks were really IOUs."

"And?" Dwight asked inexorably.

He knows me too well.

"And Billy didn't buy new tires till this afternoon. At the Kmart. Billy's wife was there, too, buying out the store. She spent almost seven hundred dollars and it barely made a dent in the stack of bills she was carrying in her purse. And there was Jamison watching them both. What was I supposed to think?"

He nodded grimly. "Just what I'm thinking. He was into Thornton for so much that he couldn't really afford to give Jap Stancil his half of the money. Now what do you think would happen if he asked Stancil to wait a little longer?"

"Mr. Jap was too fired up about refurbishing that old garage of his," I said. "He wouldn't want to wait."

"So Billy smashes him with a tire iron, keeps the money, and tells everyone he paid the old man and left him well and happy."

I shook my head. "I don't know,

Dwight. He really seemed to like Mr. Jap and his wife says he's all torn up about the murder."

"He wouldn't be the first killer that wished he could take it back as soon as he'd done it."

"Besides," I argued, "why would he break into the safe?"

"Maybe he'd signed chits for the old man."

"Then all he'd have had to do was hand the money to Mr. Jap, wait till he opened the safe, and then kill him."

"Maybe he didn't remember signing anything till it was too late. Maybe he thought there was more money in the safe. Hell, I don't know, Deb'rah. You want to stay around and ask him?"

"No," I sighed, even though his question was purely rhetorical.

Jenny Wall had seemed so happy an hour ago, buying things for their house, thinking they were out of debt, looking forward to their first Christmas together with their first baby. This was going to shatter her.

24

Many are made to believe, that in Carolina, as in Jamaica . . . the whole year is one continual summer; but this is a mistake; they have the four revolving seasons as in Britain; the transitions to each are gentle and imperceptible.

"Scotus Americanus," *1773*

As usual, Dwight had underestimated the speed with which news still travels. I hadn't opened my mouth except to say hello to my oldest brother Robert, who was starting up the steps of the funeral home just ahead of me that evening, when his wife Doris said, "You hear about Curtis Thornton? If only we'd've known, Haywood and Isabel wouldn't have had to go all the way to Atlantic City to gamble. They could've stayed right here in Colleton County."

"What you talking?" Robert laughed and gave me a hug. "I doubt Thornton had slot machines and bright colored lights or any floor shows either, and that's what Haywood loves."

"Don't forget room service," I said, hugging him back.

"What do I love?" asked Haywood, who had appeared right behind us.

"Slot machines and floor shows," I said. "Robert thinks Curtis Thornton messed up by not running a classier operation."

"Ain't that a sight?" Haywood shook his head. Organized gambling's just fine in New Jersey, but he's opposed to gambling in North Carolina, organized *or* amateur.

"And we just heard that Dwight thinks the Wall boy killed Jap Stancil so he could keep all the money to pay his gambling debts," said Isabel. She clucked her tongue at the idea.

"Well, that's what happens when you can't leave it alone," said Doris, who was one of the ones who disapproved of their trips to Atlantic City.

With a mild glance at the cigarette in Doris's hand, Isabel said, "Any kind of addiction can be real bad."

The soft dig went right past Doris. She dropped her cigarette in the ashstand just outside the door and offered around her roll of breath mints as we went inside.

A funeral home visitation is uncomfortably like the receiving line at a wedding reception except that the deceased occupies the spot usually reserved for the bride and groom. One passes through a line of lesser relatives, pauses a solemn moment before the open casket, then passes on to the immediate relatives.

Tonight, there were only three people to represent the family. Allen Stancil stood just beyond the bier, looking decidedly uncomfortable in a necktie and a too-big sports jacket that Pete Grimes had probably lent him. Merrilee Grimes stood next to him and Pete hovered protectively at her elbow.

Jap Stancil had been an ornery old man who'd outlived his wife and son. He had died without grandchildren or any church affiliation and had been considered slightly disreputable by many of his more self-righteous neighbors. As a result, the turnout at Aldcroft's tonight was rather light and most came to pay their respects to Merrilee and Pete, not because they grieved for Allen, who was relatively unknown to the community, or because they personally mourned the old man's passing.

Of those who did come for Mr. Jap's sake, Daddy and Aunt Sister were probably the only ones who remembered him from childhood although my older brothers had certainly known him in his prime.

"He kept our old 'thirty-nine Ford V-Eight running three years past its natural death," said Haywood of the first car he and Herman owned together, and they got downright lyrical about the way he'd helped them rebuild the engine of a 1950 Studebaker, a car legendary among the boys for its great heart and stamina. It was still up on cinder blocks under one of the shelters at the homeplace, like a trusty old mule let out to pasture.

Despite those memories, there was more talk about the way Jasper Stancil had died than the way he'd lived — especially after one of Merrilee's Yadkin cousins arrived. The cousin lived in the same trailer park as Billy and Jenny Wall and she described in lurid detail how a patrol car from the Sheriff's Department had come out and taken Billy Wall away in handcuffs not two hours ago.

The sedate parlor where Mr. Jap lay in unaccustomed state was electrified.

"Billy Wall? Naw, you *know* not!"

"Billy Wall? I can't believe it. Why, he was telling me just last week how grateful he was to Jap for letting him grow his corn there with no up-front money."

" 'Course you know, Billy was flashing a pretty big wad of cash down at the store yesterday."

"And I hear tell his wife's been buying stuff for the baby's room like she found the money tree."

"Won't nobody else with any cause to do him in."

When it was my turn to speak to Allen and Merrilee, I restrained myself from skewering Allen with Diana Henderson's name and expressed my formal sympathy to both Grimeses since Pete had been Merrilee's surrogate whenever she was too busy to run by there herself.

"You were mighty good to him," I told

Merrilee. "You too, Pete. I'm sure it made him rest easy knowing he could count on y'all when Dallas wasn't there."

Merrilee smiled bravely and Pete shuffled his feet in embarrassment.

The formality of the occasion had begun to dissipate beneath speculation about Billy Wall on the one hand and discussion of weekend holiday plans on the other. Conversation lost its reverent hush and occasional bursts of laughter punctuated the buzz and hum. Daddy and Aunt Sister were seated at the end of the big room beside Herman's wheelchair and I joined my sisters-in-law who were standing nearby.

Adam wasn't at the funeral home. Isabel said that he was spending the night at Zach's and would be flying out the next day. Evidently, he'd made the rounds that afternoon and said goodbye to everyone except me. There was no reference to any land sale, so I had to assume no one else knew.

"I was hoping Karen and the children could maybe fly over for our Thanksgiving get-together on Saturday," said Isabel, "but Adam says they wouldn't get enough time off from school to make it worthwhile. Beats me how it can feel like

Thanksgiving or Christmas either with palm trees and going swimming in your own backyard."

She was confusing San Diego where Frank lived with San Francisco again. In Isabel's mind, the whole of California was surf and sun three hundred and sixty days a year with earthquakes, canyon fires, and mudslides on the remaining five.

"You get the plates yet?" Doris asked me.

I assured her that I'd already taken care of it. "Plates and napkins, too."

"I thought if you didn't, I could pick them up tomorrow. I'm going to Raleigh. Start my Christmas shopping." She looked at Isabel and Nadine. "Y'all want to come?"

Nadine said she had to work. She'd promised a customer to give him an estimate on wiring a new bathroom. Isabel just smiled patiently. "Now, Doris, you know well and good that Haywood and me are driving over to Kinston tomorrow afternoon."

"Oh yes. For that plane to Atlantic City."

The devil was in me and I pulled out a twenty-dollar bill and handed it to Isabel. "Play one of the machines for me, okay?"

Isabel smiled and tucked the bill in her purse. "I'll dedicate tomorrow night to you, honey. Where you gonna be if you win a million dollars?"

"Bet she's going to New Bern," said Nadine with a sly smile.

All three of them suspect I'm sleeping with Kidd, but as long as they don't know for sure, they like it that I seem to be settling down with one man and they're keeping their fingers crossed that he'll give me a diamond for Christmas. (It's never occurred to them that I might not accept one.)

But neither Isabel nor Doris had heard her. They were facing the doorway and both of them had their mouths hanging open as Nadine and I became aware that a sudden silence had fallen over the parlor.

I turned and there was Billy Wall's wife.

This afternoon, she'd been dressed in baggy jersey warm-up pants, old sneakers, and a jacket that didn't meet across her bulging abdomen. Tonight, she wore formfitting black stretch pants, shiny black high-heeled boots, and a tunic-length black knit top with a pink-and-gold scarf tucked into the neckline. Her long brown hair was done up in a becoming twist and she had put on eye shadow and bright red lipstick. She might have used rouge, too, but it was hard to tell because she had flushed such a deep pink from her neck to her brow.

Little Jenny Wall marched across that pale gray carpet with her chin up and her eyes snapping. She could have been Hester Prynne striding the streets of Boston, only instead of a gold-embroidered scarlet A on her breast, she proudly carried Billy's unborn child.

The silence was so complete that we could hear her every word when she reached Merrilee.

"Billy told me to come, Miz Grimes. We were coming together, but they —" She gulped and almost lost it, then her chin came up again. "Billy loved Mr. Stancil. He was good to us. Billy would *never!* He *couldn't!*"

Blindly, her hand went out to Mr. Jap's casket. "If he could sit up and talk one more time, he'd tell you that himself. Billy never harmed a hair on his head. He *didn't!*"

"Of course he didn't, honey," said Merrilee and gathered Jenny Wall in her arms.

Pete rumbled something encouraging and Allen, who'd gone out for a quick cigarette and had stopped to speak to someone on his way back in, looked grateful not to be up there at the front.

Talk quickly resumed in a self-conscious attempt to smooth away the rip in the social fabric by politely pretending that nothing had happened.

"You don't reckon she's by herself, do you?" worried Isabel.

"This far along?" said Nadine. "To be sure not. Why, when I was having Reese, my doctor quit letting me drive after I was seven months gone."

Merrilee was evidently worried about that point herself because she walked Jenny Wall back across the long room. As they moved out into the hall toward the front door, we heard Jenny say that a friend was with her, that they were going back to Dobbs to see what was happening with Billy.

Now that she had faced down the community and paid their respects to Mr. Jap as Billy had asked, we could see her composure slipping again in the face of the unknown.

It was none of my businesss, of course, but I caught up with her on the front walk. "Do y'all have a family attorney?"

She shook her head. "No, ma'am. We never had the need of one before."

"If you want me to, I could call Zack Young and ask him to meet you at the Sheriff's Department. He's real good."

I didn't know if Billy was innocent or guilty, but if anybody could give Jenny's courage another shot of confidence, surely Zack could.

Jenny thanked me and after she'd driven off with her friend, I went into Duck Aldcroft's office and called Zack, who agreed to meet her at the courthouse.

Back outside, November was doing its thing again. A low front was pushing in directly from the south and the night air was already warmer here at eight-thirty in the evening than it had been even an hour ago. Mid-sixties were predicted by Thanksgiving day. As people crossed Aldcroft's wide veranda and headed for their cars, they marveled at the heavy fog rising up from the damp earth. It muffled noises, blotted out the stars, and put halos around every streetlight.

"It's pretty all right," said Doris, "but it just doesn't feel healthy."

25

Merchants in the town, and considerable planters in the country, are now beginning to have a taste for living, and some gay equipages may be seen . . .

"Scotus Americanus," *1773*

The fog was even thicker next morning and when I carried my garment bag and overnight case out to the car, I wasn't aware of Reese's truck until he pulled into the drive behind me and powered down the window.

"Ma says Dwight's arrested Billy Wall for killing Mr. Jap?"

"Yes?"

"What's going to happen to him?"

"Don't you ever watch *Matlock* or *Law and Order*?" I arranged my bags in the trunk so that things wouldn't wrinkle and closed the lid. "He'll be arraigned, the DA will present evidence to a grand jury and if they find probable cause, he'll go to trial. Depending on how the DA decides, he could be tried for anything from involuntary manslaughter right on up to murder in the first degree."

"But if they don't have any real evidence, the grand jury'll let him off, right?"

"Who knows?" I looked at him closely in the damp foggy light. "And why are you asking? I didn't know you and Billy were particular friends."

"We're not. I just hate to see somebody stuck in jail for something he didn't do."

"Now see here, Reese." I went around to the driver's side so I could look straight up into his worried blue eyes. "Was there something about Saturday morning you didn't tell me?"

"Jesus! You never quit, do you?"

He slammed the truck into reverse and roared out into the street so fast that he almost clipped Miss Sallie Anderson, who was there walking her dog, one of Hambone's littermates.

The young dog gave a startled woof and Miss Sallie said, "My goodness. He must really be late for work."

"Telephone, Deborah," Aunt Zell called from the doorway. "It's Isabel." Hambone scooted past her feet and rushed over in hopes of a frolic with his sister.

Aunt Zell handed me the phone and went out to collect her dog and exchange a few words with Miss Sallie.

"Deb'rah?" came Isabel's voice. "Now if it's not convenient, just say so and we'll do something else, but the fog's so bad and the weatherman says it's just going to get worse and I hate for Haywood to drive in it and you did say you were going to New Bern this afternoon, didn't you? And Kinston's right on the way, so if it's all right with you —"

"Sure," I said. "I have half a day of court, but I planned to leave around twelve-thirty or one o'clock if that suits you."

"Oh good! That'll get us there in plenty of time. Stevie can drive us over to Dobbs."

We settled on a meeting place and as Aunt Zell and Hambone came back into the kitchen, I told her I'd be back sometime Friday, depending on when Haywood and Isabel's plane got in. She and Uncle Ash were going to spend Thanksgiving morning picking up pecans out at his sister's farm near Cotton Grove, then come back to Portland and Avery's for a full-blown turkey dinner.

For some reason the zaniest cases seem to show up in pre-holiday court sessions. Wednesday started out normally enough, but shortly after morning recess, we got Marcus Sanders, black, sixty-nine, bone skinny and still spry.

Mr. Sanders was not a stranger to my court because he was bad for augmenting his small pension with shoplifted steaks and chickens from the Harris Teeter store at the north end of Main Street, about two blocks from his house.

More than once the same Harris Teeter security guard had sat in this same witness box and testified as to how he had stopped and searched Mr. Sanders "immediately outside the store" whereupon he had discovered the stolen meats "upon the suspect's person."

"This time, when I tried to stop Mr. Sanders, he took off like a rabbit and when I caught up to him, he was setting on his porch swing."

(Let the record show that while the witness is at least twenty years younger, he is also quite corpulent and probably does *not* run like a rabbit.)

"And did you then search the defendant?" asked Tracy Johnson, who was prosecuting today.

"Yes, ma'am. He didn't have nothing still on him, but them two packs of steaks were laying on the floor inside his screen door."

Mr. Sanders, who was representing himself, bounced up from the defense table and said, "And you didn't have no right. I was on my own premises."

I cautioned him against speaking out. "You'll get your turn."

"No more questions from me, Your Honor," said Tracy.

Mr. Sanders bounced back up. "When you catched up to me, where'd you find me, son?"

"On your porch."

"On my porch," Mr. Sanders repeated happily. "And where were them steaks?"

"Inside your screen door and fully visible."

"But not on my person?"

"Well, no."

The defendant turned to me triumphantly, his dark face aglow with righteous vindication. "See there, Your Honor? He says it himself!"

I seemed to be missing something in his logic. Tracy Johnson stood to elucidate.

"Your Honor, Mr. Sanders is under the impression that since he was not searched immediately outside the store and that since the steaks were not recovered from his physical person —"

"Home free?" I asked, disbelieving.

Sanders nodded vigorously. "Yes, ma'am, Your Honor. Home free!"

I almost hated to disillusion him. Since he'd spent the night in jail and since Harris Teeter had retrieved their steaks back intact, I sentenced him to time served and court costs.

After some public drunkenness in which all the defendants were well past fifty, the last case of the morning was larceny. Two nicely dressed white women: Josephine Reed, seventy-six, white-haired, fragile-looking; and Natalie Meadows, a sweet-faced twenty-one.

In Kmart or Wal-Mart, at Rose's or Winn-Dixie, in fact, in any store where patrons use shopping carts, Mrs. Reed and Miss Meadows were a Norman Rockwell illustration of a dutiful granddaughter there to push the cart for her failing grandmother. They usually shopped at the busiest times. On this particular occasion, however, someone noticed that after they filled their cart, they didn't bother to stop at a cash register before pushing that cart right on out to the parking lot.

Mrs. Reed used a cane and walked so slowly that store security had plenty of time to get a Dobbs police officer there before the women had fully unloaded their loot into the trunk of Mrs. Reed's car. He searched the car and found items from four different stores: cartons of cigarettes, cosmetics, toys, appliances and dozens of boxes of cold tablets, aspirin and antacids. In all, the haul was worth almost two thousand, all destined for the flea market booth the two women rented once a month when their money ran out, according to the investigating officer.

I was all set to lecture Miss Meadows for using her grandmother as stage dressing for larceny when that young woman angrily denied any kinship.

"And I didn't use her, okay? She came to *me*. Her own granddaughter was a friend of mine and when she moved to

Florida last year, Jo asked me to take her place, okay?"

"Okay," I said, and sentenced them each to jail, ten days of active time with another ninety days suspended under the usual conditions.

"Jail?" protested little Mrs. Reed, glaring at me over her bifocals. "But I'm a senior citizen."

"Sorry," I said. "No discounts for seniors."

Haywood and Isabel's son Stevie, home from college for the Thanksgiving weekend, met me in chambers after adjournment at twelve-thirty.

"You sure you don't mind driving them?" he asked. "Gayle and I were going to Raleigh, do some Christmas shopping and maybe catch a movie, but we could wait and go tomorrow."

I told him not to be silly and we went down to the parking lot where his parents were waiting. Isabel looked appropriately glitzy in gold stretch pants, gold purse and shoes, and a bright green, hip-length sweater ornamented with pearl drops, oversized rhinestones, and gold beading.

In his matching green sports jacket,

string bolo tie, and porkpie hat, Haywood looked more massive than usual as he stood beside my sleek little Firebird.

"I don't know, shug," he said doubtfully. "I'm almost afraid I might break it."

"Hey, I've got an idea," said Stevie. "Deborah could drive y'all's car and then you wouldn't have to ride all scrunched up."

"But how'll you get home?" asked Isabel.

"Don't even think about it," I told him.

Stevie laughed and just stood there. He knows he's my favorite nephew.

I sighed and handed over my keys. "If there's the least little dent, the tiniest scratch, I will personally come over to Chapel Hill and bang you out with a rubber mallet."

We transferred my things to the capacious trunk of Haywood and Isabel's living room on wheels, a ten-year-old Mercury Grand Marquis with broad leather seats and lots of legroom, which is a real necessity since Haywood has lots of leg.

As we drove through Dobbs, Haywood and Isabel asked if I'd heard anything more about Billy Wall.

"Nothing except Dwight's pretty sure he lied about paying Mr. Jap. They can prove he has a lot more cash than he ought to have."

"But he ain't said he did it?" asked Haywood.

"No. And they let him out on bond."

"Poor boy," said Isabel. "He's really messed up his life, hasn't he?"

It was hard to talk and drive, too. The fog was as bad as I could ever remember, thick and soft and cottony white. Visibility was severely limited and I couldn't relax till we finally got off the two-lane road and onto Seventy East's four lanes. Even then I didn't feel comfortable enough to go faster than fifty.

"Hope they don't cancel our plane," Isabel said anxiously from the backseat. "Zach says Adam's worried they may cancel his."

"Might not be a bad thing if they did," said Haywood. "Something's eating on that boy. I believe he loved congregating together with us this visit, but I got the feeling his life's real flusterated right now. You don't know what it is, do you?"

"What do Daddy and Seth think?" I hedged.

"They think the same thing," he answered obscurely.

"He's probably been out in California too long," said Isabel. "People out yonder just don't think like we do. It's probably messed up his judgment, don't you reckon?"

Somehow California and its citizens got her off on the people moving into a recently built subdivision over near Robert and Doris.

"I never saw such long names as is on those new mailboxes. Half of them's nothing but vowels and the other half's all consonants. They need to shake 'em up in a box and start over."

"You think maybe Adam's got a health problem?" said Haywood.

"— and of course Doris could find fault with Jesus Christ if he came back to earth, but it bothers me, too, to see people out cutting their grass on Sunday morning. 'Remember the Sabbath day, to keep it holy.' That means going to church. It *don't* mean cutting grass or building garages or painting porches. Somebody needs to tell them that's not the way we act down here."

I resisted asking why the Sabbath injunction never seemed to include cooking a big Sunday dinner and washing up the dishes afterward. Cooking and doing dishes probably fall under the ox-in-the-ditch exemption.

"Maybe it relaxes them," I said. "Some people like to cut grass better than play golf."

"I just hate to see our ways changing," said Isabel as she rummaged in her gold purse for the little notebook she uses to record their gambling wins and losses. "You see that in the paper how they're going to plunk down a Food Lion over by the Interstate, just four miles from us? And one of them new people said she was counting the days 'cause she has to drive twelve miles to shop right now. Like twelve miles is a trip to China! How come she didn't move to North Raleigh if she wants to live next door to a grocery store?"

"Or maybe things ain't like they should be between him and Karen," said Haywood. "You know, they ain't been back home together in a long time."

"Nadine said one of 'em came into the Coffee Pot the other day, ordered a breakfast plate and thought that the grits were cream of wheat. Wanted to know how he was supposed to put milk on 'em and them laying there on a flat plate. Can you believe that?"

" 'Course it might be his work. I hear tell they's lots of people losing their jobs these days."

"Tink Dupree told Nadine he was going to get him one of those T-shirts that say *We don't give a fig HOW they do it in New York*, only he didn't say 'fig,' if you know what I mean."

A little desperately, I said, "Everybody in favor of stopping for some barbecue, raise your hand."

My family will drop every other subject to discuss food. We were still about five miles from Goldsboro and one of the three most popular barbecue houses in eastern North Carolina and I figured it would take them that long to decide on whether they wanted to go inside for a plate or get sandwiches to go.

"Doesn't matter to me," I said. "Y'all are the ones catching a plane."

More conferencing.

Their plane wasn't due to leave till five. (" 'Course we're supposed to get there and get checked in.")

The Kinston airport was less than forty miles away. ("Say another hour at the rate we're going?")

"But if there's a big crowd we might have to wait and —"

By then, I was pulling into the parking lot and the smoky aroma of grilled pork laced with vinegar and red pepper, not to mention the smell of deep-fried onion-flavored hushpuppies, decided them.

"We got plenty of time to go in and set down," Haywood said happily.

Kinston is about a hundred miles east-southeast from the Raleigh-Durham Airport and visibility seemed to be better there. Radio reports said that RDU was canceling and/or diverting all flights. Not so at Kinston Airport.

"Hell, yes, we're going!" said a jovial white-haired man who seemed to know Haywood. He was also wearing an identical golf-green jacket. ("Money-green," says Haywood.)

In fact, I saw four more solid green jackets and at least twenty more gold purses.

There was a festive air at this particular gate. The revelers ranged in age from mid-fifties to late seventies and came from all over eastern Carolina. Down East accents mingled with Low Country as the regulars greeted one another.

As soon as they started boarding their chartered plane, I went and called Kidd and told him to expect me within the hour.

26

. . . The earth is rendered rich and delightful by the fine rivers and streams which glide through them. . . . It is incredible to think what plenty of fish is taken both in their salt and fresh water rivers . . .

"Scotus Americanus," *1773*

New Bern, at the confluence of the Trent and Neuse rivers, is the second-oldest town in North Carolina. As the name implies, it was founded by Swiss, English, and German colonists under the leadership of Baron Christoph von Graffenried in 1710. There were actually more English in the party than Swiss, but since the Baron was Swiss and since it was his money bankrolling the settlers, he got to name it. As a result, every gift shop in town sells souvenirs embellished by the black bear, symbol of the original Bern, and the town hall's red brick clock tower is thought to duplicate Swiss clock towers.

Despite the attempt to underline its Swiss connection, New Bern draws more tourists for its eighteenth-century English connection. Tryon Palace, the seat of royal colonial government, was built in 1770, burned in 1798, and has now been restored — overly restored some purists say — well past its original glory. Even so, this river town is an appealing mixture of old and new. Evergreen live oaks, spring-blooming dogwoods, and August-blooming crepe myrtles line the quaint streets. Expensive sailboats and sleek cruisers line the modern marinas along the badly polluted rivers. Resort hotels and restaurants fill in around the edges of the historic district to serve tourists and sailors alike. Summer can be pretty bad here, hot and humid and mosquito-laden unless the wind is blowing, but the other three seasons are pleasantly temperate.

New Bern itself is only thirty miles further east than Kinston, but since I always get lost when I try to take Kidd's back-road shortcuts, I had to go into town, cross over the Neuse River and then backtrack west a little ways until I found the dirt road that winds through the trees to Kidd's cabin on the north bank of the river.

It really is a log cabin. Kidd built it himself with the help of some friends from a kit that used passive solar design. It's warm and sunny in the winter and cool and shady in the summer. The front door is on the same level as the gravel drive, but the land drops off sharply in back where a wide plank porch runs the entire length of the cabin. Viewed from this height, the Neuse is broad and deceptively beautiful.

Kidd was laughing as he came out to meet me. "I thought you were a lost insurance salesman," he said. "This is not your father's Oldsmobile, is it?"

That first kiss after long days and longer nights alone is always sweet. He's the best kisser I've ever known anyhow, a man who takes his time and gives it serious attention.

Eventually we did get around to taking my garment bag and overnight case out of the car.

He had left the sliding glass doors to

the porch open on either side of the stone fireplace; otherwise the night would have been almost too warm for the fire crackling on the hearth. The damp river air made it welcome.

The cabin's decor is very definitely masculine, but without the spare bleakness of Mr. Jap's house. Kidd likes stone and wood and glass, but he also likes comfort and color. The sectional couch that wraps around the fireplace is a deep wine red and tossed across one corner is a bright patchwork quilt his mother pieced together when he was a little boy. Framed posters advertising various coastal attractions are clustered on one wall, another holds enlarged photographs of local birds. A musket that his great-great-grandfather carried in the Civil War hangs over the fireplace. (And carried is the operative word. According to Kidd, he spent three years in uniform and only shot birds, squirrels and rabbits for the regimental cookpot.)

In front of the couch, a low table held champagne flutes and an ice bucket.

"Are we celebrating something?"

He grinned. "Whatever you happen to feel thankful for."

"I'm sure I'll think of something."

We drank champagne and ate grilled sea bass in front of the fire, and later we made love there, too.

Later still, wrapped together in his quilt, we drank the last of the champagne and watched the fire die down to coals while the running lights of boats drifted past, far down on the river.

"Yes," I murmured sleepily.

"Yes, what?" His lips brushed my brow.

"Yes, I am thankful."

Thanksgiving Day dawned mild and foggy again with a brightness that promised sunshine by noon. Kidd's a morning person and when I slid a foot over to his side around nine-thirty, he'd been up so long that my toes found no residual warmth from his body.

But the low murmur of his voice floated up through the open window and I saw him sitting on the porch steps, talking to the dogs as he gave them a good brushing. Occasionally he'd pause to scratch their heads and gaze out over the river where the fog hung in hazy layers.

"Don't look all the pretty off the morning," I said. "Save some of it for me."

"Better hurry up then."

"I'll be down in ten minutes."

Four minutes in the bathroom, one minute to straighten the covers, another two minutes to throw on jeans and my favorite Carolina sweatshirt, and I was down the stairs with three minutes to spare, ready for coffee and juice and for standing in the kitchen with Kidd's arms around me.

Like the dogs, I need the physical contact of hands and face. I want to nuzzle and be petted, to hug and be hugged back. Next to life itself, having someone to love, having someone who loves you, is the luckiest thing in the whole world. Love doesn't have to be sexual, but it does have to be physical — touching, kissing, feeling warm skin against my skin. Or like now, standing with my head against his blue flannel shirt, feeling the beat of his heart beneath my fingers.

We seldom plan anything when I come down and we spent the morning lazing on the porch, enjoying the sun when it finally burned away the fog, and talking of this and that.

"How is Amber?" I asked dutifully when he mentioned his daughter in passing.

"Fine. Growing up too fast, though. I've got her new school pictures."

He went inside and brought back a handful of color prints.

The face that looked back at me was truly beautiful: masses of dark curly hair, flawless fair skin that showed no adolescent pimples or eruptions, intensely green eyes that crinkled a little like Kidd's in the one picture where she was smiling. Otherwise, I gathered that she generally favored her mother, a woman I hadn't met.

"She's lovely," I said truthfully, "but she looks more like eighteen than fourteen."

"Tell me about it," Kidd said, shaking his head as much in pride as in rue. "The phone never stopped the whole time she was here last weekend. I told her I didn't know why she wanted to come out when we couldn't talk ten minutes without one of her friends or some boy calling."

I knew exactly why Amber had wanted to keep him from spending the weekend with me, but not by the slightest frown or raised eyebrow would I let him know what she was up to.

So I cooed over her pictures and as Kidd talked of his daughter, I smiled and made appropriately interested noises until the conversation moved on to other topics.

After lunch, we took the dogs for a long walk along the river.

"When I was a boy," said Kidd, "the Neuse was full of fish up this way. And the brackish water a few miles down used to be so thick with crabs we could catch two or three at a time on a single chicken head."

Sunlight sparkled on the water, but instead of a fresh woodsy smell, the humid air around us held something vaguely fetid today.

Kidd tossed a pebble and the dogs perked up their ears as it plinked and sent ripples across the surface. "This used to be such a beautiful river, but now it's dying and it's killing the estuaries as well."

The troubled coastal waters were at the root of that murder down at Harkers Island where we first met.

"I see where the state's just authorized another study on the Neuse," I said. "Be simpler if we could just bus the whole legislature down here and make them swim for an hour."

"Won't happen," he said. "Too many

politicians up there in Raleigh, not enough statesmen. Greed and ignorance. They send us all their mess downriver — raw sewage, hog lagoon spills, runoffs from agri-industries — everything but the laws and the money it'll take to clean it up. We get another commission to do another study while the state spends millions to shore up the millionaires' beaches on Bald Head Island."

He plinked another pebble. We found a low spot almost level with the river and our mood lightened as we began skipping stones. I got six skips, but Kidd's a show-off and routinely got eight or ten skips out of his pebbles before they sank.

"Some of us have real jobs," I said, when he teased my lack of proficiency. "You, on the other hand, have clearly wasted too much time working on your rock-skipping skills."

The day had turned out blue-sky beautiful. As we walked through the trees, we saw several hawks kiting on thermal currents overhead. Down on the ground, the wind was such that we walked right up on a small herd of deer. Unfortunately, the dogs saw them at the same time we did and their sharp barks sent the deer dashing for the underbrush, white tails flying.

"My nephew Reese is dying to bag a nice buck," I said.

"So what's stopping him? The deer population's so swollen he shouldn't have any trouble. Or is he a bad shot?"

"No time to hunt. Now that his dad's stuck in a wheelchair, more of the work falls on him."

"Reese. He's the one with the fancy truck, right?"

I laughed. "Right. And you don't even have your scorecard."

When I first started introducing Kidd to my family, he had such a hard time keeping everybody straight that I made him a chart. He has most of my brothers and a lot of their wives down pat, especially those that live around the homeplace, but my nieces and nephews still blur together.

"You sure you don't want to come meet them all on Saturday? We're having our Thanksgiving get-together out at Daddy's."

"You sure you don't want to come backpacking around Mattamuskeet?" he countered.

"Swamp water and mud in my boots? Mice stealing my food at night? A million ducks and geese squawking in my ear?"

"No worse than a million Knotts."

I grabbed up some pine cones and pelted him, then turned and fled when he lunged at me. His legs are longer, though, and we went down in a tangle of dead grasses and fallen leaves. The dogs thought it was a game and joined in, tails wagging, to lick our faces and jump on our backs.

That evening, we drove down to Cherry Point for a Thanksgiving steak at one of the lounges with a bluesy piano. Not only does Kidd kiss good, he listens good, too. All through dinner, he listened to the developments in Mr. Jap's death since we had last talked; and on the drive back to his cabin, I curled up next to him on the van seat and told him my fears that some of my family might be involved.

"Reese must have seen something he's not telling me."

"Or somebody."

"Yeah."

"Well, you and your family do use those back lanes like turnpikes, don't you?"

"They started out as real shortcuts, but these days my brothers shuttle equipment back and forth that way every time they can — combines and tractor rigs — even when it might be quicker to go by the public road. They get a little tired of honking cars, and getting the finger from impatient commuters. Urban people move to the country and it's like, 'Gee, you mean *farmers* live in the country? And they're going to be cluttering up my road with hay balers or gang disks? Who the hell do these rednecks think they are?' Pooling equipment's the main reason Daddy and the boys are still able to make farming turn a decent living."

I sighed and Kidd put his arm around me.

Maybe it was Dallas getting killed because he wouldn't sell and move Cherry Lou back to Florida or maybe it was because of Adam's mercenary assessment, but since Mr. Jap died, I'd given a lot of thought to the varying attitudes about land.

Robert, Andrew, Haywood, Seth, and Zach will continue to farm as long as they can sit a tractor or spread manure, and each has at least one child who shares that love of farming. But Frank is in San Diego and none of his children will ever come east to live. Even if Herman weren't wheelchair-bound, he's already cast his lot in town. His older son has a white-collar job out in Charlotte. Reese enjoys hunting and fishing, he may even put a trailer out there on Herman's part, but he'll never work the land himself. Haywood's Stevie is studying liberal arts and thinking about journalism.

It's that way right on down the line with Ben, Jack and Will and their children. They rent their land to the ones that still farm, but they themselves will never be true stewards. Adam was a generation ahead of his time when he told Haywood he wanted a job where he didn't freeze in winter and broil in summer. Maybe he really was the smartest one of us, to take the money and run. Designing computers has got to be a lot less stressful than praying for rain before the crops burn up or praying the rain will stop before the crops drown and rot in the field.

Most of my brothers' children don't want to live like that. Nor do their neighbors' children. The next generation will be easier pickings for the Dick Sutterlys.

Not that there aren't a lot of the current holders with the same attitude. No sooner did Jap Stancil have the prospect of regaining his land but that *he* was ready to sell so that he could finance a state-of-the-art garage for Allen.

For Allen, the land would be a cash windfall; if Merrilee had inherited, it would have been validation of her worth. With no children to provide for, the land would have quickly converted to the clothes and jewelry Pete loved to buy for her. Maybe they'd have taken annual Caribbean cruises instead of every other winter.

And there's poor Billy Wall, hungry to farm and seeing no way he'll ever be able to buy land. Is that why he gambled so recklessly with Curtis Thornton, hoping to win enough to make a down payment on a farm?

Dick Sutterly's never lived on a farm and never wanted to, so far as I could see. Land is merely a commodity, something to buy and sell and turn a profit.

And as for G. Hooks Talbert, this particular bit of land might mean a chance to exact a little revenge on Daddy for being made to eat humble pie with a governor he disdained.

And what about Daddy?

Adam thinks I'm romantically obsessed, but I'm only a pale shadow of Daddy's fierce attachment to the land he and the boys have acquired over the years. It goes to the core of his being and I've seen how he reacts when things of lesser importance have been threatened.

There was no way to judge the situation that was building, especially when no one would give me facts.

I don't know how long we'd been sitting still in front of the cabin before I realized that we were back. I looked up into Kidd's eyes.

"Oh, good," he said. "You did come home with me. I was beginning to wonder."

As he kissed me, I gladly quit thinking and gave myself up wholly to feeling.

27

At this season, the country is very agreeable to sportsmen, having plenty of all sorts of game in the greatest perfection; such as deer, which are as numerous as sheep in Scotland . . .

"Scotus Americanus," *1773*

Airport workers were stringing lights on a tall fir tree in the main lobby of the airport next day and Haywood and Isabel were laughing like Christmas morning when they came through the gate. Their friends seemed equally jovial and there were cries of "Don't spend it all in one place, now" and "Let me know when you buy that yacht."

"Did you get lucky?" I asked.

"You might say so," they beamed.

We got their overnight bags stowed

and I tried to hand Haywood the keys to their car, but he waved them aside.

"You better drive, if you don't mind, shug. Everybody on the plane kept giving me and Isabel champagne. If I tried to drive, I reckon I'd just float on off the road."

Isabel giggled and crawled into the backseat. She pulled off her shoes and stretched her legs out along the seat. "Lordy, but my head's light as a feather."

"What'd you do, break the bank?" I asked as we buckled up.

"Near 'bout. And here's what you won."

Two fifty-dollar bills landed in my lap.

"You're kidding," I said. "My twenty dollars won?"

"On the very last quarter, won't it, Bel?" asked Haywood.

"Next to the last, so I still owe you a quarter, Deborah. Don't let me forget. Anyhow, I was talking with Joan Hadley about colleges — her last son's a senior in high school this year so I wasn't really watching and the next thing I know, the bells and lights went off and it was a hundred dollars. You didn't say whether or not to keep playing if you won, so I didn't."

"That's fine," I laughed, thinking of a

certain pair of black suede shoes on sale at Crabtree.

"Then, after I won your hundred, I switched to the machine on the other side of Joan so I could talk better, and I hadn't been sitting there ten minutes when I won eight hundred dollars more."

"She really had the St. Midas touch Wednesday night," Haywood said proudly.

"Nine hundred in one night? Hey, that's great!"

"That's not all," said Isabel. "I thought I'd run up to our room and lay down a few minutes till my heart quit beating so fast. But that night, after the buffet — they have the best lobster salad, to be sure —"

"I got the roast beef," said Haywood.

"— when we got off the elevator, there was a quarter laying on the floor. I picked it up and stuck it in the Quarter-Rama right there by the elevator and blessed if it didn't win me another twenty-five!"

"Nine hundred and twenty-five? What are you —"

"That's still not all," said Isabel. "By the time we went to bed, I'd won twenty-three hundred dollars, not counting that hundred for you."

Bemused, I said, "I'm guessing that's still not all?"

"No, wait'll you hear what Haywood did." She started giggling again. "Tell her, honey."

"Well," said Haywood, "I didn't have any luck at all Wednesday night. And it won't much better yesterday. I'd drop twenty and maybe win back five, then drop sixty and win back three. It was getting on for suppertime and like Bel says, they have them really good buffets. You don't want to be too late for 'em, if you get my whim. I was a little over my limit, but with what Bel won, we were still more'n two thousand to the good and Bel said we might as well play till six o'clock. Guess how much I won, shug?"

"I can't imagine," I told him truthfully.

"Twenty-five big ones."

"Big ones? You mean hundreds?"

"Thousands!" crowed Isabel from the backseat.

" 'Course now, the government's gonna take a good part of it," Haywood warned me.

"Twenty-eight percent right off the top," said Isabel. "Remind me to tell Seth we got to file this tax form they gave us."

(Since Seth and Minnie keep all the communal farm records on their computer, he usually does everybody's taxes, too.)

"Still and all," said Isabel, "that leaves us almost twenty thousand to the good."

Haywood sighed contentedly. "Yeah, we had us a real nice Thanksgiving. How 'bout you, shug?"

I allowed as how I'd had a right nice one myself.

By the time we hit Goldsboro, Haywood and Isabel were both sound asleep. She was curled up on the backseat, he had his head propped between the window and the headrest with his hat down over his eyes to shade them from the midday sun.

Life in the fast lane can be exhausting.

Haywood and Isabel live a little less than a mile past the homeplace. I retrieved my car from Stevie (no dings and he'd even waxed it for me) and started back to Dobbs. As I drove along the heavily wooded road that runs past Jimmy White's garage and serves as a shortcut over to Forty-Eight, I saw the blue lights of a patrol car up ahead parked on the left shoulder behind a gleaming white truck with lots of chrome.

Reese's truck.

It had straddled the ditch at a cockeyed angle that made my heart stand still. I swung my car in nose to nose with it and hit the shoulder running, almost tripping over one of those yellow road signs that was broken off at the ground. Reese's fancy chrome front bumper was crumpled and the right headlight was shattered. Despite the big wheels, the truck was far enough down in the ditch that the cab was almost level with the roadbed and both doors were open.

Reese was slumped inside the cab, still in his seat belt, head back and his eyes closed. He was covered in blood.

I pushed in beside the trooper. "What happened? Is he all right?"

"Judge Knott?"

The trooper was Ollie Harrold, someone familiar to me from traffic court. "Ma'am, you shouldn't —"

"He's my nephew. Is he alive?"

I touched Reese's face and a fresh trickle of blood ran down from a cut on his chin. "Reese?"

"Deborah?" Reese's eyes opened a crack. "Oh shit," he groaned. "Just what I need."

"What happened, honey?"

He closed his eyes and his face got that mulish look.

The exterior of the truck wasn't badly damaged, but the interior looked as if it'd been vandalized. The radio and CD player could have been hit with a hammer, and the padded dash and soft vinyl upholstery were slashed to tatters. Blood and mud were everywhere.

I looked at the trooper. "Who did this?"

"That's what I'm trying to ascertain, ma'am. I just got here myself, but he don't want to tell me."

"Reese Knott," I said sternly. "You better say what happened here and I mean it."

"Oh shit," he groaned again. When he touched his face, his hand came away with more blood. "I'm gonna have to get a goddamn tetanus shot, ain't I?"

"Reese!"

"Look, I didn't know it was going to end up like this, okay? But this buck come jumping out of the woods and fell down right in front of me." His eyes fell on his smashed CD. "Oh Jesus, look at that!

Cost me almost four hundred dollars to get it installed."

"Forget about the damn player. What about the deer? Did you hit it?"

"No. Some hunter must've shot him, and he got that far before he went down. I thought jumping the ditch must have finished him off. He had an eight-point rack, Deb'rah. The one A.K. took doesn't have but six."

"And?"

"Well, I couldn't hear nobody coming after him. Deer can run miles sometimes from where they get shot. Everybody knows that. And why should I leave him there for the buzzards to pick? So I got out my tarp and wrapped it around him and stuck him up here in the cab."

"Why not in back?"

"It's full of light fixtures I just picked up from our wholesaler in Makely." His eyes met mine and he gave a shame-faced shrug. "Besides, I was afraid the guy that shot him might come along and spot the antlers."

He closed his eyes again and I gave him a poke.

"I swear to God I thought he was dead, okay? But I hadn't hardly turned on this road when he rared up under that tarp and started tearing hell out of things. Out of me, too. You ever think about how sharp them damn hooves are?" He touched a torn and bloody spot on his upper thigh where the jeans were ripped. "Oh, God, I bet I have to get stitches. I *hate* getting stitches. He just wouldn't be still, kept kicking and raring, antlers flying — it's a pure wonder he didn't poke my eyes out with them antlers. God knows he poked me everywhere else. I tried to turn him out, but I couldn't reach around him to open the door 'cause he was trying to come through the window on my side. Next thing I know, the truck does a one-eighty into that signpost and I'm sitting here in the ditch before I finally get the damn door open."

"Oh, Reese, you idiot."

"Look at my head liner," he moaned. "Look at these seats! I'll have to get the whole inside — you know what it's gonna cost? And I bet my damn insurance —"

Trooper Harrold had trouble keeping a straight face when I turned to him.

"I observed him driving erratically," he told me as formally as if we were back in court. "Before I could put on my blue light though, he landed in the ditch and I saw a buck go bounding up the ditch bank. I thought at first he'd swerved to miss it and —"

He was interrupted by the sound of sirens and more flashing emergency lights.

Dwight Bryant pulled his departmental cruiser up behind Reese's truck and a rescue ambulance stopped a few feet away.

A tall, strongly built woman slid out from behind the wheel. A stethoscope dangled from her neck and she carried a cervical collar. "Want to give me some room here?" she said, motioning us away from the cab of the truck. "Is this the victim?"

"Victim?"

"Somebody called in and said a man out here in a white truck's been shot. He the one?"

"I reported the accident," said Harrold, "but I didn't call for an ambulance yet and he wasn't shot." He looked at the paramedic who had strapped the cervical collar around Reese's neck as a precaution before taking his vital signs. "Was he?"

"Not that I can see." She gave an exasperated twitch of her head. "People call in the wrong things all the time."

"We got the same call," said Dwight. "What happened? Reese take that curve too sharp?"

I started to tell him but we had to step back out of the road as a pickup drove slowly by. All of a sudden, it screeched on brakes and two angry hunters jumped out. Both were dressed in brown camouflage jumpsuits and bright orange hunting caps and one of them slammed the hood of Reese's truck with the flat of his hand so hard that it left a dent.

"This is the bastard, all right. See them diamond treads? Where's my buck, you dickhead?"

Dwight and Trooper Harrold both moved forward to intercept him, but the hunter banged the truck hood again. "We found where it come out of the woods and saw the blood where somebody stopped and picked him up. Same tire marks. What'd you do with it, asshole?"

His buddy pulled at his sleeve and pointed up on the bank about thirty feet away. To the casual eye, the sticklike object projecting up out of the dead weeds might've looked like fallen twigs, but the hunters recognized antlers and they headed up the bank.

The door of yet another pickup banged and I saw the familiar uniform of a wildlife officer. "You find it?" he called to the hunters.

"Yeah, this is it," they called back.

The EMS paramedic had signaled for the stretcher.

"He's probably okay," she told me as her assistant maneuvered the stretcher into place, "but that cut on his face needs stitches and so does the one on his thigh, so I want to transport him to the hospital."

"Have I got to go?" Reese asked her anxiously.

"I strongly advise it, sir," she said. "In my opinion, you may have sustained internal injuries and you could have a closed head injury. You don't want to risk a blood clot, do you?"

Reese started to argue, but about that time his eyes landed on the wildlife officer who was approaching and he clutched at the paramedic's arm. "Yeah, I'll go with you."

The officer walked over to us and he seemed surprised as he spotted me.

He'd testified in my court just this week. "You know this boy, Judge?"

"My nephew," I said as they eased Reese out of the cab and strapped him onto the stretcher.

"He able to talk to me a minute?"

The paramedic nodded and the officer leaned over and looked at Reese.

"Son," he said, "you got a permit to take deer?"

Reese moaned and closed his eyes.

"Which hospital y'all taking him to?" I asked.

"Dobbs Memorial," the paramedic said and briskly trundled the stretcher over to the waiting ambulance.

I gave the warden Reese's name and address and he scribbled out a citation.

"I need to see his driver's license," said Trooper Harrold.

"You're not going to charge him, too, are you?" I objected.

Harrold thought about it a minute. "One-vehicle accident? No property damage except to himself? I guess there's really not a whole lot I *can* charge him with unless it's operating a vehicle with a loose deer in the cab."

"Seat belt violation?" Dwight suggested helpfully. "Passengers are supposed to be fastened in."

"Naw," said Harrold. "I'll let ol' Ranger Rick here have him. That boy's got so much damage on his truck, any ticket I give him wouldn't add much to his worries."

I went over to tuck the citation in Reese's pocket and told him I'd call his parents.

He nodded in weary resignation and then he grabbed my hand. "You reckon you could get Jimmy White to tow my truck over to his place?"

"Sure," I said. "One condition, though."

"What?"

"Tell me what really happened Saturday morning."

If possible, he slumped down into the stretcher even more dispiritedly, then nodded his head toward the EMS team. "Make 'em step back?"

"Give me a minute?" I asked the paramedic.

"Okay," she said. "We'll start the paperwork."

I turned back to Reese.

He swallowed hard. "Billy Wall didn't kill Mr. Jap."

My nerves knotted in fear. "Not you?"

He shook his head impatiently and more blood oozed from the cut on his chin. "Remember how I told you nobody was there when I went past his shop the first time?"

"Yes."

"He was there when I came back out. I saw his truck and I had that sticky valve so I tooted my horn and went inside and —" He took another deep breath. "He was already dead, Deb'rah. Laying there on the floor."

"With the safe open?"

"No. Billy must've done that. It was a little after eleven-thirty. Say eleven-forty, maybe? Soon as I saw Mr. Jap laying there with that tire iron, I knew somebody'd killed him and it scared the shit out of me. I wasn't supposed to be there anyhow, so I just took off. Soon as I was out on the road and straightened up good, I looked back in my rearview mirror and I seen Billy turn in. He might've taken the money, but he never killed him."

"You'll have to tell Dwight," I said, looking around for him.

"No!" said Reese. "You tell him. Please?"

"Listen, ma'am," said the paramedic. "If we're going to transport him, we need to do it now."

Reluctantly, I stepped back and they finished loading him into the ambulance and headed back to Dobbs minus the siren and flashing lights.

I walked over to where Dwight was watching the hunters. Still muttering angrily, the two men carried the tagged and now thoroughly dead buck down across the ditch and put it in the back of their own truck.

"Eight points," Dwight said admiringly.

I nodded. "No wonder Reese was tempted."

The wildlife officer was a friend of Kidd's and apologized for having to cite my nephew for unlawful possession of a deer, but I assured him there would be no hard feelings on my part.

He and the hunters drove away. Trooper Harrold was finishing up his report in his cruiser and Dwight walked with me over to Reese's truck.

When we were alone, I told him what Reese had just told me about Saturday morning.

Dwight gave a sour laugh. "Zack

Young hauled Billy Wall down to my office last thing Wednesday evening. Billy wanted to confess that he'd kept the money and burned open the safe to get at the chits Jap was holding on him, but he said Jap was dead when he got there. I'm not real sure Zack believed him any more than I did.

"Dammit, Deb'rah! Why the hell did Reese run? And why didn't he tell me this when I first talked to him?"

"Probably for the same reason he picked up a stunned buck and put it inside his truck," I said wearily. "Congenital stupidity."

Dwight closed and locked the far door of the truck. I pulled the keys from the ignition and lifted Reese's Winchester from the gun rack.

"I'd better take this with me," I said and stowed it in the trunk of my car.

"You want me to run with you over to Jimmy's?" asked Dwight. "If he's not there —"

His radio crackled and he reached in and turned it up. "Yeah, Laurie?"

The dispatcher's voice came through clearly. "Jack just called in about that shooting. Guy in a white truck on Pleasant Road near Old Forty-Eight? He wants to know how come you're not there yet."

Dwight looked at me. We were on Pleasant Road, near Old Forty-Eight, beside Reese's white truck.

"*Where* on Pleasant Road?" Dwight asked.

"Between the west side of Old Forty-Eight and Pleasant's Crossroads."

We were on the east side of that highway.

"On my way," said Dwight. "See you, Deb'rah."

As he pulled even with Trooper Harrold's cruiser, he paused and relayed the information.

Many people would have chased right after Dwight and the trooper to see who'd been shot, but I'm a responsible adult. I did a three-point turn and drove sedately over to Jimmy's. I arranged to have Reese's truck towed. I called Nadine to say that her son was on his way to Dobbs in an ambulance.

Then I chased back toward Pleasant's Crossroads.

28

{New-comers} are apt to indulge themselves too much, tempted by such good living, and delicious fruits as abound there, which sometimes produces bad consequences.

"Scotus Americanus," *1773*

Dick Sutterly's truck was sitting in a ditch almost at the same angle as Reese's, but the damage to his truck was minimal.

There wasn't even any broken glass since the window was down when the bullet smashed into Sutterly's brain.

He'd been found by four Makely women on their way home from Christmas shopping at the malls in Raleigh. After getting their names and addresses, Detective Jack Jamison had let them go.

"They found the car in gear with the

keys in the ignition," said Dwight. "Looks like he might've had his foot on the brake, talking to the person who shot him, and then when he died, the car just rolled on into the ditch and stalled out."

I hadn't liked Dick Sutterly and I hated what he wanted to do out here, but he didn't deserve this — his body slumped over the steering wheel of his truck, with cameras flashing and crime scene technicians poking and measuring.

He had been so happy — pink-cheeked and excited about building something he could be proud of, something that would change his reputation from a penny-ante scrabbler to one of the high rollers. Now his cheeks were gray with the pallor of death and the future of his clustered village was probably just as gray.

"This is related to Mr. Jap's murder, isn't it?" I asked.

"Looks like it. Jack found a folder on the floor of the truck with a bunch of papers scattered around. There's a copy of that note Jap signed."

"That he'd sell to Sutterly?"

"Yeah. And a couple of other things."

He handed me a scrap of paper that

Jamison had slipped into a plastic bag. It looked like a note that Dick Sutterly might have scribbled to himself. There was a phone number which I recognized as Zach's. Below were the words "A.K. — Pls.Rd. lane — 2 PM."

It was 3:45 now and that 911 call had come in more than an hour ago. Sutterly's truck had run off the road less than a hundred feet from the lane that led directly to Gray Talbert's nursery.

Right past Adam's 2.9 acres.

Adam's *former* 2.9 acres, I reminded myself.

"Oh, come on, Dwight. You can't think that Adam — ? Look. There's no date on this paper," I said. "It could have been any day this week. Besides, he flew home to California Wednesday night."

I suddenly remembered the fog and all those radio reports that RDU was closing down.

"Didn't he?"

"Nope. I was out here yesterday to look at Jap's papers and have another talk with Allen."

"You worked the holiday?"

"Hey, quit looking at me like I'm an orphan or something just because Jonna wouldn't let me have Cal this weekend. I've got plenty of family — a brother and two sisters, remember? Rob and Kate had Mom and me and Nancy Faye and her family for turkey in the middle of the day. Long as I was out this way though, I thought I'd poke around a little. And Adam was there at the shop chewing the fat with Allen."

I frowned. "Never knew those two to have anything in common."

"Yeah, well, they've got one now," he said sardonically.

"Me?"

"Your name did come up a couple or forty times. They were both real pissed with you. Adam seemed to think you'd set up to pass judgment on the whole world, starting with him, and Allen kept talking about some sort of blood tests that you were going to put him through? 'Course all those empty beer cans sitting around the place might've had something to do with their attitudes."

"Both of them could stand an attitude adjustment."

"Anyhow, Adam's flight got canceled Wednesday afternoon, which means he's probably here till Monday. The TV says Thanksgiving weekend's the busiest travel time of the year."

I handed him back the bagged scrap of paper. "I still say this could have been any day last week. Maybe Tuesday. They were at the courthouse then. Maybe they met here first."

"For Adam to sell him his land?"

"You know about that?"

"And that you didn't approve. That was part of what had him going yesterday."

"It's a family matter," I said stiffly.

"And if your family's opposed, what would Adam do? Maybe try to cancel the deal? And then when Sutterly wouldn't, he —"

Someone from the crime scene unit claimed Dwight's attention and I got back into my car and drove through Adam's lane, past the nursery, across the creek and straight over to Seth's.

He and Minnie were entering farm data into the computer and double-checking the figures as they went. "Easier to put it in there right the first time than to have to go looking for the error," said Minnie.

They were shocked to hear about Dick Sutterly and when I asked them where Adam was, Seth thought he was back with Zach. "I reckon you heard his plane was canceled?"

I nodded.

"They told him not to even call the airlines again till Monday morning," said Minnie. "Every flight's sold out till then."

Zach's Lee answered the phone on the first ring and sounded disappointed that I wasn't one of his buddies calling about a double date that night. "Uncle Adam's not here," he said. "You want to talk to Dad?"

When I said I did, he hollered for Zach to pick up downstairs. "I hope y'all don't plan to talk long."

I assured him I'd be brief.

I asked Zach where Adam was and he said, "Over at the homeplace, I think. He borrowed my squirrel gun yesterday. Said he might try to pot a couple of those tree rats that were stealing Daddy's pecans. He didn't come back last night, so I just assumed he stayed over with Daddy or Seth."

Phone calls to Daddy, Haywood, Andrew and Robert were equally unproductive. So far as I could tell, Dwight and Allen were the last ones to see him.

I drove back through the lane, this time by way of Mr. Jap's place. I saw no sign of a rental car. Allen's truck was parked next to Mr. Jap's out near the shop, but the shop itself was locked and dark and nobody came to the door when I blew long and loud on my horn over at the house.

When I got back to the highway, they were just loading Dick Sutterly's body onto the ambulance and Dwight was about ready to pack it in.

His eyes narrowed when I told him I couldn't find Adam nor Allen either.

"Adam's running around with a gun? What caliber?"

"I don't know. A .22 probably. Why?"

"We think Sutterly was shot with a small-bore gun," Dwight said grimly.

29

. . . They are in no danger, but may be out late or early, travel by night or day, go the same lengths, and use the same freedoms they were accustomed to at home with equal safety.

"Scotus Americanus," *1773*

As word spread through the family that Adam seemed to be missing, everyone turned out to look for him. We scoured the land until darkness forced us to call off the search. Not just our land and along Possum Creek, but both the Stancil and Pleasant farms in case he'd forgotten the old boundaries and strayed across them. Zach thought Adam might have remembered that he was renting a farm on the west side of Cotton Grove and he took some of the kids to search over there as well.

I called Merrilee and Pete, and someone even stopped past Cherry Lou's. So far though, Dwight was the last person to see either man since the afternoon before.

The last person to admit it anyhow.

Minnie phoned Karen out in California to see if he'd called home by any chance. "And didn't I sound like an idiot?" she said afterwards. "Saying I forgot to ask him before he went off hunting if he was still going to be here for our get-together tomorrow. But I really don't think she noticed."

We couldn't agree on the details of the car Adam was driving except that it was a blue Taurus. Luckily, Zach found the rental papers in Adam's carry-on bag. Because it'd been twenty-four hours since any of us had seen Adam, Dwight stretched a point and put it on the wire. After that, there was nothing to do except wait.

And speculate, of course.

A hunting accident?

Murder?

Had Adam seen Allen shoot Dick Sutterly?

Had both of them seen someone else shoot Sutterly?

"What if it's just something dumb, like

pulling a drunk?" asked Seth. "Maybe Adam went juking last night and he's holed up somewhere drinking or hung over."

"Never knew Adam to do much catting around," said Will. "He always walked the straight and narrow."

All this was over sandwiches at Minnie and Seth's.

"Well, being back here, off his chain, maybe he's finally broke loose," said Isabel as she rummaged in Minnie's refrigerator. "Anybody want pickles while I have them out?"

Haywood was back to worrying over Adam's state of mind. "You don't reckon he's got money troubles, do you?"

"Don't know if it's money or his marriage, but something's eating at him," Zach said, taking a huge bite of his cold meatloaf sandwich.

Daddy kept his own counsel and I kept my mouth shut except to nibble at some tangerines a cousin had shipped from Florida for the holidays.

By nine o'clock, we were ready to call it a night.

"If y'all hear anything —"

"— don't matter how late —"

"Call us."

"Let us know."
"We'll call."

I drove back through the lane one more time, half expecting to see Adam's car parked in front of Mr. Jap's shop, but except for that single dim light bulb that burned day and night on the back porch of the house, all was dark and silent.

As I looked at the shop in frustration, it occurred to me that no one had actually searched inside since it was locked from the outside.

I stopped, turned on my overhead light so I could find Merrilee's number in my address book, then reached for my cell phone.

"Hello?"

"Merrilee?"

"Deb'rah? Did y'all find them?"

"Not yet. What I was wondering is, do you have a key to Mr. Jap's shop?"

"Oh, sure. I keep spares of all his keys, just in case. Why?"

"Well, I just realized that we didn't check inside here. I know it's after nine and a long shot, but since I'm here, would it be much trouble to let me take a look?"

She sighed. "Well, no, not really."

"I know I'm imposing, but if Adam *is* in there, he might be hurt."

"Or Allen," she said, tartly defending family honor, even if Allen was family only by marriage. "He's missing, too, isn't he, and his truck's right there? He wouldn't go far, not if he's walking." She sighed again. "Oh, all right. Let me put on some clothes. I'll have the key up there in five minutes."

As I sat alone in the darkness, waiting for Merrilee, it was the first time I'd had to think about Dick Sutterly's death even though my family had turned the known facts inside out and upside down trying to figure if it involved Adam.

If this killing was linked to Mr. Jap's, why on a public road, so seemingly spur of the moment?

Sutterly had been all over this section of land last Saturday morning. His own death would seem to clear him of Mr. Jap's, but what if he'd seen someone entering or leaving the shop? And what if he tried to pressure that someone?

Allen?

Allen's alibi was Katie Morgan and her

brother. They'd probably lie for him in a heartbeat.

So say it *was* Allen that Sutterly saw. What does he do? See Allen out there on the road and say, "I'll tell unless you — ?"

"Unless he what?" asked my pragmatist.

Pays blackmail?

"Sutterly didn't need small money and Allen hasn't got big."

Of course, when (if) Cherry Lou's convicted, Allen will have the land. Big money potential there. And don't forget that promissory note Dwight found in Sutterly's truck. Why was it on top, if not to shake in someone's face? Maybe Sutterly said he'd keep silent if Allen would honor the terms Mr. Jap had negotiated.

"But Allen thought that was a good deal. He was hoping Sutterly would be legally bound to pay off on that note when he got title. Your trouble is you just don't want to think Adam's involved."

Whoever shot Sutterly killed Mr. Jap first, and Adam had no reason to do that.

"If Cherry Lou had signed the land back to Mr. Jap, he could have sold part of the road frontage right away and then

Adam's land would have been less valuable. No sixty thousand for him."

That argument thankfully ended when a car turned into the drive over beyond the house and circled around through the yard to park a few yards behind me.

By tilting my watch to the headlights, I saw it was closer to ten minutes than the five Merrilee had promised. I also saw that she'd sent Pete instead of coming herself.

I might have known. All she needed to do was pout a little about having to go traipsing up to Uncle Jap's shop and good ol' Pete would insist upon coming for her, anything to save Merrilee the least bit of aggravation.

Automatically, I pulled my keys from the ignition and met him at the shop door.

"Sorry to drag you out," I apologized, "but Dwight Bryant said Adam and Allen were here together yesterday afternoon and since nobody's seen them again —"

"It's okay," Pete said. "I don't blame you for worrying. If Allen and Adam got to fussing, no telling what might happen. Allen used to be worse'n me for drinking and then getting in fights."

He opened the padlock and left it

hanging on the staple. Inside, we found the light switch and lit up the shabby old shop. Beer cans littered the workbench and floor beside two broken-down chairs, but there was nothing to indicate a fight of any kind.

"That Adam's rifle?" asked Pete, pointing to the .22 propped against the old air compressor.

"Actually, it's Zach's." And I was really glad to see it. "I've been worrying that he was lying out in the woods somewhere in a hunting accident."

"Still could be," said Pete. "Allen could have brought the rifle back and then took off in Adam's car."

"And Dwight did say Sutterly was shot with a small-bore weapon," I said reluctantly. "Maybe I'd better leave it here till we know better. There might be fingerprints."

"I hear Billy Wall's out on bail. Don't you reckon he killed Dick Sutterly, too?"

I suppose I could have told him. It would be all over this end of the county by next day anyhow, but I just shook my head.

"Sure he did," said Pete. "He killed Uncle Jap, stole his money, and then he probably shot Dick Sutterly because

Dick saw him here."

"I grant you that's probably why Sutterly was shot, but not by Billy Wall. Sutterly was up and down all the lanes Saturday. He must've seen —"

My mouth was in gear but my brain was on idle. I hesitated, abruptly made uneasy by something feral in the way Pete had gone absolutely still and unblinking, like a cat that suspects a vole beneath the leaves. And just as abruptly, I remembered how he'd tried to prevent Merrilee from coming in here that morning. "Aw, now, honey," he'd said. "You don't want to go in there and remember him there like that."

Like how?

Pete?

He saw it in my face, let out a roar of denial and lunged at me. He was twice my size and if he ever caught me in that bear hug, I'd be dog meat.

He grabbed my arm and swung me around. I raked his face with my car keys and tried to knee him in the groin. I must have missed the main target, but it did loosen his grip for an instant and I snatched up a hammer from the workbench. By then, he had a lug wrench in his beefy hand, and he swung so hard that both my keys and the hammer went flying. A second swing landed a glancing blow on my hip and I fell to the concrete floor.

As he moved in for the kill, I grabbed Allen's creeper board and shoved it toward him. He stepped down heavily on it and both feet went out from under him.

I didn't wait to see how he landed, just sprinted for the door as fast as I could, slammed it and rammed the padlock home.

Oh God, for a car key! There was a spare set in a magnetic case under the fender but Pete was already banging against the door and I knew the hasp wouldn't hold long enough for me to find them and drive away. The way my hip throbbed from where he'd hit me, I also knew I couldn't run far.

Thanking the Lord for the moonless night, I dashed down the lane straight for the barn shelter fifty feet away and dived under the wrecked Maverick just as Pete burst through the door. There wasn't much room and I wiggled through the powdery dry sand till I was under the furthest hulk, a car that rode a lot higher than the Maverick.

From where I lay in pitch darkness, I could see Pete rush around his car and mine, looking for me. Car doors banged and I heard something crash against the shop wall, then he reached into his car and my heart sank as he pulled out a powerful flashlight and began searching more carefully. As he pointed the beam under the cars and all around the shop, I saw that he held the flash in his left hand.

His right hand held a pistol.

I wiggled right up against the cinder block supporting the left front wheel, oblivious to black widows, brown recluses or snakes of any color that might be hibernating in the cracks and crevices. All I wanted was a crack or crevice myself. Or better yet, a deep dark hole.

Instead, I realized that space had opened up above me. Of course! The motor on this old car had been pulled years ago, probably before I was even born. I pushed my hand up through cobwebs and waved it around. There was plenty of room up under the hood, although my hand encountered so many dangling wires and sharp ends of copper tubing, I wasn't sure if I could get past the axle and the radiator without tearing my clothes — not to mention my skin — to shreds.

But then Pete's flashlight turned toward the shed and shelters and damned if I didn't find that terror makes a real good lubricant. I slipped up into the motor housing like a greased monkey and my foot left the ground just as the light swept a long low arc under all the cars.

Pete was so close I could hear his heavy grunts as he stooped to look under each car.

Panicked, I realized there was a gaping hole under the dash where the floorboards had rusted through into the motor housing, and I quickly turned my head so that my face wouldn't shine back should the light hit it.

Fortunately, it was only a hasty inspection and the light didn't linger. Through the broken window, I heard Pete move around to the vehicles on the other side of the shelter, then the vibration of running feet, as if it had suddenly dawned on him that I might have headed for my daddy's house.

I pushed my way through the hole, up into the front seat, and found that I was inside the Hudson Hornet whose racing virtues Allen had sung when Kidd and I met him out here last month. The upholstery was filthy and probably riddled with mouse nests, but all I cared about was keeping tabs on Pete. Maybe if he went far enough down the lane, I could risk a run for my car, at least grab the cell phone and call for the cavalry.

I crawled over the high front seat and into the back. The seat here was hard as a rock, more like a thinly padded church pew than the cushiony springs of the front seat. I knelt on it though and peered through the tiny dirty rear windows.

I might never know why Pete killed Mr. Jap — momentary rage at hearing Merrilee slighted for Allen? Or merely the greedy assumption that Merrilee would split the estate with Allen if Mr. Jap died? — but I was pretty sure the same assumption was what sent Dick Sutterly over to Pete this afternoon with that promissory note. "Don't tell the Grimeses or Allen Stancil," he'd said Wednesday afternoon when he was so gleeful over securing Adam's land. And I'd been too weary of the whole subject to try to educate anyone else about the laws of inheritance. In view of how quickly Pete had attacked me, I had to wonder if Dick Sutterly had really seen Pete last Saturday or if Pete's guilty conscience led him to believe that Sutterly's proposition was a prelude to blackmail?

Out in the field, the powerful beam of that flashlight swept across the fallow field, up and down both sides of the lane. If he would just go on over the rise and down toward the creek —

The light disappeared. I waited a few seconds, but saw nothing. Just as I reached for the door handle, there was a burst of light, then darkness. He was coming back, straight across the field to Mr. Jap's house, trying to catch my silhouette between the lane and the dim porch light, hoping to flush me with his flashlight.

The old frame house sat up on low brick pilings with a lattice skirting that gapped in places. Pete circled the house, shining the light up under every corner.

Eventually he stood up and I rejoiced to see the slump of defeat in his shoulders as he trudged back over to his car. I was just starting to take big breaths of relief when his hand banged down on the hood and he straightened purposefully.

Oh, dear Lord, he was heading back toward the sheds! There was no way I could scrabble across the front seat and under the hood in time. As I ducked down below the windows, my weight shifted, the seat tilted and I was almost dumped to the floor.

I instantly remembered all the bootlegging lore I'd ever heard. Praying it would be empty, I tilted the padded board all the way over and a darker crevice appeared. In the old days, the hollowed-out backseat would have held at least four dozen half-gallon Mason jars of my daddy's best white lightning. No reason it wouldn't hold his daughter now.

I slid inside and pulled the padded board back over me like a coffin lid.

A moment later, I felt the car rock as Pete stepped on the running board and ran the light over every inch of the Hornet's interior. His breathing was ragged from exertion.

I myself had quit breathing and had no intention of starting again any time soon.

There was a thin crack where I hadn't quite pushed the board into the backrest as far as it was meant to go and so much light after such darkness terrified me. Any second now I would hear his triumphant cry and feel the explosion as he fired down through the board.

Then the car rocked violently as Pete jumped from the running board. I heard his feet pounding across the lane as a wash of headlights played across the shed and I came up out of my hidey-hole just in time to see Pete's car roar across the yard and turn out onto Old Forty-Eight on two wheels. At the same moment, car doors opened and slammed over at the shop.

Two male figures circled my car and called my name through the open shop door.

The adrenaline high that had kept me at fever pitch for the last half-hour abruptly evaporated and I was almost too weak to wrest open the rusty hinges and totter down to the shop.

I must have looked like the devil's playmate, torn, scratched, filthy dirty, but my appearance sent Adam and Allen into gales of raucous laughter.

Both of them clutched beer cans and both were drunk as skunks, but I couldn't see what was so damn funny.

"Reckon we showed you, darlin'," said Allen.

"Take the wind out of *your* sails," Adam said. A sudden hiccup made him giggle.

I hadn't seen my uptight, upright brother this wrecked since the night of his bachelor party.

"Where've you been?" I demanded. "You scared the hell out of us, disappearing like that."

He gave me a foolish grin. I spotted my car keys on the floor, grabbed them and headed outside. I didn't get three steps toward my car though when I saw my smashed cell phone. Damn that Pete Grimes!

Allen and Adam followed me, still strutting and bragging.

"Thought you'd sic the law on me 'cause of that phony blood test Diana did?" asked Allen. "Ha-ha on you, darlin'. She called me yesterday, told me all about what you done to her."

He was slurring his S sounds and that struck Adam as even funnier than the look on my face.

"Me and Adam, we drove up to Greensboro last evening and Katie and me got married today in Fort Mill, South Carolina."

Adam beamed at me. "Bes' man," he said happily. "Chauffeur, too."

"I'm just here to get my truck, pick up my stuff and head on back to Greensboro tomorrow."

"Don't let the door hit you on the way out," I said as I loaded my sodden brother into my car and dumped my smashed phone in his lap.

Five minutes later, Seth was putting Adam to bed on the couch in the den and I was phoning Dwight.

30

Mean time they have abundance, nay affluence, and enjoy independence, which, we all know, is a great sweetener of life and every blessing, and makes up for many superfluous refinements in what is called polite society . . .

"Scotus Americanus," *1773*

The phone kept ringing Saturday morning as half my family called to exclaim or condole about my close brush with danger, Pete's arrest, Adam's safe return. If I'd planned to sleep in, I could just forget it.

I had a bruise the size of Rhode Island on my hip and it was tender, but I seemed to be able to walk okay.

By ten o'clock, I had stuck the blue paper plates and napkins and the ten pounds of roasted peanuts in the trunk of my car and was driving over to Andrew's house. Dinner was to be at the homeplace at two o'clock, but Daddy had suggested that my brothers and I might want to come out early and watch some of his new puppies go through their paces in the training pen at Andrew's.

The temperature had dropped thirty degrees during the night and was barely expected to hit forty. Despite the sun, there was a stiff wind out of the north. Not a good day to stand around outside, but something in Seth's tone when he called to relay Daddy's message made me think I ought to be there. So I put on wool socks, boots, and a white turtleneck sweater under a sapphire blue warm-up suit that looked like crushed silk. My silver earrings were set with small blue topazes. I felt festive, yet I was still casual enough for the jeans and flannel shirts and sweaters my brothers would be wearing. For safe measure, I took along gloves and a blue-gray wool car coat that had a hood in case I got chilly.

Andrew's land is next to Seth's. The house is a comfortable old white clapboard built in the twenties by one of April's uncles over in Makely. When a new supermarket bought the lot, her cousin said April and Andrew could have it as a wedding present if they wanted to move it. It's been much remodeled since then — April rearranges walls the way some women rearrange furniture — and the kitchen is huge and modern now.

And smelled like Thanksgiving when I stuck my head in the back door. Isabel was bringing a ham and Nadine and Minnie were each roasting a turkey, but April always makes her succulent smoked oyster dressing and she was just putting the big pans in the oven, enough for fifty people.

April is Andrew's second wife and considerably younger than he, closer to my age, in fact, than his. She got her B.A. after A.K. was born and teaches sixth grade at Cotton Grove's middle school.

"Need any help?" I asked.

"Oh, Deborah!" She rushed over to hug me. "You could have been killed. Pete Grimes." She shook her head. "Have you heard how Merrilee's taking it?"

"I think she's retained Zack Young, but when Dwight called me last night, he said he's pretty sure they'll find that Dick Sutterly was killed with a bullet from Pete's gun."

"Thank goodness he didn't shoot you."

I looked around the kitchen. "You sure there's nothing I can do?"

"No, everything's done except I may mix up a little crabapple relish. And maybe make another gallon of tea. If you want coffee, here's a mug. They've got the pot plugged in down at the dog pen."

"Holler if you change your mind about needing help," I told her and went on down the slope where at least six pick-ups were parked, half with dog cages in the back.

Bert, Robert's four-year-old grandson, came running to meet me holding a beagle pup so young it didn't yet have its eyes open.

"Better bring him on back, little man," called Robert. "His mama's getting worried."

I swung Bert and the puppy both up in my arms. "I haven't had any sugar all week," I said, kissing him under his chin till he was giggling all over.

Haywood's granddaughter Kim is three and she wanted me to pick her up, too, so she could tell me all about a new litter of piglets that Seth's Jessica had taken her to see that morning.

Jess and A.K. and Adam's twin, Zach, were inside the quarter-acre training pen distributing fresh branches over the logs and pipes so the rabbits would have enough bolt spaces, and they all had plenty to say about my close call. As did Daddy when I saw him. The younger children were racing up and down along the outside perimeter with Blue and Ladybelle and a couple of other pet dogs, squealing with excitement and waiting for the fun to begin.

Reese and Annie Sue drove up and the kidding started before he even got out of her car good.

"Hey, Reese," Zach called. "Heard you got hold of a deer yesterday."

"Naw," said A.K. "I heard it was the other way 'round."

"Yeah, yeah," said Reese. "Y'all have fun. Get it out of your system."

"Let me buy you a cup of coffee," I said, taking pity on his bruised and stitched face.

"Hell, from what I hear, I ought to be buying you one." He looked me up and down. "Gotta say though, you're looking pretty good this morning for an old lady that spent time scrunched up in a wrecked car."

"Old lady?"

He ducked my punch and slipped through the door ahead of me.

The boys got together a few years ago and salvaged enough building scraps to put up a one-room shack right beside the training yard, complete with a big picture window, a small potbellied woodstove, and several cast-off chairs, including an old rump-sprung recliner that Isabel was going to make Haywood take to the dump. Now Daddy can sit out there with them and watch the training sessions even when it's cold and rainy.

The fire was welcome today, and so was the coffee Haywood poured for Reese and me. Adam was sitting in there with a mug between his hands, looking like something the dogs had dragged around in the mud.

I grinned. "Best man, huh?"

"Don't say it," he groaned.

Reese laughed and went outside.

As I stood watching through the picture window, Haywood said in the lowest, most confidential tone he could muster, "Uh, say, Adam? Me'n Isabel, we was wondering if you could use this?"

There was a rustle of paper, then Adam said, "Huh? Ten thousand dollars? What's this for?"

Haywood's whisper was like everybody else's normal level and I heard the awkwardness in his voice. "Well, I knowed you was worried about something and if it's just money, well, shootfire! I got lucky Thursday. You can pay me back when it's convenient."

I didn't wait to hear Adam's reply. My eyes were stinging as I took my coffee out into the crisp morning air. We might be going to have a real winter after all.

"Cold weather feels good, don't it, shug?" asked Daddy. He'd already asked me twice was I sure Pete hadn't seriously hurt me? Once again, I promised him that I was just fine. He had on a fleece-lined brown jacket and the beige felt Stetson that he wears in winter, and he was watching Andrew buckle a training collar around the neck of a pup he'd paid twelve hundred for.

Some people think an electronic training collar is a cruel device and I suppose it is if wrongly used. On the other hand, if you're out in the woods and your dogs won't come when you call or whistle, they can follow a rabbit trail halfway across the county and wind up footsore and lost. It's sad to see a couple of slab-sided hunting dogs wandering the back roads in winter. They give you such a hopeful look when your car passes, as if wondering if this car, this time, will finally hold their owner. Yet if you stop to try and read their tags, they skitter away and often can't be caught.

Daddy and my brothers believe a few mild electric shocks are worth preventing that.

This little dog had already caught the whiff of rabbits and was wiggling with anticipation. Daddy led her inside, got her settled, then gave the command to seek. She found the scent immediately and started yipping and singing. The other dogs in the cages started barking, too. Rabbits were zinging every which way, and the grandbabies were tumbling all over each other, laughing and pointing as a rabbit sailed right over the young dog's head.

Daddy let her run till she was almost tired enough to stop on her own, then gave a sharp call. When she didn't break off the chase, he gave her a quick zap at the same split second that he called again. She yelped once and instantly went to him for praise and petting.

He repeated the drill twice more and by the third try, she broke off the chase as soon as he called out to her the first time.

"She's gonna be a good'un," Daddy said, pleased. He rubbed her ears and praised her some more before A.K. carried her back to her box in Daddy's pickup.

The process was repeated with three more dogs, then Andrew decided one of his rabbit dogs needed reinforcement about ignoring deer scents.

"Where's that piece of deerskin?" he called.

"You don't need it, Uncle Andrew," said Jessica. "Just turn Reese in and let him run around the pen."

Reese rolled his eyes at me. "I'm gonna hear about that damn buck till the day I die, ain't I?"

"Till the day I die, at least," I promised, squeezing his shoulder.

Eventually, four or five young littermates were put in the pen to get used to the smell of rabbits. Supervision of the little kids was turned over to some of the nieces and nephews as we joined Daddy inside the shack.

It was a bit crowded: Robert, Andrew, Haywood, Seth, Will, Adam, Zach and me. Young Bert was perched sleepily on Daddy's lap.

"You want me to take him out?" asked Jessica.

"No, let him stay. You can stay, too, if you keep what's said here in the family."

Jess nodded solemnly and sat down on the arm of Seth's chair.

Daddy looked around the small room. "Who's missing?"

"Herman," said Haywood, "and I reckon I can tell him what happens."

"I wish Frank and Benjamin and Jack was here, too," said Daddy, "but they ain't."

His eyes traveled around and met each of ours in turn. "Now, y'all know how things been changing around here. What some of y'all *don't* know is that G. Hooks Talbert's planning to develop all that land across the creek. He's bought out Leo Pleasant, he's bought Adam's —"

There was some surprised and resentful muttering at that bit of news, but Daddy sailed on.

"— and he'll probably buy Jap Stancil's land once the title's clear on who owns it. Best we can find out, he wants to dredge out the creek, build a lake and put up lots of big fancy houses for rich people."

I was not the only one who sighed.

"I know, I know," he said. "I don't like it neither. But Talbert's set on doing this. Best we can hope for is a chance to help make it into something we can live with."

Lulled by the rumble of his great-grandfather's voice, little Bert lay back against Daddy's chest and fell asleep.

"Now, nothing's gonna happen till after Cherry Lou's trial, so we got us a little time to talk about what we want to let's do."

"Seems to me like Adam went ahead and decided all by hisself," said Robert. "He ain't got nothing more to sell, have you, Adam?"

Before Adam could answer, Daddy said, "No, not right now, he ain't, but he will when I'm gone, when what's mine gets split up equal between all of y'all."

There was an uncomfortable stirring. The boys don't like to think of that day any more than I do.

"Besides," said Daddy, looking at Robert, "he didn't decide all by hisself.

He asked my advice and his need was great and I didn't see as it'd make any difference in the long run."

Andrew and Haywood snorted at the idea of Adam being in need. I knew what was running through their heads — a million-dollar house in California, swimming pool, kids in private schools?

Adam took a deep breath and finally swallowed his pride. "You guys think I'm loaded, right? Sorry. I got downsized in February," he said in a tone that dared them to offer sympathy. "No golden parachute, no job, no income. Dick Sutterly was fronting for G. Hooks Talbert and they wanted my three acres so badly that they gave me sixty thousand for it."

"Sixty thousand!" Will was incredulous.

Each of us owns outright between a hundred and two hundred acres and I could almost hear my brothers mentally multiplying their own land by twenty thousand an acre even though it was unlikely Talbert would be offering that much on land that was less strategic.

Adam's chin came up defiantly. "I needed the money and I took it."

"That's how we know for sure that Talbert's serious about developing that whole section," said Seth.

"Maybe we ought to've talked it over with all of y'all first," said Daddy, "but it won't gonna change Adam's need."

Haywood was distressed. "How come you didn't say nothing, son? We'd've helped your ox out of any hole you was in. Right, boys?"

"That's what family's for," Robert said gruffly.

Before everybody got so uncomfortable that we all wound up in one of those sloppy group hugs, I said, "You talk like we have options, Daddy. G. Hooks doesn't give a d—"

Daddy cut his eyes at me. He does not like to hear a lady use strong language and he particularly doesn't like it used around small children, even if the small child in question is sound asleep.

"— doesn't give a darn whether we can live with his plans or not. In fact, he probably hopes we'll hate it enough to sell out."

"Well, that's one of our options, ain't it, shug?" he said mildly. "If any y'all want to quit farming and cash out, sell to G. Hooks, I'm saying right now, far as I'm concerned, you can do it and I won't say a word. You boys, 'specially you older boys, helped work this land out — I wouldn't have half what I've got without y'all working hard back then, even before Annie Ruth died."

By all accounts, Daddy's first wife had been a harder worker than even he himself and she had imbued her sons with that ethic. Haywood and Robert and Andrew seemed shocked at the very idea of breaking up the farm, but Will and Zach, my mother's sons, had speculative looks in their eyes.

I was really, really hating this.

"You said we had options," I said hotly. "That doesn't sound like much of one to me."

Daddy smiled like the crafty old fox he is.

"What?" I said, feeling a small shaft of hope.

"Well, now, G. Hooks thinks he owns the south side of the creek," said Daddy. "He don't. We do. When I was buying from the Pleasant children and grandchildren all those years ago, I always bought both sides of the creek. G. Hooks' deed may say something like 'thence in common with the Keziah Knott line along Possum Creek,' but mine says 'to and *including* the south bank of Possum Creek.' "

"You mean we can keep him off the creek?" asked Andrew. "Stop him from dredging out a fancy lake?"

"We could. But if we get horsey with him, he's liable to forget about fancy and go for common. If he fills that piece with the kind of crackerboxes like Dick Sutterly built over on Forty-Eight, we could have hundreds of young'uns swarming over the creek anyhow. No, I was thinking maybe we tell him we can work with him, but then he has to maybe do some things like we want."

The sound level went up as my brothers all started talking at once. "Well, *I* ain't selling!"

"Me neither!"

"Talbert'n go to hell 'fore he gets —"

"— put up barbed wire and fence the whole creek —"

"Twenty thousand a acre? You know how much that comes to?"

"I've been thinking," said Seth, and the others gradually quit talking.

Seth stands halfway between us and not just in age. He hasn't had as much formal education as Adam and Zach and I, but he reads and ponders and keeps his mind more open than some of the older ones. He respects where they're coming from, though, and he's always been a conciliator. The boys listen to Seth. I do, too.

"In exchange for access to the creek, maybe we can get G. Hooks to agree to a buffer zone, so we don't have to see and hear everything over there," he said. "If we agree to lay back a few hundred feet on this side of the creek, and he lays back the same distance —"

"A greenbelt?" I asked.

"Huh?" said Robert.

"Like a park or a wilderness area," I said. "Instead of building right up to the creek, make him leave a wide strip of trees and bushes where people can walk or ride bicycles or have picnics."

It was just like down at the coast. I might not like to see our homeplace changing, but Daddy was right. Best we could hope for was to have a say in *how* it changed.

"Something like that could increase the value of land over here," said Adam. "If Talbert does a good job over there —"

"Yeah," said Will. "And no reason to say we couldn't form a development company ourselves someday."

The older boys were looking hostile

again and Jess touched Seth's sleeve. "I don't want to give up Silver Dollar, Daddy."

"Nobody's asking you to give up your horse or anything else," Seth said. "We've got plenty of time, plenty of land. We're just talking out loud right now."

Annie Sue opened the door and a blast of cold November air swept across the room. "Aunt April says tell y'all it's almost two o'clock and everybody's started coming in over at the home-place."

The mention of food, and a Thanksgiving feast at that, eased the tension that had built up in this room.

"Well, y'all think on it," Daddy said, as we stirred to go.

He looked down at his great-grandson asleep on his chest. What we were talking about would affect the rest of little Bert's life. Years from now, when he was an old, old man, would he and his cousins remember this day? And would they bless it or curse it?

Daddy touched that smooth cheek with his workworn finger.

"Y'all just think on it," he said.

The employees of Thorndike Press hope you have enjoyed this Large Print book. All our Large Print titles are designed for easy reading, and all our books are made to last. Other Thorndike Large Print books are available at your library, through selected bookstores, or directly from us.

For information about titles, please call:

(800) 223-2336

To share your comments, please write:

Publisher
Thorndike Press
P.O. Box 159
Thorndike, Maine 04986